William A. Knight, William Wordsworth

The English Lake District

As interpreted in the poems of Wordsworth

William A. Knight, William Wordsworth

The English Lake District
As interpreted in the poems of Wordsworth

ISBN/EAN: 9783337406882

Printed in Europe, USA, Canada, Australia, Japan

Cover: Foto ©Andreas Hilbeck / pixelio.de

More available books at **www.hansebooks.com**

THE ENGLISH LAKE DISTRICT

As INTERPRETED IN THE

POEMS OF WORDSWORTH

Printed at The Edinburgh Press, 9 & 11 Young Street,

FOR

DAVID DOUGLAS

LONDON . .	SIMPKIN, MARSHALL, HAMILTON, KENT, AND CO., LIM.
CAMBRIDGE .	MACMILLAN AND BOWES.
GLASGOW . .	JAMES MACLEHOSE AND SONS.

THE

ENGLISH LAKE DISTRICT

AS INTERPRETED IN THE

POEMS OF WORDSWORTH

BY

WILLIAM KNIGHT

PROFESSOR OF MORAL PHILOSOPHY AND POLITICAL ECONOMY
IN THE UNIVERSITY OF ST. ANDREWS

.

SECOND EDITION
Revised and Enlarged

EDINBURGH: DAVID DOUGLAS

1891

CONTENTS.

PREFACE.

THIS little book is not a new attempt at criticism. It does not try to estimate the genius, or weigh the merits, of the poetry of Wordsworth. Its aim is much humbler: viz., to interpret the poems, by bringing out the singularly close connection between them, and the district of the English lakes, and by explaining Wordsworth's numerous allusions to the locality. As such, it is only one small stone added to the cairn, that is being raised to the memory of the poet, by the devotion of successive generations.

It aims at being a guide to the Poems, as much as to the District; and to the District, only in so far as it is reflected in, and interpreted by, the Poems. It necessarily takes for granted a certain knowledge of both. The Poems, however, are no longer "caviare to the general." The number of those who can trace to their influence much of what is highest and best within them is multiplying with the spread of culture, and almost in proportion to the complexity of our civilisation; while the peculiar charm of the District is increasingly felt by Englishmen.

Many of Wordsworth's allusions to Place are obscure; and the exact localities, as well as individual objects, are difficult to identify. It is doubtful if he cared whether they could be afterwards

B

traced out or not; and in reference to one (see p. 58), when asked by a friend to indicate the particular spot, he refused to localise it, saying, "Oh, yes; that, or any other that will suit." Besides, in some of his most realistic passages, he avowedly weaves together a description of places remote from each other. Numerous instances of this will occur as we proceed.

It is true that "poems of places" are not meant to be photographs; and were they simply to reproduce the features of a particular district, and be an exact transcript of reality, they would be literary photographs and not poems. Poetry cannot, in the nature of things, be a mere register of phenomena appealing to the eye or the ear. (No imaginative writer, however, within the range of English literature, is so peculiarly identified with locality as Wordsworth is; and there is none on the roll of poets, the appreciation of whose writings is more aided by an intimate knowledge of the district in which he lived.) Homer can be understood without a visit to the Troad, or the Ægean; but the *power* of Wordsworth cannot be fully known by one who is a stranger to Westmoreland. The wish to be able definitely to associate his poems with the places which suggested them, and which they interpret, is natural to every one who has ever felt the spell of his genius. It is indispensable to all who would know the peculiar charm of a Region which he characterised as "a national property," and of which he, beyond all other men, may be said to have effected the literary "conveyance" to posterity.

On July 1833, Henry Crabbe Robinson wrote in his diary at Grasmere: "One charm of this district is its infinite variety, as one of the great excellences of Wordsworth's poems, and also his prose-writing, is the perfect discrimination between them

all. The sweet repose of Grasmere is heightened
to elegance in Windermere; the romantic beauties
of Ullswater are enhanced to savage wildness in
Wastwater; while Crummock Water is fantastic,
and Derwentwater is sublime. But these epithets
by no means exclusively apply, and may be often
interchanged."

These poems are the best, and, in one sense, the
only needed, "guide" to the whole of that classic
ground. It is ground which they have *made*
classic. They have done more for the north of
England than the novels and metrical romances
of Sir Walter Scott have done for Scotland: and
Scott's are the only works which, in this connection, can be even remotely compared with Wordsworth's. There is, however, another and a most
interesting scientific work, in reference to Scotland, with which the poetic interpretation of the
English Lakes may be contrasted. It is Professor
Geikie's book on *The Scenery and Geology of Scotland*, in which he endeavours to interpret the present physical character of the country, by explaining
the forces that have been moulding it for centuries,
shaping its valleys, and determining the form of its
mountains and coast lines. It is by far the best
guide to Scottish scenery, because it contains a
scientific exposition of the processes by which the
country has come to be what it now is. The poetry
of Wordsworth fulfils a yet nobler, though quite a
kindred, function for Cumberland and Westmoreland; interpreting the scenery as it now is, by lay-
ing hold of its inner meaning, its perennial spirit,
and embodying its deep underlying significance, in
imaginative forms of unparalleled grace and power.
This, apart from everything else, will give perma-
nence to his poetry.

It will doubtless be asked, What is the use of a
minute identification of all these places? Is not

the general fact that Wordsworth described this
district of Mountain, Vale, and Mere sufficient,
without any further attempt at localisation? The
question is more important, and has wider bearings
than may appear upon the surface.

On the one hand, it must be admitted, that the
discovery of the precise point of every local allusion
is not necessary to an understanding or appreciation of the poems ; and in some instances it is
unattainable. It must also be admitted that
Wordsworth was never contented with simply
copying what he saw in Nature. Even in reference
to his early poem, *The Evening Walk*, written
in his eighteenth year, he tells us that the plan of
the poem was "not confined to a particular walk or
an individual place ; a proof (of which I was unconscious at the time) of my unwillingness to submit
the poetic spirit to the chains of fact and real circumstance. The country is idealised rather than
described in any one of its local aspects."[1]

In *The Excursion* he leaps from Langdale to
Grasmere, over to Patterdale, back to Grasmere,
and again to Haweswater, without warning : and
in one of the Duddon Sonnets even he intro-
duces a description taken direct from Rydal. Mr.
Aubrey de Vere tells us of a conversation he had with
Wordsworth, in which he passionately condemned
the ultra-realistic poets, who went out into the
presence of Nature, with "pencil and note-book,
and jotted down whatever struck them most ;"
adding, "Nature does not permit an inventory to
be made of her charms! He should have left his
pencil and note-book at home ; fixed his eye, as he
walked, with a reverent attention on all that surrounded him, and taken all into a heart that could
understand and enjoy. Afterwards he would have

[1] Fenwick note to the poem.

discovered that while much of what he had admired was preserved to him, much was also most wisely obliterated. That which remained, the picture surviving in his mind, *would have presented the ideal and essential truth of the scene, and done so, in large part, by discarding much which, though in itself striking, was not characteristic.* In every scene many of the most brilliant details are but accidental."[1]

In these sentences, and especially in the one I have italicised, a thought is expressed which lies very near the centre of the philosophy of creative art. It will no doubt depend upon the power of the "inward eye," and of the reproducing, idealising mind, whether the poetic result is a travesty of Nature, or the expression of a truth higher than Nature yields. But in keeping with what Wordsworth so felicitously expressed to Mr. de Vere, it is obvious that a mere inventory of places mentioned by him, however accurate, would afford no real help to the understanding of his poetry.

On the other hand, it is equally certain that in many instances the identification of a particular place casts sudden light upon obscure passages in the poems, and is by far the best commentary that can be given. It is a great thing to be able to compare the actual scene, which suggested the ideal creation, with the latter, which arose out of it, and was both Wordsworth's reading of the text of Nature, and his interpretation of it. In his seventy-third year, looking back on the *Descriptive Sketches* written at school—and during his first two college vacations —he said that there was not an image in the poem which he had not observed, and that he "recollected the time and place when most of them were noticed." In the notes dictated to Miss Fenwick,

---

[1] *The Prose Works of Wordsworth*, vol. iii. p. 487.

he frequently says, "The fact occurred strictly as recorded;" and, very often, the "fact" involves the accessories of Place. I cannot doubt that, in the case of one so faithful to detail as Wordsworth was, the discovery of his minutest allusions will prove an aid to the understanding and appreciation of the poems.

Nor will the work which this volume attempts to do be deemed superfluous by those who know the district well, and associate it pre-eminently with this poet, if they have ever tried to trace out the allusions in the "Poems on the naming of Places," or even to discover *Michael's sheepfold*, to identify *Ghimmer Crag*, or *Thurston-mere;* not to speak of the individual "rocks" and "recesses" described in *The Excursion*, near Blea Tarn, at the head of Little Langdale. Every one knows Kirkstone Pass, Aira Force, Dungeon Ghyll, and Helm Crag; but where is *Emma's Dell*, or "the meeting point of two highways" described so characteristically in the twelfth Book of *The Prelude*, and who will determine for us the pool in Rydal Upper Park, immortalised in the poem to M. H. (see p. 71), or identify *Joanna's Rock?*

Much has already been done in the direction indicated, but more remains to reward intelligent and zealous inquiry. The notes and illustrations of the poems, dictated by Wordsworth himself to Miss Fenwick, are the most valuable of all existing memoranda, and are in themselves a singularly precious literary relic. But some of his most characteristic poems require further commentary, which can be obtained only after minute study of the places mentioned. Many of these are themselves undergoing change, and becoming more difficult to identify every year. Such a memorial, for example, as "the Rock of Names," on the shore of Thirlmere, is threatened with immersion fathoms

deep below the waters of a Manchester reservoir.[1]
Others are perishing through the wear and tear of
time, the decay of old buildings, the alteration of
roads, the cutting down of trees, and the modern-
ising or "improving" of the district generally. All
this is inevitable. But as the poet wrote for posterity, it is a matter for thankfulness that many of
the natural objects, over and around which the
light of his genius lingers, are out of the reach of
"improvements," and are indestructible even by
machinery.

The attempt to identify localities, which some
might prefer to leave undisturbed in the realm of
imagination, is undertaken only for those who find
their interest in the poems intensified by such
realistic detail—those who already feel grateful for
the work which Miss Fenwick undertook. If it be
objected, that some of the places which we now
try to identify, in the earlier poems, were purposely
left unrevealed in the Fenwick notes, it may be
replied that Death and Time have removed probable reasons for reticence, especially in poems
alluding to domestic and friendly ties. By dictating the notes for the gratification of a small and
private circle. Wordsworth himself sanctioned the
principle, which is now carried out only more fully;
and much of his own descriptive detail is more
minute and runs farther into matters of secondary
interest, than that attempted in this volume. All
experience shows, moreover, that posterity takes a
great and growing interest in exact topographical
illustrations of the works of great authors—witness
the labour recently bestowed upon localities associated with Shakespeare, and with Burns, and
the success which has attended it.

The localities most deeply and permanently iden-

---

[1] See pp. 217-18.

tified with Wordsworth are the following :--Gras-
mere, where he lived during the years of his "poetic
prime," and where he is buried ; Lower Easdale,
where he spent so many days with his sister, by
the side of the brook, and on the terraces at
Lancrigg (where *The Prelude* was written); Rydal
Mount, where he spent the latter half of his life,
and where he found one of the most perfect
retreats in England ; and the old (upper) path
between Rydal and Grasmere, under Nab Scar,
his favourite walk during his later years, where he
composed hundreds of verses.   There is scarcely
a rock or mountain-summit, a stream or tarn, or
even a well, a grove, or a forest-side in all that
neighbourhood, which is not imperishably associated with this poet, who at once (as I hope to
show) interpreted them, as they had never been
interpreted before, and added

> The gleam,
> The light, that never was on sea or land,
> The consecration, and the poet's dream.

Most persons are aware that Wordsworth himself wrote a *Guide through the District of the
Lakes in the North of England, with a description
of the Scenery, etc.*   It appeared as early as 1810;
a fifth edition was published in 1835.   Totally
unlike ordinary "Guide-books," this unpretending
volume is weighted with reflections on aspects of
Nature missed by the ordinary eye, and contains
many profound glances into the heart of those
familiar things "that border the highway."
   Of the district generally, Wordsworth remarks :
"I do not know any tract of country in which,
within so narrow a compass, may be found an
equal variety in the influences of light and shadow
upon the sublime and beautiful features of landscape. . . .   Though clustered together, every

valley has its distinct and separate character : in
some instances as if they had been formed in
studied contrast to each other, and in others with
the differences and resemblances of a sisterly
rivalship" (sect. 1). He goes on to point out,
in a singularly striking and original manner, the
peculiar features which make this region unique,
not only in England but in Europe, alluding in
succession to the mountains, both in their form
and colouring, to the vales, the lakes, the islands,
the tarns, the rivers, and the woods. As there
is no finer delineation of the district, except in
his own poetry, I may quote a few sentences from
this *Guide*. Referring to the lake, he says :
" Its form is most perfect when it least resembles
that of a river, . . . a body of still water under
the influence of no current ; reflecting, therefore,
the clouds, the light, and all the imagery of the
sky and surrounding hills ; expressing, also, and
making visible, the changes of the atmosphere
and motions of the lightest breeze, and subject to
agitation only from the winds." Alluding to the
tarns, round the margin of which large boulders
lie scattered—"some defying conjecture as to the
means by which they came hither, and others
obviously fallen from on high, the contribution of
ages" (and this, it must be remembered, was
written before the rise of modern geology, and
while the glacial theory was unknown)—he adds,
characteristically, "A not unpleasing sadness is
induced by this perplexity, and these images of
decay." Speaking of the climate of the district,
and of the skiey influences generally, he remarks :
"The rain comes down here *heartily*, and is frequently succeeded by clear, bright weather, when
every brook is vocal, and every torrent sonorous,
brooks and torrents which are never muddy, except
after a drought. Days of unsettled weather, with

partial showers, are frequent; but the showers,
darkening or brightening as they fly from hill to
hill, are not less grateful to the eye than finely
interwoven passages of gay and sad music are
touching to the ear. Vapours exhaling from the
lakes and meadows after sunrise in a hot season,
or in moist weather brooding upon the heights,
or descending towards the valleys with inaudible
motion, give a visionary character to everything
around them, and are in themselves so beautiful
as to dispose us to enter into the feelings of those
simple nations by whom they are taken for the
Guardian Deities of the mountains; or to sym-
pathise with others who have fancied these delicate
apparitions to be the spirits of their departed
ancestors. Akin to these are fleecy clouds, resting
upon the hill tops. Such clouds, cleaving to their
stations, or lifting up suddenly their glittering
heads from behind rocky barriers, or hurrying
out of sight with speed of the sharpest edge, will
often tempt an inhabitant to congratulate himself
on belonging to a country of mists, and clouds,
and storms, and make him think of the blank
sky of Egypt, and the cerulean vacancy of Italy,
as an unanimated and even a sad spectacle."
Finally, he says that as "in human life there
are moments worth ages, so in the climate of England there are, for the lover of Nature, days which
are worth whole months, I might even say years.
. . . It is in autumn that days of such affecting
influence most frequently intervene; the atmosphere seems refined, and the sky rendered
more crystalline, as the vivifying heat of the
year abates; the lights and shadows are more
delicate; the colouring is richer, and more finely
harmonised; and in this season of stillness, the
ear being unoccupied, or only gently excited, the
sense of vision becomes more susceptible of its

appropriate enjoyments. A resident in a country like this which we are treating of, will agree with me that the presence of a lake is indispensable to exhibit in perfection the beauty of one of these days ; and he must have experienced, while looking on the unruffled waters, that *the imagination, by their aid, is carried into recesses of feeling otherwise impenetrable.* The reason of this is that the heavens are not only brought down into the bosom of the earth, but that the earth is necessarily looked at, and thought of, through the medium of a purer element."[1]

Perhaps Wordsworth's finest description (in prose) of the outward features of any single object in Nature is that contained in a letter to Coleridge,[2] giving an account of his visit to the waterfall near Hardrane in Yorkshire, on his way to Grasmere, to settle down there in 1799.

In that chapter of his *Guide*, in which he speaks of the best time for visiting the district, he mentions successively certain features of Nature — which afford a good illustration of the way in which he passed from the external features of a scene, or those of which the senses takes cognisance, to its underlying spirit. He first refers to "the tender green of the after-grass upon the meadows, interspersed with islands of gray or mossy rock." He then alludes to the notes of birds, which, "when listened to, by the side of broad, still waters, or heard in unison with the murmuring of mountain brooks, have the compass of their powers enlarged accordingly;" next, of the "imaginative influence of the voice of the cuckoo, when that voice has taken possession of a deep mountain valley." Again he writes : "He is the most fortunate, who chances to

---

[1] *Guide*, section I.
[2] *Memoirs*, vol. I. p. 150, etc.

be involved in vapours which open and let in an
extent of country partially, or, dispersing suddenly,
reveal the whole region from centre to circumference."[1]

In order to show what Wordsworth saw in
Nature, and *how* he saw it, I must, of necessity,
quote very largely from the Poems ; and, in doing
so, I shall depart from the poet's own arrangement
of them, and follow an order partly chronological
and partly topographical.   It seems natural to
begin with Cockermouth, his birthplace, and to
pass thence to Hawkshead, where his wonderful
"school-time" was passed, and where his spirit
received the most powerful influences of Nature;
going on to Grasmere, where he settled at the end
of last century; and with Grasmere as our centre,
to radiate in different directions, to Langdale, Patterdale, and Keswick.

The poems in this volume are grouped together
according to the districts to which they refer, and
which they describe.   This leads of necessity to
their partial dismemberment.   But only those
which allude to localities in the Lake country are
quoted, with the relevant portions of the I. F. MS.,
and extracts from the Journal of Dorothy Wordsworth. They cast a flood of light upon the whole
district, and on the poet's work in connection with
it ; and any value which this book may have will
be in proportion to the ease with which the commentary is forgotten in the realisation of the poems
themselves.

It remains for me to express my obligations in
past years in the sometimes difficult task of identifying obscure places, and tracing out obscure
allusions, to the late Dr. Cradock, Principal of
Brasenose College, Oxford—who knew more of the

------

[1] *Guide*, section 4.

district, in connection with Wordsworth, than any one I ever met with—to the late Lady Richardson of Lancrigg; to the Reverend H. D. Rawnsley, of Crosthwaite Vicarage, Keswick, who is probably the most learned of all men now alive in the topography of the Wordsworth country; also, through the medium of Dr. Cradock, to the Cookson family—neighbours and friends of the poet during a large portion of his life. The extent of my indebtedness to Dr. Cradock is apparent throughout the volume. I often wished that he could have been himself induced to undertake the work.

WILLIAM KNIGHT.

St. Andrews, October 1878.

PREFACE TO THE SECOND EDITION.

THIRTEEN years have elapsed since the first edition of this little book was published. In the present issue the lecture on Wordsworth, with which the former one concluded, is omitted; and in its place are printed many additional memoranda of the district by Wordsworth and his sister Dorothy.

I have not thought it necessary to make reference to any special edition of the poet's works in quoting from them. The text will be found to be accurate, but it is unnecessary to state from what particular edition each extract is taken.

In one or two instances, the localisations in the former edition have been slightly altered by a subsequent study of the places described.

In addition to the new material supplied by the Grasmere Journals of the poet's sister, there are several localities in the Lake Country, not referred to in the previous volume, which are embraced within this one,—especially the Penrith district, and the Duddon Valley. I have especially to thank Mr. Gordon Wordsworth, for permission to give extracts from the Journal of his great aunt, and Mr. Herbert Rix, assistant-secretary of the Royal Society, for permission to use his notes on the Duddon.

It was my original intention to include, along with what is now published (but in a second volume), the localisation of every reference in

Wordsworth's poems to Yorkshire, Somersetshire, Dorsetshire, Wales, the Isle of Man, Scotland, Switzerland, and Italy—in short, all the places memorialised by him. The materials for such a volume are collected, and indeed lie ready to hand in the notes I have already given in the library edition of the Poems (1883-1889), and other data brought together in previous years. It has been thought desirable, however, to limit the present volume—like its predecessor—to the District of the English Lakes alone.

The portrait prefixed to this volume has a special interest. Mr. Leonard C. Wyon, after reading a paper on thirty-eight portraits of the poet, which was read to the Wordsworth Society, and published in its *Transactions*, wrote to me that there was a thirty-ninth, taken by himself at Rydal, in 1847, in Wordsworth's seventy-seventh year, and that he would gladly show it to me. On calling next day, I found it to be one of the best—perhaps the most characteristic—of all the portraits. It is a small crayon profile, and although there is a noticeable feebleness in the lower part of the face, due as much to age as to anything else, the expression is one of remarkable strength and tenderness combined. Mr. Wyon has most generously consented to its reproduction in this volume.

The sketch on the outside cover of the book is from a drawing of Dove cottage, as it was in 1800, given to me by Miss Richardson of Heughfolds, Grasmere.

Since the first edition was published, there have been several books added to our Wordsworth Literature : The *Transactions* of " The Wordsworth Society ;" a chronological edition of the poet's *Works*, with notes descriptive and critical, in eight volumes ; and, as its sequel, the *Life of Wordsworth*, in three volumes. The *Transactions* were issued privately to members of the Society.

The *Works* and *Life* were published by Mr. William Paterson, 1882-86. In 1879, Messrs. Macmillan issued a little book called *Poems of Wordsworth, chosen and edited by Matthew Arnold*, with an admirable preface ; and in 1888, a volume of *Selections* was published by Messrs. K. Paul, Trench, & Co., to which Mr. Browning, and many other members of the Wordsworth Society, contributed.

For more precise information as to the poems, and what suggested them; to the localities memorialised, and some points in the allusions themselves; as well as to scattered folk-lore, antiquarian details, and historical facts connected with them, I must refer to the notes in the Chronological (Library) Edition of the poet's *Works*.

Perhaps the most interesting event, in connection with Wordsworth's influence on the present generation, is the recent purchase—for the world and for posterity—of Dove Cottage, his residence from December 1799 to May 1808 (see page 54).

WILLIAM KNIGHT.

Edgecliffe, St. Andrews,
April 1891.

CHAPTER I.

COCKERMOUTH, ETC.

IT is to his autobiographical poem, *The Prelude*, that one naturally turns to find out how Wordsworth felt towards Cockermouth, the place of his birth; and how he interpreted the surrounding district in which his childhood was spent.

There are many allusions in *The Prelude* to the old house in which he was born, its garden, and the river which passed it. In the first book, he says, alluding to the Derwent, that

> One, the fairest of all rivers, loved
> To blend his murmurs with my nurse's song,
> And from his alder shades and rocky falls,
> And from his fords and shallows, sent a voice
> That flowed along my dreams. For this, didst
>   thou,
> O Derwent! winding among grassy holms
> Where I was looking on, a babe in arms,
> Make ceaseless music that composed my thoughts
> To more than infant softness, giving me
> Amid the fretful dwellings of mankind
> A foretaste, a dim earnest, of the calm
> That Nature breathes among the hills and groves?
> When he had left the mountains and received
> On his smooth breast the shadow of those towers
> That yet survive, a shattered monument
> Of feudal sway, the bright blue river passed

1   C

Along the margin of our terrace walk ;
A tempting playmate whom we dearly loved.
Oh, many a time have I, a five years' child,
In a small mill-race severed from his stream,
Made one long bathing of a summer's day ;
Basked in the sun, and plunged and basked again
Alternate, all a summer's day, or scoured
The sandy fields, leaping through flowery groves
Of yellow ragwort ; or when rock and hill,
The woods, and distant Skiddaw's lofty height,
Were bronzed with deepest radiance, stood alone
Beneath the sky, as if I had been born
On Indian plains, and from my mother's hut
Had run abroad in wantonness, to sport
A naked savage, in the thunder shower.[1]

The "mill-race" may easily be guessed, but is too vaguely described to be known with accuracy ; and the "sandy fields" must be those close to the "race" itself. The "towers" are, of course, those of Cockermouth Castle. The "terrace walk" is at the foot of the garden attached to the old mansion in the town in which he was born, and in which his father, who was law-agent of the Lonsdale family, resided.

Two of the sonnets composed in 1833 refer to his birthplace; the first, suggested *In sight of the Town of Cockermouth (where the Author was born, and his Father's remains are laid);* the second, *An Address from the Spirit of Cockermouth Castle.* Neither of them need be quoted ; but another in the same series, and of the same date, addressed *To the River Derwent,* is as follows :—

Among the mountains were we nursed, loved
    Stream !
Thou near the eagle's nest—within brief sail,

---

[1] *The Prelude,* book i. p. 41.

I, of his bold wing floating on the gale,
Where thy deep voice could lull me !   Faint the
      beam
Of human life when first allowed to gleam
On mortal notice.--Glory of the vale,
Such thy meek outset, with a crown, though frail,
Kept in perpetual verdure by the steam
Of thy soft breath !— Less vivid wreath entwined
Nemæan victor's brow; less bright was worn,
Meed of some Roman chief—in triumph borne
With captives chained ; and shedding from his car
The sunset splendours of a finished war
Upon the proud enslavers of mankind !

It was in reference to this home of his childhood
that, in 1801, he wrote the poem he called *The
Sparrow's Nest :* the " sister Emmeline" referred to
in it being his only sister, Dorothy.   In a note written
in 1801, he says : " At the end of the garden of my
father's house at Cockermouth was a high terrace,
that commanded a fine view of the river Derwent
and Cockermouth Castle.   This was our favourite
playground. The terrace wall, a low one, was covered
with closely-clipt privet and roses, which gave an
almost impervious shelter to birds who built their
nests there.   The following stanzas allude to one
of those nests.

Behold, within the leafy shade,
These bright blue eggs together laid !
On me the chance-discovered sight
Gleamed like a vision of delight.
I started—seeming to espy
The home and sheltered bed,
The Sparrow's dwelling, which, hard by
My Father's house, in wet or dry
My sister Emmeline and I
      Together visited.

> She looked at it, and seemed to fear it:
> Dreading, tho' wishing to be near it:
> Such heart was in her, being then
> A little Prattler among men.
> The Blessing of my later years
> Was with me when a boy:
> She gave me eyes, she gave me ears;
> And humble cares, and delicate fears:
> A heart, the fountain of sweet tears;
>   And love, and thought, and joy.

Though written in the Dove Cottage orchard, Grasmere, the poem, *To a Butterfly*, refers to the days of Wordsworth's childhood at Cockermouth, before 1778.

> Stay near me: do not take thy flight!
> A little longer stay in sight!
> Much converse do I find in thee,
> Historian of my infancy!
> Float near me: do not yet depart.
> Dead times revive in thee:
> Thou bring'st, gay creature as thou art!
> A solemn image to my heart,
>   My father's family!
>
> Oh! pleasant, pleasant were the days,
> The time, when, in our childish plays,
> My sister Emmeline and I
> Together chased the butterfly!
> A very hunter did I rush
> Upon the prey: with leaps and springs
> I followed on from brake to bush;
> But she, God love her! feared to brush
>   The dust from off its wings.

Of this poem Dorothy Wordsworth wrote, March 14, 1802: "While we were at breakfast, W. wrote the poem, *To a Butterfly.* The thought came upon him as we were talking about the pleasure we both always felt at the sight of a butterfly. I told him that I used to chase them a little, but that I was afraid of brushing the dust off their wings, and did not catch them."

In the thirteenth book of *The Prelude* there is an allusion to an experience of childhood, which must refer to Cockermouth, and which I do not think any one has hitherto traced out :—

> Who doth not love to follow with his eye
> The windings of a public way? the sight,
> Familiar object as it is, hath wrought
> On my imagination since the morn
> Of childhood, when a disappearing line
> One daily present to my eyes, that crossed
> The naked summit of a far-off hill
> Beyond the limits that my feet had trod,
> Was like an invitation into space
> Boundless, or guide into eternity.[1]

For a hint in reference to this road, I have been indebted to Dr. Henry Dodgson of Cockermouth. Referring to a suggestion that it might be the road leading to Bridekirk, Dr. Dodgson writes (July 1878) : "I scarcely think that the road answers to the description. The hill over which it goes is not naked, but well wooded, and has probably been so for many years. Besides, it is not visible from Wordsworth's house, nor from the garden behind it. This garden extends from the house to the river Derwent, from which it is separated by a wall, with a raised terraced walk on the inner side, and nearly on a level with the top. I understand that this terrace was in existence in the poet's

---

[1] *The Prelude*, book xiii. p. 341.

time. . . . Its direction is nearly due east and
west; and looking eastwards from it, there is a
hill which bounds the view in that direction, and
which fully corresponds to the description in *The
Prelude.* It is from one and a half to two miles
distant, is of considerable height: is bare and
destitute of trees: and has a road directly over its
summit, as seen from the terrace in Wordsworth's
garden. The road is now used only as a footpath;
but fifty or sixty years ago it was the highroad to
Isel, a hamlet on the Derwent, about three and a
half miles from Cockermouth, in the direction of
Bassenthwaite Lake. The hill is locally called
'The Hay;' but on the Ordnance map it is marked
'Watch Hill.'"

There can be no doubt, I think, as to the
accuracy of this suggestion. No other hill-road is
visible from the house or garden at Cockermouth.
The view from the front of the old mansion is
limited by houses, doubtless more so now than in
last century; but there is no hill towards the
Lorton Fells on the south or south-east with a road
over it, visible from any part of the town. Besides,
this must have been a very early experience of
Wordsworth's childhood (he had not as yet walked
two miles), and the road was one "*daily* present to
his eyes." It must, therefore, have been seen
either from the house or the garden. It is almost
certain that he is referring to that path over the
Hay, or Watch Hill, which he and his "sister
Emmeline" could see daily, from the terrace at the
foot of their garden.

CHAPTER II.

HAWKSHEAD, WINDERMERE, CONISTON, ETC.

PASSING to Hawkshead, where Wordsworth was sent to school in his ninth year, we find much more than at Cockermouth that speaks to us of the poet, and is immortalised by his description or allusion. The old market town of Hawkshead, where he spent more than eight years (1778 to 1786), is one of the quaintest in the Lake District. The irregular outline of the narrow winding streets; the pavement of single slates covering "the famous brook," which gives the name of Flag Street to one of them; the low archways; the picturesque frontages of the houses, with their many-paned windows and primitive chimneys; the open court in the centre of the town; the Church upon the hill, with its winding approach; and the ancient Grammar-School below it, for three centuries a famed academy;—all these things give a visitor to Hawkshead a succession of quaint surprises. It is in *The Prelude* that Wordsworth has written most about his school life and summer vacations at Hawkshead, and of that wonderful spring-time which he there enjoyed.

> The snow-white church upon the hill
> Sits like a thronèd lady, sending out
> A gracious look all over her domain.[1]

[1] *The Prelude*, book iv. p. 86.

7

This old Norman Church, built in 1160—the same year as that in which Furness Abbey was erected—is no longer snow-white, a "restoration" having taken place within recent years, on architectural principles ! The plaster is stripped from the outside of the Church, which is now of a dull stone colour. Archbishop Sandys private chapel is, perhaps, its most interesting feature to the visitor. "Apart from poetic sentiment," says Dr. Cradock, "it may be doubted whether the pale colour still preserved at Grasmere and other churches in the district does not better harmonise with the scenery and atmosphere of the Lake country." The Church, however, is still a conspicuous object as you approach Hawkshead by the Ambleside Road or from Sawrey. It is the latter approach that Wordsworth describes, in his account of his return to Hawkshead from Cambridge during a summer vacation.

The school in which the poet was taught (founded by Archbishop Sandys in 1585) is still very much as it was in Wordsworth's time. The main schoolroom is on the ground floor. One small chamber on the first floor was used in his day by the head master for teaching a few advanced pupils. In another room is a library, formed in part by the donations of the scholars ; it being the custom for each pupil to present a volume on leaving school, or to send one afterwards. On the wall of this room is a tablet recording the names of several masters ; and there, in an old oak chest, is kept the original charter of the school. In the oak benches downstairs the names and initials of some of the boys are deeply cut ; and amongst them "W. Wordsworth" may be seen.

Within recent years some ornamental scrolls have been put up on the walls of the schoolroom. The idea was Mr. Rawnsley's, and they were designed by Mrs. Rawnsley. The suggestion of the particular mottoes came from several sources. There are four of them, and they are as follows :—

"Small service is true service while it lasts."

"The child is father to the man,
And I could wish my days to be
Bound each to each by natural piety."

"Books, we know,
Are a substantial world, both pure and good,
Round these, with tendrils strong as flesh and blood,
Our pastime and our happiness will grow."

"We live by admiration, hope, and love."

Towards the close of last century, when Wordsworth and his three brothers were educated at this school, it was one of the best educational institutions in the north of England. The pupils boarded in the houses of the village dames.

Ye lowly cottages, wherein we dwelt,
A ministration of your own was yours ;
Can I forget you, being as you were
So beautiful among the pleasant fields
In which ye stood? or can I here forget
The plain and seemly countenance with which
Ye dealt out your plain comforts? Yet had ye
Delights and exultations of your own.[1]

Wordsworth lived with one Anne Tyson, for whose memory he cherished the warmest regard. Her cottage, the young poet's residence for nine eventful years, remains unaltered externally; and little, if at all, changed in the interior. It is well known, and easily found. It now belongs to Mr. Thomas Atkinson, Hawkshead Hill. It is reached through a picturesque archway, nearly opposite the principal

[1] *The Prelude*, book i. p. 23.

village inn (the Lion), and stands on the right of a
small open yard which you enter through this archway ; while to the left a lane leads westwards to the
open country. It is a humble dwelling of two stories;
the floor of the basement flat, paved with the blue
flags of Coniston slate, is not likely to have been
changed since Wordsworth's time. On the upper
flat there are two bedrooms to the front, with oaken
flooring, one of which must have been occupied
by Wordsworth, as he could not otherwise have
written of

> That lowly bed whence I had heard the wind
> Roar, and the rain beat hard ; where I so oft
> Had lain awake on summer nights to watch
> The moon in splendour couched among the leaves
> Of a tall ash, that near our cottage stood ;
> Had watched her with fixed eyes while to and fro
> In the dark summit of the waving tree
> She rocked with every impulse of the breeze.[1]

The ash-tree is gone, but there is no doubt as
to the place where it grew. Mr. Watson, whose
father owned and inhabited the house immediately
opposite Mrs. Tyson's cottage in Wordsworth's
time, and who was himself born in it, tells me that
the ash-tree grew on the proper right front of the
cottage, where an outhouse is now built. If this be
so, Wordsworth's room must have been that on the
proper left, with the smaller of the two windows.
The cottage faces nearly south-west. Referring to
the "old dame so kind and motherly," and her
humble dwelling, with its garden, etc., Wordsworth
writes :—

> The thoughts of gratitude shall fall like dew
> Upon thy grave, good creature ! While my heart

---

[1] *The Prelude*, book iv. p. 88.

Can beat never will I forget thy name.
Heaven's blessing be upon thee where thou liest
After thy innocent and busy stir
In narrow cares, thy little daily growth
Of calm enjoyments, after eighty years,
And more than eighty, of untroubled life,[1]
Childless, yet by the strangers to thy blood
Honoured with little less than filial love.
What joy was mine to see thee once again,
Thee and thy dwelling, and a crowd of things
About its narrow precincts all beloved,
And many of them seeming yet my own !
Why should I speak of what a thousand hearts
Have felt, and every man alive can guess?
The rooms, the court, the garden were not left
Long unsaluted, nor the sunny seat
Round the stone table under the dark pine,
Friendly to studious or to festive hours;
Nor that unruly child of mountain birth,
The famous brook, who, soon as he was boxed
Within our garden, found himself at once,
As if by trick insidious and unkind,
Stripped of his voice and left to dimple down
(Without an effort and without a will)
A channel paved by man's officious care.[2]

There can be little doubt as to the identity of
"the famous brook" within our garden.   "Persons
have visited the cottage," says Dr. Cradock, "without discovering it; and yet it is not forty yards
distant, and is still exactly as described.   On the
opposite side of the lane already referred to, a few
steps above the cottage, is a narrow passage through

---

[1] "Anne Tyson of Colthouse, widow, died May 25th,
1796; buried 28th, in churchyard; aged 83," is the
entry in the Hawkshead parish register.

[2] *The Prelude*, book iv. p. 87.

some new stone buildings. On emerging from this you meet a small garden, the farther side of which is bounded by the brook, confined on both sides by large flags, and also covered by flags of the same Coniston formation, through the interstices of which you may see and hear the stream running freely.[1] The upper flags are now used as a footpath, and lead by another passage back into the village. No doubt the garden has been reduced in size, by the use of that part of it fronting the lane for building purposes. The stream, before it enters the area of buildings and gardens, is open by the lane side, and seemingly comes from the hills to the westwards. The large flags are extremely hard and durable, and it is probable that the very flags which paved the channel in Wordsworth's time may be still doing the same duty."

The only difficulty in this identification of the garden is that the adjoining house, to which it would naturally be attached, was not Dame Tyson's but Mr. Watson's; and, unless it was let to Mrs. Tyson, or unless Wordsworth was inaccurate in this detail, he may possibly be describing another part of the brook farther up the stream. A good way above the village, at a place called Walker Ground, the same brook is certainly "boxed within a garden;" and there it is literally "stript of its voice" for a considerable distance. The present house at Walker Ground is comparatively recent; but in two adjoining cottages boys attending the Grammar-School were boarded in the beginning of the century, just as at Mrs. Tyson's. Wordsworth *may* be describing a garden at Walker Ground; but, on the whole, I think it was the garden in the village. In reference to the cottage he lived in, he says there was "a crowd of things about its

[1] Therefore, not quite "stripped of its voice."

narrow precincts all beloved." The garden was, I think, close at hand.

There is neither trace nor tradition, however, of the "dark pine" with the "stone table" under it. They have disappeared as completely as the

> rude mass
> Of native rock left midway in the square
> Of our small market village,[1]

which was

> the goal,
> Or centre of our sports.[2]

In the fifth book of *The Prelude* Wordsworth tells us—

> Well do I call to mind the very week
> When I was first entrusted to the care
> Of that sweet Valley; when its paths, its streams,
> And brooks were like a dream of novelty
> To my half-infant thoughts.[3]

It is thus that he describes the "fair seed-time" of his soul:—

> Fair seed-time had my soul, and I grew up
> Fostered alike by beauty and by fear :
> Much favoured in my birthplace, and no less
> In that beloved Vale to which ere long
> We were transplanted—there were we let loose
> For sports of wider range.   Ere I had told
> Ten birthdays, when among the mountain slopes
> Frost, and the breath of frosty wind, had snapped
> The last autumnal crocus, 'twas my joy
> With store of springes o'er my shoulder hung

---

[1] *The Prelude*, book ii. p. 34.   [2] *Ibid.*

[3] *Ibid.* book v. p. 124.

To range the open heights where woodcocks run
Along the smooth green turf. Through half the
    night,
Scudding away from snare to snare, I plied
That anxious visitation; moon and stars
Were shining o'er my head. I was alone,
And seemed to be a trouble to the peace
That dwelt among them. Sometimes it befel
In these night wanderings, that a strong desire
O'erpowered my better reason, and the bird
Which was the captive of another's toil
Became my prey; and when the deed was done
I heard among the solitary hills
Low breathings coming after me, and sounds
Of undistinguishable motion, steps
Almost as silent as the turf they trod.
    Nor less when spring had warmed the cultured
        Vale,
Moved we as plunderers where the mother-bird
Had in high places built her lodge; though mean
Our object and inglorious, yet the end
Was not ignoble. Oh! when I have hung
Above the raven's nest, by knots of grass
And half-inch fissures in the slippery rock
But ill sustained, and almost (so it seemed)
Suspended by the blast that blew amain,
Shouldering the naked crag, oh, at that time
While on the perilous ridge I hung alone,
With what strange utterance did the loud dry wind
Blow through my ear! the sky seemed not a sky
Of earth—and with what motion moved the
    clouds![1]

The concluding lines of this passage, in which he
describes the effect of Nature over him, when, with
his school companions, he harried the ravens' nests,
might be thought to refer to the same vale—that of

[1] *The Prelude*, book ii. p. 15.

Esthwaite—to which the earlier part of the extract alludes.   But the scene of these exploits cannot have been that "cultured vale."   No ravens build there, or could build in Wordsworth's time ; and there are no "naked crags" with "half-inch fissures in the slippery rock" in Esthwaite.   The locality must have been the Holme Fells, above Yewdale, to the north of Coniston, and only a few miles from Hawkshead, where a *Raven's Crag* now divides Tiberthwaite from Yewdale.   In confirmation of this, in his *Epistle to Sir George Beaumont*, Wordsworth speaks of Yewdale as a plain

> spread
> Under a rock, too steep for man to tread,
> Where, sheltered from the north, and black north
>   west,
> Aloft the raven hangs a visible nest,
> Fearless of all assaults that would her brood molest.

It was in these days, and in holiday rambles to more distant valleys and mountain ranges (quite as much as at a later stage when he visited the Wye), that

> the tall rock,
> The mountain, and the deep and gloomy wood,
> Their colour and their forms, were then to him
> An appetite : a feeling, and a love,
> That had no need of a remoter charm,
> By thought supplied, nor any interest
> Unborrowed from the eye.

Almost the precise spot of another of his youthful experiences at Hawkhead, recorded in *The Prelude*, can easily be identified.   He tells us how one summer evening he

> found
> A little boat tied to a willow tree
> Within a rocky cove, its usual home.

Straight I unloosed her chain, and stepping in
Pushed from the shore.   It was an act of stealth
And troubled pleasure, nor without the voice
Of mountain-echoes did my boat move on;
Leaving behind her still, on either side,
Small circles glittering idly in the moon,
Until they melted all into one track
Of sparkling light.   But now, like one who rows,
Proud of his skill, to reach a chosen point
With an unswerving line, I fixed my view
Upon the summit of a craggy ridge,
The horizon's utmost boundary; far above
Was nothing but the stars and the grey sky.
She was an elfin pinnace; lustily
I dipped my oars into the silent lake,
And, as I rose upon the stroke, my boat
Went heaving through the water like a swan;
When, from behind that craggy steep till then
The horizon's bound, a huge peak, black and huge,
As if with voluntary power instinct
Upreared its head.   I struck and struck again,
And growing still in stature the grim shape
Towered up between me and the stars, and still,
For so it seemed, with purpose of its own
And measured motion like a living thing,
Strode after me.   With trembling oars I turned,
And through the silent water stole my way
Back to the covert of the willow tree;
There in her mooring-place I left my bark,—
And through the meadows homeward went, in grave
And serious mood; but after I had seen
That spectacle, for many days, my brain
Worked with a dim and undetermined sense
Of unknown modes of being; o'er my thoughts
There hung a darkness, call it solitude
Or blank desertion.   No familiar shapes
Remained, no pleasant images of trees,
Of sea or sky, no colours of green fields;

But huge and mighty forms, that do not live
Like living men, moved slowly through the mind
By day, and were a trouble to my dreams.[1]

Any one rowing across Esthwaite Lake, or walking along the eastern shore, can see the very spot
to which this refers. The "craggy steep, till then the
horizon's bound," is the ridge of Ironkeld ; while
the "huge peak, black and huge, as if with
voluntary power instinct" (which every one who
understands Wordsworth recognises as he would a
living thing), is the summit of Wetherlam.

A still more characteristic passage from *The
Prelude* may be here given in full, as it describes,
in immortal verse, the influence of Nature over the
poet, subduing, moulding, and educating him—in
these early days. It is his own record of the

> first virgin passion of the soul
> Communing with this glorious universe.

It has been often quoted, and is well known; but it
is unrivalled in the picture it gives of the idealism
that springs out of real fellowship with Nature.
The "silent bays" into which he retired from the
tumultuous throng of his school companions to
"cut across the reflex of a star" while skating on
Esthwaite water may be easily guessed. There are
comparatively few of them in this lake.

> Wisdom and Spirit of the universe !
> Thou Soul that art the eternity of thought,
> That givest to forms and images a breath
> And everlasting motion, not in vain
> By day or star light thus from my first dawn

[1] *The Prelude*, book i. p. 18.

Of childhood didst thou intertwine for me
The passions that build up our human soul;
Not with the mean and vulgar works of man,
But with high objects, with enduring things—
With life and nature—purifying thus
The elements of feeling and of thought,
And sanctifying, by such discipline,
Both pain and fear, until we recognise
A grandeur in the beatings of the heart.
Nor was this fellowship vouchsafed to me
With stinted kindness.   In November days,
When vapours rolling down the valley made
A lonely scene more lonesome, among woods,
At noon and 'mid the calm of summer nights,
When, by the margin of the trembling lake,
Beneath the gloomy hills homeward I went
In solitude, such intercourse was mine ;
Mine was it in the fields both day and night,
And by the waters, all the summer long.

    And in the frosty season, when the sun
Was set, and visible for many a mile
The cottage windows blazed through twilight gloom,
I heeded not their summons : happy time
It was indeed for all of us—for me
It was a time of rapture !   Clear and loud
The village clock tolled six,—I wheeled about,
Proud and exulting like an untired horse
That cares not for his home.   All shod with steel,
We hissed along the polished ice in games
Confederate, imitative of the chase
And woodland pleasures,—the resounding horn,
The pack loud chiming, and the hunted hare.
So through the darkness and the cold we flew,
And not a voice was idle ; with the din
Smitten, the precipices rang aloud ;
The leafless trees and every icy crag
Tinkled like iron ; while far distant hills

Into the tumult sent an alien sound
Of melancholy not unnoticed, while the stars
Eastward were sparkling clear, and in the west
The orange sky of evening died away.
Not seldom from the uproar I retired
Into a silent bay, or sportively
Glanced sideway, leaving the tumultuous throng,
To cut across the reflex of a star
That fled, and, flying still before me, gleamed
Upon the glassy plain; and oftentimes,
When we had given our bodies to the wind,
And all the shadowy banks on either side
Came sweeping through the darkness, spinning
    still
The rapid line of motion, then at once
Have I, reclining back upon my heels,
Stopped short; yet still the solitary cliffs
Wheeled by me—even as if the earth had rolled
With visible motion her diurnal round!
Behind me did they stretch in solemn train,
Feebler and feebler, and I stood and watched
Till all was tranquil as a dreamless sleep.[1]

Probably this skating scene on Esthwaite is the one most vividly associated, by the majority of the readers of *The Prelude*, with the youth of the poet; but who, except Wordsworth, would have noticed "the alien sound of melancholy" sent into the tumult from "far distant hills?" Who but he would have observed (as in the former part of the above extract), that "vapours rolling down a valley" made "a lonely scene more lonesome?"

Every one who has been taught by him must feel a special interest in the surroundings of the Hawkshead district, and the vale of Esthwaite, where he tells us that, in his tenth year, he

---

[1] *The Prelude*, book i. p. 19.

Held unconscious intercourse with beauty
Old as creation,

and where he saw

Gleams, like the flashings of a shield, the earth
And common face of Nature spake to him
Rememberable things.

In reference to these days, and haunts, he thus
addresses the Soul of Nature :—

O Soul of Nature ! excellent and fair !
That didst rejoice with me, with whom I, too,
Rejoiced through early youth, before the winds
And roaring waters, and in lights and shades
That marched and countermarched about the hills
In glorious apparition, Powers on whom
I daily waited, now all eye and now
All ear; but never long without the heart
Employed, and man's unfolding intellect : [1]

To many it is a better education to endeavour

to retrace
The simple ways in which his childhood walked,
Those chiefly that first led him to the love
Of rivers, woods, and fields, [2]

and to find out the force of the following lines as
they bear upon the poet's childhood, than to recall
and meditate upon similar experiences of their
own :—

These recollected hours that have the charm
Of visionary things, these lovely forms

[1] *The Prelude*, book xii. p. 321.   [2] *Ibid.* book ii. p. 33.

And sweet sensations that throw back our life,
And almost make remotest infancy
A visible scene, on which the sun is shining.[1]

The islands in Windermere, which were visited
on summer half-holidays, are easily identified. The
two last referred to in the following extract are
certainly the Lily of the Valley Island and Lady
Holme respectively.   The first may have been
House Holme or Thomson's Holme.   It is less
likely to have been Belle Isle, from the greater
size of the latter, and from its hardly being a "sister
isle" to the one where the lily of the valley still
grows "beneath the oaks' umbrageous covert."
The "ruins of the shrine" have now disappeared
as completely from Lady Holme in Windermere as
from St. Herbert's Island in Derwentwater.

> When summer came,
> Our pastime was, on bright half-holidays,
> To sweep along the plain of Windermere
> With rival oars; and the selected bourne
> Was now an Island musical with birds
> That sang and ceased not; now a Sister Isle
> Beneath the oaks' umbrageous covert, sown
> With lilies of the valley like a field;
> And now a third small Island, where survived
> In solitude the ruins of a shrine
> Once to Our Lady dedicate, and served
> Daily with chaunted rites.[2]

The description of the inn,

> Midway on long Winander's eastern shore,
> Within the crescent of a pleasant bay,[3]

[1] *The Prelude*, book i. p. 29.   [2] *Ibid.* book ii. p. 35.
[3] *Ibid.* book ii. p. 39.

calls for no special remark; but one of the incidents
in the return home of the youthful party, with its
allusion to Robert Greenwood, the "minstrel of
the troop," afterwards Senior Fellow of Trinity,
Cambridge, is too characteristic to be passed over.

> But, ere nightfall,
> When in our pinnace we returned at leisure
> Over the shadowy lake, and to the beach
> Of some small island steered our course with one,
> The Minstrel of the Troop, and left him there,
> And rowed off gently, while he blew his flute
> Alone upon the rock—oh, then, the calm
> And dead still water lay upon my mind
> Even with a weight of pleasure, and the sky,
> Never before so beautiful, sank down
> Into my heart, and held me like a dream!
> Thus were my sympathies enlarged, and thus
> Daily the common range of visible things
> Grew dear to me: already I began
> To love the sun; a boy I loved the sun,
> Not as I since have loved him, as a pledge
> And surety of our earthly life, a light
> Which we behold and feel we are alive;
> Nor for his bounty to so many worlds—
> But for this cause, that I had seen him lay
> His beauty on the morning hills, had seen
> The western mountain touch his setting orb,
> In many a thoughtless hour, when, from excess
> Of happiness, my blood appeared to flow
> For its own pleasure, and I breathed with joy.[1]

For his teacher in the Hawkshead school, the
Reverend William Taylor, Wordsworth cherished
the warmest affection. It was the farewell which
this master took of his pupils on his deathbed (of

---

[1] *The Prelude*, p. 40.

whom the poet was one) that suggested the lines
addressed to the scholars of Hawkshead, which
are inseparably associated with that village school.
The following lines occur in the poem.

> Here did he sit confined for hours;
> But he could see the woods and plains,
> Could hear the wind and mark the showers
> Come streaming down the streaming panes.
> Now stretched beneath his grass-green mound
> He rests a prisoner of the ground.
> He loved the breathing air,
> He loved the sun, but if it rise
> Or set, to him where now he lies,
> Brings not a moment's care.

The three poems, respectively entitled, *Matthew*,
The Two April Mornings, and *The Fountain*,
are full of allusions to Hawkshead, and his
teachers; though Wordsworth tells us that the
"schoolmaster was made up of several, like the
wanderer in *The Excursion*" (I. F. MS.) I have
found no tradition of a "Leonard's Rock."

There are many streams in the neighbourhood to
which the following stanza may refer—which is
finer than the refrain of Tennyson's *Brook*—

> Men may come, and men may go,
> But I go on for ever.

The particular stream has not been identified.
It is most likely, however, that it is the "famous
brook" of *The Prelude* at a point higher up
amongst the fells.

> No check, no stay, this streamlet fears;
> How merrily it goes !
> 'Twill murmur on a thousand years,
> And flow as now it flows.

The following sonnet, composed in 1806, is a reminiscence of the Vale of Hawkshead, and its brooks :—

"Beloved Vale !" I said, "When I shall con
Those many records of my childish years,
Remembrance of myself and of my peers
Will press me down : to think of what is gone
Will be an awful thought, if life have one."
But, when into the Vale I came, no fears
Distressed me; from mine eyes escaped no tears;
Deep thought, or dread remembrance, had I none.
By doubts and thousand petty fancies crost
I stood, of simple shame the blushing Thrall;
So narrow seemed the brooks, the fields so small!
A Juggler's balls old Time about him tossed;
I looked, I stared, I smiled, I laughed; and all
The weight of sadness was in wonder lost.

Those who have tried to realise Wordsworth's life at Hawkshead will remember that his

                         morning walks
   Were early.   Oft before the hour of school
   I travelled round our little lake, five miles
   Of pleasant wandering.[1]

He also tells us—

                    I would walk alone,
Under the quiet stars, and at that time,
Have felt whate'er there is of power in sound
To breathe an elevated mood, by form
Or image unprofaned; and I would stand,
If the night blackened with a coming storm,
Beneath some rock, listening to notes that are
The ghostly language of the ancient earth,
Or make their dim abode in distant winds.
Thence did I drink the visionary power;[2]

   .   .   .   .   .   .

[1] *The Prelude*, book v. p. 46.   [2] *Ibid.* book ii. p. 45.

Nor seldom did I lift our cottage latch
Far earlier, ere one smoke-wreath had risen
From human dwelling, or the vernal thrush
Was audible; and sate among the woods
Alone upon some jutting eminence,
At the first gleam of dawn-light, when the Vale,
Yet slumbering, lay in utter solitude.
How shall I seek the origin ! where find
Faith in the marvellous things which then I felt?
Oft in these moments such a holy calm
Would overspread my soul, that bodily eyes
Were utterly forgotten, and what I saw
Appeared like something in myself, a dream,
A prospect in the mind.[1]

A passage follows this in *The Prelude* which
refers to the way in which, even in his seventeenth
year, he received the influences of Nature, and
dealt with them.   It gives us a key to all that is
most distinctive in Wordsworth's poetry, and is so
superior to the vagueness of Goethe's sentence
about the Poet, and

The stream of song that out of his bosom springs,
And to his heart the world back coiling brings,

that I may quote it also.
                        An auxiliar light
Came from my mind, which on the setting sun
Bestowed new splendour ; the melodious birds,
The fluttering breezes, fountains that run on
Murmuring so sweetly in themselves, obeyed
A like dominion, and the midnight storm
Grew darker in the presence of my eye :[2]

.   .   .   .   .

From Nature and her overflowing soul,
I had received so much, that all my thoughts

---

[1] *The Prelude*, book ii. p. 47.   [2] *Ibid.* book ii. p. 48.

Were steeped in feeling ; I was only then
Contented, when with bliss ineffable
I felt the sentiment of Being spread
O'er all that moves and all that seemeth still
O'er all that, lost beyond the reach of thought ;
And human knowledge, to the human eye
Invisible, yet liveth to the heart ;
O'er all that leaps and runs, and shouts and
        sings,
Or beats the gladsome air ; o'er all that glides
Beneath the wave, yea, in the wave itself,
And mighty depth of waters.   Wonder not
If high the transport, great the joy I felt,
Communing in this sort through earth and
        heaven
With every form of creature, as it looked
Towards the Uncreated with a countenance
Of adoration, with an eye of love.
One song they sang, and it was audible,
Most audible, then, when the fleshly ear,
O'ercome by humblest prelude of that strain,
Forgot her functions, and slept undisturbed.[1]

We do not know the precise situation of the
house in the vale of Esthwaite, or of Yewdale,
where, during a summer vacation,

                              'mid a throng
Of maids and youths, old men and matrons staid,
A medley of all tempers, he had passed
A night in dancing, gaiety, and mirth.

There is more than one such mountain farm in
the district.   It cannot have been far from Hawkshead, and must have been somewhere between it
and Coniston.   He may have looked down either

[1] *The Prelude*, book ii. p. 49.

into Yewdale to the right, or Esthwaite to the south, or across to Latterbarrow to the left. His unequalled description of his return homeward at early morning, and the effect produced upon him by the calm and the splendour of the dawn, must be quoted.

>   Magnificent
> The morning rose, in memorable pomp,
> Glorious as ere I had beheld—in front,
> The sea lay laughing at a distance; near,
> The solid mountains shone, bright as the clouds,
> Grain-tinctured, drenched in empyrean light;
> And in the meadows and the lower grounds
> Was all the sweetness of a common dawn—
> Dews, vapours, and the melody of birds,
> And labourers going forth to till the fields.
> Ah! need I say, dear Friend! that to the brim
> My heart was full; I made no vows, but vows
> Were then made for me; bond unknown to me
> Was given, that I should be, else sinning greatly,
> A dedicated Spirit.   On I walked
> In thankful blessedness, which yet survives.[1]

The "labourers" in the fields were probably in the arable valley of Esthwaite to the left, and the "solid mountains" were probably Coniston, Old Man, and Wetherlam to the right; the sea "laughing at a distance" being seen across Duddon sands.

Dr. Cradock suggested the following as to that morning walk: "All that can be safely said as to the course of that memorable morning walk is this, that in the neighbourhood a view of the sea can only be obtained at a considerable elevation; also that if the words, 'in front the sea lay laughing,' are to be taken as rigidly exact, the poet's progress

---

[1] *The Prelude*, book iv. p. 98.

towards Hawkshead must have been in a direction mainly southwardly, and therefore from the country north of that place; these, and all other conditions of the description, are answered in several parts of the range of hills lying between Esthwaite and Hawkshead."

In the fourth book of *The Prelude* he describes the road from Windermere to Hawkshead, past Sawrey, by which he returned from a regatta on Windermere; and the place on that road where he met the old dismissed soldier travelling homewards, may be easily guessed.

> .   .   .   a long ascent,
> Where the road's watery surface, to the top
> Of that sharp rising, glittered to the moon,
> And bore the semblance of another stream,
> Stealing with silent lapse to join the brook
> That murmured in the vale.[1]

There is no difficulty in identifying this spot. The brook is Sawrey beck; and the "long ascent" is the second of the two, in crossing from Windermere to Hawkshead, which goes over the ridge between the two Sawreys. It is only there that a brook could be heard "murmuring in the vale."

Another poem, composed in part while at school at Hawkshead, is entitled, cumbrously enough, *Lines left upon a seat on a Yew-tree, which stands near the Lake of Esthwaite, on a desolate part of the shore, commanding a beautiful prospect.* In 1843 Wordsworth said: "The tree has disappeared, and the slip of common on which it stood, that ran parallel to the lake and lay open to it, has long been enclosed, so that the road has lost much of its attraction. This spot was my favourite walk in the

---

[1] *The Prelude*, book ii. p. 100.

evenings during the latter part of my school-time."
The exact place where the yew-tree stood may
be found without difficulty.   It was about three-
quarters of a mile from Hawkshead, on the eastern
shore of the lake as you go towards Sawrey, a
little above the highway.   Mr. Bowman, the son of
Wordsworth's last teacher at the grammar school,
tells me that it stood about forty yards nearer
Hawkshead than the yew which now stands on the
roadside and is sometimes called " Wordsworth's
yew."   In his school-days the road passed right
through the unenclosed common, and the tree was
a conspicuous object.   It was removed, he says,
owing to the popular belief that its leaves were
poisonous, and might injure the cattle grazing in
the common.   I heard some persons in Hawkshead
call the present tree Wordsworth's yew; and doubtless its proximity to the place where the tree of
the poem grew has given rise to the tradition.

Nay, Traveller! rest. This lonely Yew-tree stands
Far from all human dwelling: what if here
No sparkling rivulet spread the verdant herb?
What if the bee love not these barren boughs,
Yet, if the wind breathe soft, the curling waves,
That break against the shore, shall lull thy mind
By one soft impulse saved from vacancy.
.   .   .   .   .   Who he was
That piled these stones and with the mossy sod
First covered, and here taught this aged Tree
With its dark arms to form a circling bower,
I well remember.—He was one who owned
No common soul.   In youth by science nursed,
And led by nature into a wild scene
Of lofty hopes, he to the world went forth
A favoured Being, knowing no desire
Which genius did not hallow; 'gainst the taint
Of dissolute tongues, and jealousy, and hate,

And scorn,—against all enemies prepared,
All but neglect. The world, for so it thought
Owed him no service ; wherefore he at once
With indignation turned himself away,
And with the food of pride sustained his soul
In solitude.—Stranger! these gloomy boughs
Had charms for him; and here he loved to sit,
His only visitants a straggling sheep
The stone-chat, or the glancing sand-piper:
And on these barren rocks, with fern and heath,
And juniper and thistle, sprinkled o'er,
Fixing his downcast eye, he many an hour
A morbid pleasure nourished, tracing here
An emblem of his own unfruitful life:
And, lifting up his head, he then would gaze
On the more distant scene,—how lovely 'tis
Thou seest,—and he would gaze till it became
Far lovelier, and his heart could not sustain
The beauty, still more beauteous! Nor, that time,
When Nature had subdued him to herself,
Would he forget those Beings to whose minds,
Warm from the labours of benevolence
The world, and human life, appeared a scene
Of kindred loveliness: then he would sigh,
Inly disturbed, to think that others felt
What he must never feel; and so, lost Man!
On visionary views would fancy feed,
Till his eye streamed with tears. In this deep vale
He died,—this seat his only monument.

    If Thou be one whose heart the holy forms
Of young imagination have kept pure,
Stranger! henceforth be warned; and know that
        pride,
Howe'er disguised in its own majesty,
Is littleness; that he who feels contempt
For any living thing, hath faculties
Which he has never used; that thought with him

Is in its infancy.   The man whose eye
Is ever on himself doth look on one,
The least of Nature's works, one who might move
The wise man to that scorn which wisdom holds
Unlawful ever.   O be wiser, Thou !
Instructed that true knowledge leads to love ;
True dignity abides with him alone
Who, in the silent hour of inward thought,
Can still suspect, and still revere himself,
In lowliness of heart.

The following sonnet, which refers to his return
to Hawkshead, and to the scenes of his youth, years
afterwards, is very characteristic :—

" Beloved Vale ! " I said, " When I shall con
Those many records of my childish years,
Remembrance of myself and of my peers
Will press me down : to think of what is gone
Will be an awful thought, if life have one."
But, when into the Vale I came, no fears
Distressed me ; from mine eyes escaped no tears ;
Deep thought, or dread remembrance, had I none.
By doubts and thousand petty fancies crost
I stood, of simple shame the blushing Thrall :
So narrow seemed the brooks, the fields so small !
A Juggler's balls old Time about him tossed ;
I looked, I stared, I smiled, I laughed ; and all
The weight of sadness was in wonder lost.

Perhaps, however, the most remarkable reference
to Hawkshead in *The Prelude* has yet to be
quoted.   It occurs in the twelfth book, and its
significance is enhanced by these prefatory
words :—

There are in our existence spots of time,
That with distinct pre-eminence retain

A renovating virtue, whence, depressed
.   .   .   .   . our minds
Are nourished and invisibly repaired;
A virtue, by which pleasure is enhanced,
That penetrates, enables us to mount,
When high, more high, and lifts us up when fallen.
.   .   .   .   . Such moments
Are scattered everywhere, taking their date
From our first childhood. [1]

He gives an illustration of this from a weird
experience on the hills near Cockermouth, where
he was riding with "an ancient servant of his
father's house," when a mere child, and "could
scarcely hold a bridle." He parted from his guide,
dismounted through fear, led his horse over "a
rough and stony moor," and came to a "bottom,"
where, "in former times, a murderer had been
hung in iron chains." The monumental letters or
his name were carved on the turf; and the boy fled,
and saw, as he re-ascended the bare common,

A naked pool that lay beneath the hills,
A beacon on the summit, and more near,
A girl who bore a pitcher on her head.

He says—

                    It was, in truth,
An ordinary sight; but I should need
Colours and words that are unknown to man,
To paint the visionary dreariness
Which, while I looked all round for my lost guide,
Invested moorland waste, and naked pool,
The beacon crowning the lone eminence,
The female and her garments vexed and tossed
By the strong wind. [2]

[1] *The Prelude*, book xii. p. 325.   [2] *Ibid.* p. 327.

The use he makes of this experience is most
characteristic, but the place, I fear, cannot be
identified.   It may have been amongst the Lorton
Fells, or the north-western slopes of Skiddaw.   He
then proceeds to give another of these memorials
of his youth, and one still more noteworthy :—

                                    One Christmas-time,
On the glad eve of its dear holidays,
Feverish, and tired, and restless, I went forth
Into the fields, impatient for the sight
Of those led palfreys that should bear us home ;
My brothers and myself.   There rose a crag,
That, from the meeting-point of two highways
Ascending, overlooked them both, far stretched ;
Thither, uncertain on which road to fix
My expectation, thither I repaired,
Scout-like, and gained the summit ; 'twas a day
Tempestuous, dark, and wild, and on the grass
I sate half-sheltered by a naked wall ;
Upon my right hand couched a single sheep,
Upon my left a blasted hawthorn stood ;
With those companions at my side, I watched,
Straining my eyes intensely, as the mist
Gave intermitting prospect of the copse
And plain beneath.   Ere we to school returned,—
That dreary time,—ere we had been ten days
Sojourners in my father's house, he died,
And I and my three brothers, orphans then,
Followed his body to the grave.   The event,
With all the sorrow that it brought, appeared
A chastisement ; and when I called to mind
That day so lately past, when from the crag
I looked in such anxiety of hope ;
With trite reflections of morality,
Yet in the deepest passion, I bowed low
To God, who thus corrected my desires ;
And, afterwards, the wind and sleety rain,

E

And all the business of the elements,
The single sheep, and the one blasted tree,
And the bleak music from that old stone wall,
The noise of wood and water, and the mist
That on the line of each of those two roads
Advanced in such indisputable shapes;
All these were kindred spectacles and sounds
To which I oft repaired, and thence would drink,
As at a fountain; and on winter nights,
Down to this very time, when storm and rain
Beat on my roof, or, haply, at noon-day,
While in a grove I walk, whose lofty trees,
Laden with summer's thickest foliage, rock
In a strong wind, some working of the spirit,
Some inward agitations thence are brought,
Whate'er their office, whether to beguile
Thoughts over busy in the course they took,
Or animate an hour of vacant ease.[1]

The precise time of this second experience is easily ascertained from the date of his father's death; and though the locality is difficult to determine, it must, I think, be one of two places. His father died at Penrith, and it was there that the sons went for their Christmas holiday. The road from Penrith to Hawkshead was by Kirkstone Pass and Ambleside; and the "led palfreys" sent to carry the boys home would certainly come through the latter town. Now there are only two roads from Ambleside to Hawkshead, which meet at a point about a mile north of Hawkshead, called in the Ordnance map "Outgate." The eastern road is now chiefly used by carriages, being less hilly and better made than the western one, which passes the little public-house at the cross roads, and then joins the coach road between Ambleside and

---

[1] *The Prelude*, book xii. p. 329.

Coniston. The western road is not longer, and would be quite as convenient as the other for horses. Supposing one to walk out from Hawkshead, reach the point at which the roads separate at " Outgate," and then to ascend the ridge between them, he would come to several points from which he could overlook *both* roads "far stretched," if his view were not partly intercepted by numerous plantations. Dr. Cradock, to whom I am indebted for this suggestion, thinks that "a point marked in the map as ' High Crag,' between the two roads, and about three-quarters of a mile from their point of divergence, answers the description as well as any other. It may be nearly two miles from Hawkshead, a distance of which an eager, active schoolboy would think nothing. ' The blasted hawthorn,' and ' the naked wall,' are probably things of the past as much as the ' single sheep.' "

Undoubtedly this may be the spot ; a green, rocky knoll with a steep face to the north, where a quarry is wrought, and with a plantation to the east. It commands a view of both roads. The other possible place is a crag, not a quarter of a mile from Outgate, a little to the right of the place where the two roads divide. A low wall runs up across it to the top, dividing a plantation of oak, hazel, and ash from the firs that crown the summit. These firs, which are larch and spruce, seem all of this century. The summit may have been bare when Wordsworth lived at Hawkshead. But at the foot of the path, along the dividing wall, there are a few (possibly older) trees ; and a solitary walk beneath them at noon or dusk is almost as solemn and suggestive as repose under the yews of Borrowdale, listening to the "mountain flood" on Glaramara. The "loud dry wind" may still be heard whistling through the underwood, and moaning amongst the fir-trees ; and at the summit of the crag

there is a very old blackthorn tree.   But the same
may be said of High Crag, which certainly
commands a *further* view of the two roads, it
being more than half a mile nearer Ambleside.   I
entertain no doubt that the precise spot to which
the boy Wordsworth climbed on that eventful day,
which impressed itself so deeply upon the tablets
of his memory, was either one or other of these
two crags.

One reason of the difficulty we find in identifying places referred to in *The Prelude*, is due to
its having been a posthumous publication.   Had
Miss Fenwick been able to cross-question the poet
about it, as she did about the other poems, many
obscure allusions would have been cleared up, and
much invaluable commentary supplied.

In the fine fragment from the same poem, written
in Germany in 1797, and first published in the
Lyrical Ballads, 1800—though afterwards inserted
in *The Prelude*—we have another reference to the
Hawkshead district.

> There was a Boy: ye knew him well, ye cliffs
> And islands of Winander!—many a time
> At evening, when the earliest stars began
> To move along the edges of the hills,
> Rising or setting, would he stand alone
> Beneath the trees or by the glimmering lake,
> And there, with fingers interwoven, both hands
> Pressed closely palm to palm, and to his mouth
> Uplifted, he, as through an instrument,
> Blew mimic hootings to the silent owls,
> That they might answer him; and they would
>   shout
> Across the watery vale, and shout again,
> Responsive to his call, with quivering peals,
> And long halloos and screams, and echoes long
> Redoubled and redoubled, concourse wild

Of jocund din ; and, when a lengthened pause
Of silence came and baffled his best skill,
Then sometimes, in that silence while he hung
Listening, a gentle shock of mild surprise
Has carried far into his heart the voice
Of mountain torrents ; or the visible scene
Would enter unawares into his mind,
With all its solemn imagery, its rocks,
Its woods, and that uncertain heaven, received
Into the bosom of the steady lake.

This Boy was taken from his mates, and died
In childhood, ere he was full twelve years old.
Fair is the spot, most beautiful the vale
Where he was born ; the grassy churchyard hangs
Upon a slope above the village school,
And through that churchyard when my way has led
On summer evenings, I believe that there
A long half-hour together I have stood
Mute, looking at the grave in which he lies![1]

The only information we get as to this poem
in the I. F. MS. is the brief intimation, that of all
the poet's schoolfellows, one, William Raincock of
Rayrigg, took the lead in the art of making a
musical instrument of his own fingers ! but whether
he is the same immortal boy whom the cliffs and
islands of Windermere knew so well, and whether
it is he who is buried in Hawkshead churchyard,
"above the village school," on whose grave the
poet used to gaze so raptly, cannot even be
conjectured. No visitor, however, to that "grassy
churchyard" will fail to recall these lines about
"the gentle shock of mild surprise," in reference to
which Coleridge said, that had he met with them
while traversing the deserts of Arabia, he would
immediately have shouted out "Wordsworth."

[1] *The Prelude*, book v. p. 122.

The following seems at first sight to refer to the Hawkshead cottage; but I have been unable to identify the "smooth rock wet with constant springs"—

<blockquote>

               A diamond light
(Whene'er the summer sun, declining, smote
A smooth rock wet with constant springs) was seen
Sparkling from out a copse-clad bank that rose
Fronting our cottage.   Oft beside the hearth
Seated, with open door, often and long
Upon this restless lustre have I gazed,
That made my fancy restless as itself.
'Twas now for me a burnished silver shield
Suspended over a knight's tomb, who lay
Inglorious, buried in the dusky wood:
An entrance now into some magic cave
Or palace built by fairies of the rock;
Nor could I have been bribed to disenchant
The spectacle, by visiting the spot.
Thus wilful Fancy, in no hurtful mood,
Engrafted far-fetched shapes on feelings bred
By pure imagination; busy Power
She was, and with her ready pupil turned
Instinctively to human passions, then
Least understood.[1]

</blockquote>

Nothing corresponding to this can be seen from Anne Tyson's cottage. There is no "copse-clad bank" fronting it, and no "smooth rock wet with constant springs," where the "restless lustre" of the sunlight could give rise to fancies so subtle as those recorded in this passage. I am almost inclined to think that in this passage Wordsworth is referring to what he saw from his Grasmere cottage at sunset, long afterwards, on the slopes of Loughrigg or Silver How. In any case, the way in which the fancy of the boy poet dealt with this "restless lustre," will recall the way in which his

---

[1] *The Prelude*, book vii. p. 223.

maturer imagination worked amongst the yews of
Borrowdale.

There is a singularly interesting passage in the
same book of *The Prelude*, entitled "Retrospect,"
in which he quotes and recasts some lines he wrote
when a boy at Hawkshead. Every one who knows
anything of Wordsworth must remember the
*Conclusion of a Poem composed in anticipation of
leaving School*. It was written in his sixteenth year,
and the extract from it, with which every edition
of his poems after 1815 begins, is as follows :—

> Dear native regions, I foretell,
> From what I feel at this farewell,
> That, wheresoe'er my steps may tend,
> And whensoe'er my course shall end,
> If in that hour a single tie
> Survive of local sympathy,
> My soul will cast the backward view,
> The longing look alone on you.
>
> Thus, while the Sun sinks down to rest
> Far in the regions of the west,
> Though to the vale no parting beam
> Be given, not one memorial gleam,
> A lingering light he fondly throws
> On the dear hills where first he rose.

This was recast, in the blank verse of *The Prelude*, thus—

> A grove there is whose boughs
> Stretch from the western marge of Thurston-mere,
> With lengths of shade so thick that whoso glides
> Along the line of low-roofed water, moves
> As in a cloister. Once—while in that shade
> Loitering, I watched the golden beams of light
> Flung from the setting sun, as they reposed
> In silent beauty on the naked ridge
> Of a high eastern hill—thus flowed my thoughts
> In a pure stream of words fresh from the heart:

Dear native Regions, wheresoe'er shall close
My mortal course, there will I think on you;
Dying, will cast on you a backward look;
Even as this setting sun (albeit the Vale
Is nowhere touched by one memorial gleam)
Doth with the fond remains of his last power
Still linger, and a farewell lustre sheds
On the dear mountain-tops where first they rose.[1]

Though the former was the impromptu utterance of a boy of sixteen, some will prefer its fresh simplicity to the new version written in the poet's manhood. The reference to "Thurston-mere" has puzzled many readers of *The Prelude*, and it is a good illustration of the need of some topographical commentary to the poems. The I. F. note is as follows : "The image with which this poem concludes suggested itself to me while I was resting in a boat along with my companions, under the shade of a magnificent row of sycamores, which then extended their branches from the shore of the promontory upon which stands the ancient, and at that time more picturesque, Hall of Coniston."[2] Now there is nothing in the poem definitely to connect "Thurston-mere" with Coniston, though their identity is suggested. I find, however, that Thurston was the ancient name of Coniston.[3] The site of that grove "on the shore of the promontory" is easily identified, though the grove itself is gone.

Another extract from *The Prelude* may be given here, as it describes a district close at hand, the estuary of the Leven, Morecambe Bay, the ruins of a Roman chapel on a rocky islet, and a

---

[1] *The Prelude*, book viii. p. 226.

[2] *Prose Works*, vol. iii. p. 4.

[3] See Lewis's *Topographical Dictionary of England*, vol. i. p. 662; also the *Edinburgh Gazetteer* (1822), articles *Thurston* and *Coniston*.

characteristic incident in the poet's life, in his
twenty-fourth year, shortly after his return to
England from his one year's residence in France.
The "honoured teacher of his youth" was the
Rev. William Taylor, who was buried in Cartmell
churchyard, and to visit whose grave the pupil
turned aside that morning, from his route over
the Ulverstone sands.[1]

> O Friend! few happier moments have been mine
> Than that which told the downfall of this Tribe
> So dreaded, so abhorred.   The day deserves
> A separate record.   Over the smooth sands
> Of Leven's ample estuary lay
> My journey, and beneath a genial sun,
> With distant prospect among gleams of sky
> And clouds, and intermingling mountain tops,
> In one inseparable glory clad,
> Creatures of one ethereal substance met
> In consistory, like a diadem
> Or crown of burning seraphs as they sit
> In the empyrean.   Underneath that pomp
> Celestial, lay unseen the pastoral vales
> Among whose happy fields I had grown up
> From childhood.   On the fulgent spectacle,
> That neither passed away nor changed, I gazed
> Enrapt; but brightest things are wont to draw
> Sad opposites out of the inner heart,
> As even their pensive influence drew from mine.
> How could it otherwise? for not in vain
> That very morning had I turned aside
> To seek the ground where, 'mid a throng of graves,
> An honoured teacher of my youth was laid,
> And on the stone were graven by his desire
> Lines from the churchyard elegy of Gray.
> This faithful guide, speaking from his deathbed,
> Added no farewell to his parting counsel,

[1] *Memoirs*, vol. i. p. 38.

But said to me, " My head will soon lie low ; "
And when I saw the turf that covered him,
After the lapse of full eight years, those words,
With sound of voice and countenance of the Man,
Came back upon me, so that some few tears
Fell from me in my own despite.   But now
I thought, still traversing that widespread plain,
With tender pleasure of the verses graven
Upon his tombstone, whispering to myself :
He loved the Poets, and, if now alive,
Would have loved me, as one not destitute
Of promise, nor belying the kind hope
That he had formed, when I, at his command,
Began to spin, with toil, my earliest songs.

  As I advanced, all that I saw or felt
Was gentleness and peace.   Upon a small
And rocky island near, a fragment stood
(Itself like a sea rock) the low remains
(With shells encrusted, dark with briny weeds)
Of a dilapidated structure, once
A Romish chapel, where the vested priest
Said matins at the hour that suited those
Who crossed the sands with ebb of morning tide.
Not far from that still ruin all the plain
Lay spotted with a variegated crowd
Of vehicles and travellers, horse and foot,
Wading beneath the conduct of their guide
In loose procession through the shallow stream
Of inland waters ; the great sea meanwhile
Heaved at safe distance, far retired.   I paused
Longing for skill to paint a scene so bright
And cheerful, but the foremost of the band
As he approached, no salutation given
In the familiar language of the day,
Cried, " Robespierre is dead ! " .   .   .
Great was my transport, etc.[1]

  [1] *The Prelude*, book x. p. 228.

CHAPTER III.

DOVE COTTAGE.

THE cottage at Grasmere, to which Wordsworth came with his sister in one of the last days of last century (December 21, 1799), is, even more than Rydal Mount, "identified with his poetic prime." It had once been a public-house, bearing the sign of the Dove and Olive Bough, from which circumstance it was for a long time, and is still occasionally, named "Dove Cottage." It is a small two-storied house. "The front of it faces the lake; behind is a small plot of orchard and garden ground, in which there is a spring and rocks; the enclosure shelves upwards towards the woody sides of the mountain above it."[1]

> This plot of orchard ground is ours;
> My trees they are, my sister's flowers.

He writes thus of his settlement at Grasmere, and of his sister—

> On Nature's invitation do I come,
> By Reason sanctioned. Can the choice mislead,
> That made the calmest, fairest spot on earth,
> With all its unappropriated good,
> My own, and not mine only, for with me

---

[1] *Memoirs*, vol. i. p. 156.

Entrenched, say rather peacefully embowered,
A younger orphan of a home extinct,
The only daughter of my parents, dwells;
Ay, think on that, my heart, and cease to stir;
Pause upon that, and let the breathing frame
No longer breathe, but all be satisfied.

.   .   .   .   .   .

Where'er my footsteps turned,
Her voice was like a hidden bird that sang;
The thought of her was like a flash of light
Or an unseen companionship, a breath,
A fragrance independent of the wind.

.   .   .   .   .   .

Embrace me, then, ye hills, and close me in,
Now in the clear and open day I feel
Your guardianship: I take it to my heart:
'Tis like the solemn shelter of the night.
But I would call thee beautiful; for mild
And soft, and gay, and beautiful thou art,
Dear valley, having in thy face a smile,
Though peaceful, full of gladness. Thou art
        pleased,
Pleased with thy crags, and woody steeps, thy
        lakes,
Its one green island, and its winding shores,
The multitude of little rocky hills,
Thy church, and cottages of mountain stone,
Clustered like stars some few, but single most,
And lurking dimly in their shy retreats,
Or glancing at each other cheerful looks,
Like separated stars with clouds between.[1]

The above reference to his "sole sister" Dorothy
is so exquisite, and hers was a nature so rarely
endowed, while their relationship as brother and
sister was in many respects unique, that three other

[1] *Memoirs*, vol. i. pp. 157, 158.

references to her from *The Prelude*, which need
no commentary, may here be quoted—

> And yet I knew a maid,
> A young enthusiast, who escaped these bonds;
> Her eye was not the mistress of her heart;
> Far less did rules prescribed by passive taste,
> Or barren intermeddling subtleties,
> Perplex her mind; but, wise as women are,
> She welcomed what was given, and craved no
> more;
> Whate'er the scene presented to her view
> That was the best, to that she was attuned
> By her benign simplicity of life.
> Birds in the bower, and lambs in the green field,
> Could they have known her, would have loved;
> methought
> Her very presence such a sweetness breathed,
> That flowers, and trees, and even the silent hills,
> And everything she looked on should have had
> An intimation how she bore herself
> Towards them, and to all creatures.[1]

Again—

> I turned to abstract science, and there sought
> Work for the reasoning faculty enthroned
> Where the disturbances of space and time
>
> .   .   .   .   .
>
> . . . Find no admission.   Then it was—
> Thanks to the bounteous Giver of all good!—
> That the beloved Sister in whose sight
> Those days were passed, now speaking in a voice
> Of sudden admonition—like a brook
> That did but *cross* a lonely road, and now
> Is seen, heard, felt, and caught at every turn
> Companion never lost through many a league--

[1] *The Prelude*, book xii. p. 323.

Maintained for me a saving intercourse
With my true self;   .   .   .
She, in the midst of all, preserved me still
A Poet, made me seek beneath that name,
And that alone, my office upon earth;
And, lastly,   .   .   .
Led me back through opening day
To those sweet counsels between head and heart
Whence grew that genuine knowledge, fraught
        with peace. [1]

Again—

        Child of my parents! Sister of my soul!
Thanks in sincerest verse have been elsewhere
Poured out for all the early tenderness
Which I from thee imbibed: and 'tis most true
That later seasons owed to thee no less;
For, spite of thy sweet influence and the touch
Of kindred hands that opened out the springs
Of genial thought in childhood, and in spite
Of all that unassisted I had marked
In life or nature of those charms minute
That win their way into the heart by stealth,
Still, to the very going-out of youth,
I too exclusively esteemed that love,
And sought that beauty, which, as Milton sings,
Hath terror in it.   Thou didst soften down
This over-sternness; but for thee, dear Friend!
My soul, too reckless of mild grace, had stood
In her original self too confident,
Retained too long a countenance severe:
A rock with torrents roaring, with the clouds
Familiar, and a favourite of the stars:
But thou didst plant its crevices with flowers,
Hang it with shrubs that twinkle in the breeze,

---

[1] *The Prelude*, book xi. p. 309.

And teach the little birds to build their nests
And warble in its chambers.   At a time
When Nature, destined to remain so long
Foremost in my affections, had fallen back
Into a second place, pleased to become
A handmaid to a nobler than herself,
When every day brought with it some new sense
Of exquisite regard for common things,
And all the earth was budding with these gifts
Of more refined humanity, thy breath,
Dear Sister! was a kind of gentler spring
That went before my steps.[1]

With these extracts may be associated some
stanzas of his *Farewell* to the cottage, written
when he left it in 1802 to be married to Mary
Hutchinson—

Farewell, thou little Nook of mountain ground,
Thou rocky corner in the lowest stair
Of that magnificent temple which doth bound
One side of our whole vale with grandeur rare ;
Sweet garden orchard, eminently fair,
The loveliest spot that man hath ever found,
Farewell! we leave thee to Heaven's peaceful care,
Thee, and the Cottage which thou dost surround.
Our boat is safely anchored by the shore,
And there will safely ride when we are gone ;
The flowering shrubs that deck our humble door
Will prosper, though untended and alone:
Fields, goods, and far-off chattels we have none :
These narrow bounds contain our private store
Of things earth makes, and sun doth shine upon:
Here are they in our sight—we have no more.

Sunshine and shower be with you, bud and bell!
For two months now in vain we shall be sought;

---

[1] *The Prelude,* book xiv. p. 362.

We leave you here in solitude to dwell
With these our latest gifts of tender thought;
Thou like the morning in thy saffron coat,
Bright gowan, and marsh-marigold, farewell!
Whom from the borders of the lake we brought,
And placed together near our rocky Well.

We go for One to whom you will be dear;
And she will prize this Bower, this Indian shed,
Our own contrivance, Building without peer!
—A gentle Maid, whose heart is lowly bred,
Whose pleasures are in wild fields gathered,
With joyousness, and with a thoughtful cheer,
Will come to you; to you herself will wed;
And love the blessed life that we lead here.

Dear Spot! which we have watched with tender
      heed,
Bringing these chosen plants and blossoms blown
Among the distant mountains, flower and weed,
Which thou hast taken to thee as thy own,
Making all kindness registered and known
Thou for our sakes, though Nature's child indeed,
Fair in thyself and beautiful alone,
Hast taken gifts which thou dost little need.

.   .   .   .   .   .

O happy Garden! whose seclusion deep
Hath been so friendly to industrious hours;
And to soft slumbers, that did gently steep
Our spirits, carrying with them dreams of flowers,
And wild notes warbled among leafy bowers;
Two burning months let summer overlead,
And, coming back with Her who will be ours,
Into thy bosom we again shall creep.

The following is De Quincey's description of Dove
Cottage as he saw it in the summer of 1807:—"A
white cottage, with two yew-trees breaking the

glare of its white walls" (these yews still stand on the eastern side of the cottage). "A little semi-vestibule between two doors prefaced the entrance into what might be considered the principal room of the cottage. It was an oblong square, not above eight and a half feet high, sixteen feet long, and twelve broad ; wainscotted from floor to ceiling with dark polished oak, slightly embellished with carving. One window there was, a perfect and unpretending cottage window, with little diamond panes, embowered at almost every season of the year with roses, and in the summer and autumn with a profusion of jasmine and other shrubs. . . I was ushered up a little flight of stairs, fourteen in all, to a little drawing-room, or whatever the reader chooses to call it. Wordsworth himself has described the fireplace of this room as his

'Half-kitchen and half-parlour fire.'

It was not fully seven feet six inches high, and in other respects pretty nearly of the same dimensions as the rustic hall below. There was, however, in a small recess, a library of perhaps 300 volumes, which seemed to consecrate the room as the poet's study and composing room, and such occasionally it was. But far oftener he both studied, as I found, and composed on the highroad."[1]

The orchard ground behind the cottage, mostly in grass, slopes upwards, with bits of natural rock seen through it, in which some rough stone steps were cut by Wordsworth and a near neighbour of his, John Fisher, to reach an upper terrace, where he built an arbour. It is not much altered since 1800. This short terrace walk is curved, with a sloping bank of grass above, shaded by apple-trees, hazel, laburnum, holly, laurel, and mountain-ash.

[1] *Recollections of the Lakes*, pp. 130 and 137 (*Works*, vol. ii. Edition 1862).

Below the terrace is the well which supplied the
cottage in Wordsworth's time, where rich large-
leaved primroses still grow, doubtless the successors
of those planted by him and his sister.

> Here, thronged with primroses, the steep rock's
>   breast
> Glittered at evening like a starry sky;
> And in this bush our sparrow built her nest,
> Of which I sang one song that will not die.

Above, in the rocks, are the daffodils which they
also brought to their "garden ground;" the Christmas roses which they planted near the well have
been removed to the eastern side of the garden,
where they flourish luxuriantly.   The boxwood
planted by the poet grows close to the house.   The
arbour is gone ; and in the place where it stood
a seat is erected.   The hidden brook still sings its
undersong as it used to do, "its quiet soul on all
bestowing :"

> If you listen, all is still,
> Save a little neighbouring rill,
> That from out the rocky ground
> Strikes a solitary sound.

As the poem on *The Green Linnet* gives perhaps
the very best idea of the orchard and garden-ground.

> Beneath these fruit-tree boughs that shed
> Their snow-white blossoms on my head
> With brightest sunshine round me spread
>   Of spring's unclouded weather,
> In this sequestered nook how sweet
> To sit upon my orchard seat !
> And birds and flowers once more to greet,
>   My last year's friends together.

One have I marked, the happiest guest
In all this covert of the blest:
Hail to Thee, far above the rest
    In joy of voice and pinion!
Thou, Linnet! in thy green array,
Presiding Spirit here to-day,
Dost lead the revels of the May;
    And this is thy dominion.

While birds, and butterflies, and flowers,
Make all one band of paramours,
Thou, ranging up and down the bowers,
    Art sole in thy employment:
A Life, a Presence like the Air,
Scattering thy gladness without care,
Too blest with any one to pair;
    Thyself thy own enjoyment.

Amid yon tuft of hazel trees,
That twinkle to the gusty breeze,
Behold him perched in ecstacies,
    Yet seeming still to hover;
There! where the flutter of his wings
Upon his back and body flings
Shadows and sunny glimmerings,
    That cover him all over.

My dazzled sight he oft deceives,
A Brother of the dancing leaves;
Then flits, and from the cottage-eaves
    Pours forth his song in gushes;
As if by that exulting strain
He mocked and treated with disdain
The voiceless Form he chose to feign,
    While fluttering in the bushes.

The second in the first series of the *Miscellaneous Sonnets* may also refer to Dove Cottage,

although some of the details are scarcely applicable.
There is no "brook" within the cottage grounds, and
scarcely anything in the garden to warrant the
phrase, "its own small pasture."

> Well may'st thou halt—and gaze with brighten-
>   ing eye!
> The lovely Cottage in the guardian nook
> Hath stirred thee deeply; with its own dear brook,
> Its own small pasture, almost its own sky!
> But covet not the Abode :—forbear to sigh,
> As many do, repining while they look;
> Intruders—who would tear from Nature's book
> This precious leaf, with harsh impiety.
> Think what the Home must be if it were thine,
> Even thine, though few thy wants!— Roof,
>   window, door,
> The very flowers are sacred to the Poor,
> The roses to the porch which they entwine:
> Yea, all, that now enchants thee, from the day
> On which it should be touched, would melt away.

Here, too, in the arbour he watched *the Redbreast
chasing the Butterfly*, on which he wrote the lines.

> Art thou the bird whom Man loves best,
> The pious bird with the scarlet breast,
>   Our little English Robin;
> The bird that comes about our doors
> When autumn winds are sobbing? etc.

and those addressed to *The Kitten and the falling
Leaves*, sporting with them as they fell from the
lofty elder-tree; with the description of the blue-
cap:—

> . . . blest as bird could be,
> Feeding in the apple-tree;
> Making wanton spoil and rout,
> Turning blossoms inside out.

In this poem (as in *The Green Linnet*), in dealing
with the simplest and most familiar of sights, there
is all the fine spiritual sense and unerring imaginative insight of the poet.   He knows that

> .   .   .   enjoyments dwell
> In the impenetrable cell
> Of the silent heart, which Nature
> Furnishes to every creature.

He sees that there is "a light of gladness" in the
freaks of the kitten; and that it imparts "a living
force" to the countenance of his infant child, and
he says—

> I will have my careless season
> Spite of melancholy reason,
> Will walk through life in such a way
> That, when time brings on decay,
> Now and then I may possess
> Hours of perfect gladsomeness,
> —Pleased by any random toy;
> By a kitten's busy joy,
> Or an infant's laughing eye
> Sharing in the ecstacy;
> I would fare like that or this,
> Find my wisdom in my bliss;
> Keep the sprightly soul awake,
> And have faculties to take,
> Even from things by sorrow wrought,
> Matter for a jocund thought,
> Spite of care and spite of grief,
> To gambol with Life's falling Leaf.

Here, too, he wrote the stanzas in his pocket
copy of Thomson's *Castle of Indolence*, in which
occurs the description of his friend Coleridge, of
which Hartley said, that "his father's character
and history are preserved in a livelier way, than
in anything that has been written about him."

Dove Cottage has now been purchased for the nation and for posterity, as Shakespeare's home at Stratford was secured. It is to the Rev. Stopford Brooke and his brother, Mr. William Brooke of Dublin, that the entire credit of this is due. The proposal had been made long ago, but no steps were taken to realise it. As far back as 1862, it was thought of, and in 1876 Dr. Cradóck and I went over the house, with a view to see what would require to be done to it in the event of its purchase. Later, Mr. Rawnsley took up the idea. It was brought forward at meetings of the Wordsworth Society, but Mr. Rawnsley's later idea was to secure Greta Hall, Keswick, the house of Coleridge and Southey, also classic ground, and make it a sort of Valhalla for memorials of the poets of the Lake Country. In 1884 it was examined carefully, with this end in view, but the difficulty of raising funds was insuperable. At last Mr. Brooke and his brother visited the district of Grasmere in 1889, and, after inspecting the cottage and the surrounding places memorialised in the poems, made up his mind that it should be secured "for those who love English poetry all over the world." He wrote to the owner, who offered to sell it for £650; and a Committee was formed to carry out the project. A sum of nearly £1000 was soon raised, and the cottage and its garden purchased. The property is to be conveyed to a Board of Trustees, who will appoint an Executive Committee of Management.

Mr. Brooke has written an excellent little book on Dove Cottage, in which he has managed, with rare skill, to weave into his pages almost every point of interest in Dorothy Wordsworth's Grasmere Journal, and to vivify the whole.

The following passages from that Journal contain their very best commentary.

"*June* 2, 1800.—I sat a long time to watch the

hurrying waves" (on Rydal), "and to hear the
regularly irregular sound of the dashing waters.
The waves round about the little island seemed
like a dance of spirits that rose out of the water,
round its small circumference of shore.

"*July* 26.—The lake was now most still, and
reflected the yellow, blue, purple, and grey colours
of the sky. We heard a strange sound in the
Bainriggs wood as we were floating on the waters :
it seemed in the wood, but it must have been above
it, for presently we saw a raven very high above us.
It called out, and the dome of the sky seemed to
echo the sound. It called again and again as it
flew onwards, and the mountains gave back the
sound, seeming as if, from their centre, a musical,
bell-like answering to the bird's hoarse voice. We
heard both the call of the bird, and the echo, after
we could see him no longer.

"*October* 11. — Walked up Green-head Gill in
search of a sheepfold.[1] The colour of the mountain,
soft, and rich with orange fern ; the cattle pasturing
upon the hill tops ; kites sailing in the sky above
our heads ; sheep bleating, and feeding in the water
courses, scattered over the mountains. They come
down to feed, in the little green islands in the beds
of the torrents, and so may be swept away. The
sheepfold is falling away. It is built nearly in the
form of a heart unequally divided. Looked down
the brook, and saw the drops rise upwards and
sparkle in the air at the little falls. The higher
sparkled the tallest.

"*Nov.* 24.—We heard the wind everywhere about
us as we went along the lane. We were stopped at
once at the distance of fifty yards from our favourite birch-tree. It was yielding to the gusty wind
with all its tender twigs. The sun shone upon it,

---

[1] Michael's sheepfold.

and it glanced in the wind like a flying sun-shiny shower. It was a tree in shape, with stem and branches, but it was like a spirit of water. The sun went in, and it resumed its purplish appearance, the twigs still yielding to the wind, but not so visibly to us. The other birch-trees that were near it looked brighter and cheerful, but it was a creature by its own self amongst them.

"*Feb.* 23, 1801.—We walked to the top of the hill, then to the bridge. The sykes[1] made a sweet sound everywhere; and in the twilight that little one above Mr. Oliff's house, a ghostly, white serpent line, made a sound most distinctly heard of itself. 23*rd*.—When we came out of our doors, the thrush was singing upon the topmost of the smaller branches of the ash tree at the top of the orchard. How long it had been perched I cannot tell, but we heard its dear voice in the orchard all the day through, along with a cheerful undersong made by our winter friends the robins. We went to John's Grove, and sate, looking at the fading landscape. The lake, though the objects on the shore were fading, seemed brighter than when it is perfect day, and the island, pushed itself upwards, distinct and large. There was a sweet, sea-like sound in the trees above our heads.

"*April* 29.—We went to John's Grove. William and I lay in the the trench under the fence, he with eyes shut, listening to the waterfall and the birds. There was now one waterfall above another—it was a sound of waters in the air—the voice of the air. We were unseen by one another. We thought it would be so sweet thus to be in the grave, to hear the peaceful sounds of the earth, and just to know that our dear friends are near. The lake was still: there was a boat out. Silver How reflected with

---

[1] Small streams, almost runlets.

delicate purple and yellowish hues, as I have seen spar: lambs on the island, and running races together by the dozen in the round field near us. As I lay down on the grass, I observed the glittering silver line on the ridge of the backs of the sheep, owing to their situation respecting the sun, which made them look beautiful, but with something of strange-ness, like animals of another kind, as if belonging to a more splendid world.

"*May* 6.—We have put the finishing stroke to our bower, and here we are sitting in the orchard. It is one o'clock. We are sitting upon a seat under the wall, which I found my brother building up when I came to him. He had intended that it should have been done before I came. It is a nice, cool, shady spot. The small birds are singing, lambs bleating, cuckoos calling, the thrush sings by fits; Thomas Ashburnam's axe is going quietly, without passion, in the orchard; hens are cackling, flies humming, the women talking together at their doors, plum and pear trees are in blossom, apple trees greenish, the opposite woods green, the crows are cawing, we have heard ravens, the ash trees are in blossom, birds flying all about us, the stitchwort is coming out, there is our budding lychnis, the primroses are passing their prime, celandine, violets, and wood-sorrel for ever more, little geraniums and pansies on the wall. The moon a perfect boat, a silver boat; the birch tree all over green in small leaf, more light and elegant than when it is full out. It bent to the breezes as if for the love of its own delightful motions. Sloethorns and hawthorns in the hedges."

These are samples of the wonderful *Grasmere Journal* of Dorothy Wordsworth, for a fuller idea of which readers of this book must be referred to the first volume of the *Life of William Words-worth*, by the present writer, published in 1889.

CHAPTER IV.

GRASMERE, ETC.

THE poems that most naturally recur to one's memory, in thinking of Wordsworth as the interpreter of Grasmere, are those in that exquisite series of seven *On the Naming of Places*. In an "advertisement" to this series, Wordsworth said: "By persons resident in the country and attached to rural objects, many places will be found unnamed or of unknown name, where little incidents must have occurred, or feelings been experienced, which will have given to such places a private and peculiar interest. From a wish to give some sort of record to such incidents, and renew the gratification of such feelings, Names have been given to Places by the author and some of his friends, and the following poems written in consequence."

While the third, fourth, sixth, and seventh of these "places" are easily identified, I think it possible that the poet did not wish the other three to be known with absolute accuracy. In reference to the second—entitled *To Joanna*—when walking with some friends, and asked to name the rock referred to, he gave an evasive answer. They were passing Butterlip How at the time, and he replied, "Any place that will suit; that as well as any other." I cannot think that he made his answer vague—and his note dictated to Miss Fenwick still vaguer—with the view of "puzzling posterity;" but

perhaps he did not care to localise everything, and
he may have disliked to be cross-examined upon
such personal matters.

The first of these *Poems on the Naming of Places*
is as follows:—

It was an April morning: fresh and clear
The Rivulet, delighting in its strength,
Ran with a young man's speed; and yet the voice
Of waters which the winter had supplied
Was softened down into a vernal tone.
The spirit of enjoyment and desire,
And hopes and wishes, from all living things
Went circling, like a multitude of sounds,
The budding groves seemed eager to urge on
The steps of June; as if their various hues
Were only hindrances that stood between
Them and their object: but, meanwhile, prevailed
Such an entire contentment in the air
That every naked ash, and tardy tree
Yet leafless, showed as if the countenance
With which it looked on this delightful day
Were native to the summer.—Up the brook
I roamed in the confusion of my heart,
Alive to all things and forgetting all.
At length I to a sudden turning came
In this continuous glen, where down a rock
The Stream, so ardent in its course before,
Sent forth such sallies of glad sound that all
Which I till then had heard appeared the voice
Of common pleasure: beast and bird, the lamb,
The shepherd's dog, the linnet and the thrush
Vied with this waterfall, and made a song
Which, while I listened, seemed like the wild
     growth
Or like some natural produce of the air,
That could not cease to be. Green leaves were
     here;

But 'twas the foliage of the rocks—the birch,
The yew, the holly, and the bright green thorn,
With hanging islands of resplendent furze:
And, on a summit, distant a short space,
By any who should look beyond the dell,
A single mountain-cottage might be seen.
I gazed and gazed, and to myself I said,
"Our thoughts at least are ours; and this wild
    nook,
My EMMA, I will dedicate to thee."
——Soon did the spot become my other home,
My dwelling, and my out-of-doors abode,
And, of the Shepherds who have seen me there,
To whom I sometimes in our idle talk
Have told this fancy, two or three, perhaps,
Years after we are gone and in our graves,
When they have cause to speak of this wild place,
May call it by the name of EMMA'S DELL.

In reference to it, Wordsworth said to Miss
Fenwick, "This poem was suggested on the banks
of the brook that runs through Easdale, which is,
in some parts of its course, as wild and beautiful
as brook can be. I have composed thousands of
verses by the side of it."[1] The brook is therefore
Easdale beck. But where is "Emma's Dell?" In
the autumn of 1877, Dr. Cradock took me to a
place of which he writes: "I have a fancy for a spot
just beyond Goody Bridge to the left, where the
brook makes a curve, and returns to the road two
hundred yards further on. But I have not discovered a trace of authority in favour of the idea,
further than that the wooded bend of the brook
with the stepping-stones across it, connected with
a field-path recently stopped, was a very favourite
haunt of Wordsworth's. At the upper part of this
bend, near to the place where the brook returns to

[1] *Prose Works*, vol. iii. p. 29.

the road, is a deep pool at the foot of a rush of
water.   A sad accident occurred there many years
ago.   A man named Wilson was drowned in the
pool.   He lived at a house on the hill, called Score
Crag, which, if my conjecture as to Emma's Dell is
right, is the 'single mountain cottage' on a 'summit,
distant a short space.'   Wordsworth, happening to
be walking at no great distance, heard a loud
shriek.   It was that of old Wilson, the father, who
had just discovered his son's body in the beck."

In the *Reminiscences* of the poet, by the Hon.
Mr. Justice Coleridge,[1] he tells us of a walk they
took up Easdale to this very place, entering the
field just at the spot which Dr. Cradock concludes
to be "Emma's Dell."   "He turned aside at a
little farmhouse, and took us into a swelling field,
to look down on the tumbling stream which bounded
it, and which we saw precipitated at a distance, in
a broad white sheet, from the mountain."   (This of
course refers to Easdale Force.)   "Then, as he
mused for an instant, he said, ' I have often thought
what a solemn thing it would be could we have
brought to our mind at once all the scenes of dis-
tress and misery which any spot, however beautiful
and calm before us, has been witness to since the
beginning.   That water-break, with the glassy quiet
pool beneath it, that looks so lovely, and presents
no images to the mind but of peace—there, I
remember, the only son of his father, a poor man
who lived yonder, was drowned."[2]   This walk and
conversation took place in October 1836.   If any
one is surprised that the poet, if then standing
opposite, and looking down into "Emma's Dell" (of
which he had said such exquisite things in 1800)
did not name it as such to Mr. Coleridge, he must

[1] *Prose Works*, p. 423.

[2] *Ibid*. vol. iii p. 431.

remember that thirty-six years is a long interval;
and that, in 1836, Wordsworth's " sister Emmeline "
had for a year been a confirmed invalid at Rydal.
I have repeatedly followed the Easdale beck all the
way up from its junction with the Rothay to the Tarn,
and found no spot corresponding so closely to the
minute realistic detail of this poem as that suggested
by Dr. Cradock.   There are two places farther up,
where " sallies of glad sound " are audible, but they
are not at a " sudden turning," as is the spot above
Goody Bridge.   If one leaves the Easdale road at
this bridge, and keeps to the side of the beck for a
few hundred yards, till he reaches the " sudden
turning," remembering that this path by the brook
was a favourite haunt of Wordsworth and his sister,
the probability of Dr. Cradock's conjecture will
be apparent.   Lady Richardson concurred in this
identification of the " dell."

Of the next poem in the series, addressed *To
Joanna* (Hutchinson), Wordsworth said : " The
effect of her laugh is an extravagance, though the
effect of the reverberation of voices in some parts
of these mountains is very striking.   There is in
The Excursion an allusion to the bleat of a lamb
thus rendered and described, without any exaggeration, as I heard it on the side of Stickle Tarn,
from the precipice that stretches on to Langdale
Pike " (I. F. MS.)[1]   This echo at the foot of
Harrison Stickle is easily found.   The " precipice "
referred to is Pavey Ark.

Omitting an introductory passage, the poem is
as follows :—

While I was seated, now some ten days past
Beneath those lofty firs, that overtop
Their ancient neighbour, the old steeple tower,

[1] *Prose Works*, vol. iii. p. 29.

The Vicar from his gloomy house hard by[1]
Came forth to greet me ; and when he had asked,
" How fares Joanna, that wild-hearted Maid ;
And when will she return to us ?" he paused ;
And, after short exchange of village news,
He with grave looks demanded, for what cause,
Reviving obsolete idolatry,
I, like a Runic Priest, in characters
Of formidable size had chiselled out
Some uncouth name upon the native rock,
Above the Rotha, by the forest-side.
—Now, by those dear immunities of heart
Engendered between malice and true love,
I was not loth to be so catechised,
And this was my reply :—" As it befel,
One summer morning we had walked abroad
At break of day, Joanna and myself.
—'Twas that delightful season when the broom,
Full-flowered, and visible in every steep,
Along the copses runs in veins of gold.
Our pathway led us on to Rotha's banks ;
And when we came in front of that tall rock
That eastward looks, I there stopped short—and
    stood
Tracing the lofty barrier with my eye
From base to summit ; such delight I found
To note in shrub and tree, in stone and flower,
That intermixture of delicious hues,
Along so vast a surface, all at once,
In one impression, by connecting force
Of their own beauty, imaged in the heart.
—When I had gazed perhaps two minutes' space,
Joanna, looking in my eyes, beheld
That ravishment of mine, and laughed aloud.

[1] The Rectory at Grasmere, "gloomy" enough to
Wordsworth by-and-by, where he lived from 1811 to
1813, and where two of his children died.

The Rock, like something starting from a sleep,
Took up the Lady's voice, and laughed again;
That ancient Woman seated on Helm-crag
Was ready with her cavern; Hammer-scar,
And the tall Steep of Silver-how, sent forth
A noise of laughter; southern Loughrigg heard,
And Fairfield answered with a mountain tone;
Helvellyn far into the clear blue sky
Carried the Lady's voice—old Skiddaw blew
His speaking trumpet;—back out of the clouds
Of Glaramara southward came the voice;
And Kirkstone tossed it from his misty head.
—Now whether (said I to our cordial Friend,
Who in the hey-day of astonishment
Smiled in my face) this were in simple truth
A work accomplished by the brotherhood
Of ancient mountains, or my ear was touched
With dreams and visionary impulses
To me alone imparted, sure I am
That there was a loud uproar in the hills
And, while we both were listening, to my side
The fair Joanna drew, as if she wished
To shelter from some object of her fear.
—And hence, long afterwards, when eighteen
        moons
Were wasted, as I chanced to walk alone
Beneath this rock, at sunrise, on a calm
And silent morning, I sat down, and there,
In memory of affections old and true,
I chiselled out in those rude characters
Joanna's name deep in the living stone :—
And I, and all who dwelt by my fireside,
Have called the lovely rock, JOANNA'S ROCK."

The firs referred to stood by the road side scarcely
twenty yards north-west from the steeple. Their
site is now included in the road which has been
widened at that point. They were Scotch firs of

unusual size, and might justly be said to overtop
"their neighbour" the tower— no very great feat!

Mr. Fleming Green, who well remembers the
trees, gave me the information, which is confirmed
by other inhabitants. When the road was enlarged,
not many years ago, the roots of the trees were
found by the workmen.

The "tall rock that eastward looks" by "Rotha's
banks," with a "lofty barrier from base to summit,"
is, I cannot doubt, some portion of Helm Crag.   It
is clear, however, that there are several deviations
from accuracy in the details of this poem.   It was
written in 1800, and was published that year in the
second edition of the *Lyrical Ballads*.   It is addressed to Joanna Hutchinson, who is said to have
been absent from Grasmere for two years, and
Wordsworth says that he carved the Runic characters, *in memoriam*, eighteen months after that
summer morning, when he heard the echo of her
laugh.   But he only took up his residence at
Grasmere in 1799.   The full effect, however, of
this highly imaginative poem is not impaired—it
may even be enhanced — by our inability to fix
the locality. Can Wordsworth have read Michael
Drayton's description of this district?[1]

---

[1] Which Copeland scarce had spoke, but
        quickly every hill.
    Upon her verge that stands, the neighbour-
        ing vallies fill :
    Helvillion from his height, it through the
        mountain threw,
    From whence as soon again, the sound
        Dunbalrase drew,
    From whose stone-trofied head, it on the
        Wendrosse went,
    Which, tow'rds the sea, resounded it to
        Dent,

The third poem in this series is as follows : —

There is an Eminence,—of those our hills
The last that parleys with the setting sun ;
We can behold it from our orchard-seat ;
And, when at evening we pursue our walk
Along the public way, this Peak, so high
Above us, and so distant in its height,
Is visible ; and often seems to send
Its own deep quiet to restore our hearts.
The meteors make of it a favourite haunt :
The star of Jove, so beautiful and large
In the mid heavens, is never half so fair
As when he shines above it.   'Tis in truth
The loneliest place we have among the clouds.
And She who dwells with me, whom I have loved
With such communion that no place on earth
Can ever be a solitude to me,
Hath to this lonely Summit given my Name.

This is the hill, called "Stone Arthur," which
rises to the east of the road from Grasmere up
Dunmail Raise, between Green Head Ghyll and
Tongue Ghyll. "It is not accurate," Wordsworth
himself naïvely said to Miss Fenwick, "that the
eminence could be seen from our orchard-seat."
It is visible from their garden.

The fourth poem begins thus :—

A narrow girdle of rough stones and crags,
A rude and natural causeway, interposed

> That *Brodwater*, therewith within her banks
>   astound,
> In sailing to the sea, told it to *Egremound*,
> Whose buildings, walks, and streets, with
>   echoes loud and long,
> Did mightily commend old *Copland* for her
>   song.
>   *Polyolbion*, Song xxx. ll. 155-164.

Between the water and a winding slope
Of copse and thicket, leaves the eastern shore
Of Grasmere safe in its own privacy :
And there myself and two beloved Friends,
One calm September morning, ere the mist
Had altogether yielded to the sun,
Sauntered on this retired and difficult way.
——Ill suits the road with one in haste ; but we
Played with our time ; and, as we strolled along,
It was our occupation to observe
Such objects as the waves had tossed ashore—
Feather, or leaf, or weed, or withered bough,
Each on the other heaped, along the line
Of the dry wreck.   And, in our vacant mood,
Not seldom did we stop to watch some tuft
Of dandelion seed or thistle's beard,
That skimmed the surface of the dead calm lake,
Suddenly halting now—a lifeless stand !
And starting off again with freak as sudden ;
In all its sportive wanderings, all the while,
Making report of an invisible breeze
That was its wings, its chariot, and its horse,
Its playmate, rather say, its moving soul.
——And often, trifling with a privilege
Alike indulged to all, we paused, one now,
And now the other, to point out, perchance
To pluck, some flower or water-weed, too fair
Either to be divided from the place
On which it grew, or to be left alone
To its own beauty.   Many such there are,
Fair ferns and flowers, and chiefly that tall fern,
So stately, of the queen Osmunda named ;
Plant lovelier, in its own retired abode
On Grasmere's beach, than Naiad by the side
Of Grecian brook, or Lady of the Mere,
Sole-sitting by the shores of old romance.

In Wordsworth's early days at Grasmere, a wild

woodland path of quiet beauty led from Dove Cottage along the margin of the lake to this "point," leaving the eastern shore truly "safe in its own privacy,"—a "retired and difficult way." The only road for conveyances went at that time over White Moss Common.

The late Dr. Arnold gave the following names to the three roads from Rydal to Grasmere: the highest, "Old Corruption;" the intermediate, "Bit by Bit Reform;" the lowest and most level, "Radical Reform." Wordsworth was never quite reconciled to the radical reform effected on a road that used to be so delightfully wild and picturesque. How could he?

The two friends alluded to in this poem were his sister Dorothy and Coleridge. The rest of it need not be quoted. The spot, which they rather infelicitously named "Point Rash-judgment," is easily identified; although, as Wordsworth remarks, "the character of the shore is changed, by the public road being carried along its side." The three friends were quite aware that this "memorial name" of theirs was "uncouth." In spite of its awkwardness, the name will probably survive, though scarcely for Browning's reason—

> The better the uncouther :
> Do roses stick like burrs ?

The fifth poem is the following—

TO M. H.

Our walk was far among the ancient trees ;
There was no road, nor any woodman's path ;
But a thick umbrage—checking the wild growth
Of weed and sapling, along soft green turf
Beneath the branches—of itself had made

A track, that brought us to a slip of lawn,
And a small bed of water in the woods.
All round this pool both flocks and herds might
      drink
On its firm margin, even as from a well,
Or some stone basin, which the herdsman's hand
Had shaped for their refreshment; nor did sun,
Or wind from any quarter ever come,
But as a blessing to this calm recess,
This glade of water and this one green field.
The spot was made by Nature for herself;
The travellers know it not, and 'twill remain
Unknown to them; but it is beautiful;
And if a man should plant his cottage near,
Should sleep beneath the shelter of its trees,
And blend its waters with his daily meal,
He would so love it that in his death-hour
Its image would survive among his thoughts :
And therefore, my sweet MARY, this still Nook,
With all its beeches, we have named from You!

Of this poem Wordsworth says, "To Mary
Hutchinson, two years before our marriage. The
pool alluded to is in Rydal Upper Park" (I. F. MS.).
To find this pool, I have carefully examined the
course of the beck, all the way up to the foot of
Rydal Fell. There is a pool beyond the enclosures
of the Hall property, when you have ascended about
500 feet above Rydal Mount, which partly corresponds to the description, but there is wood around
it ; and the trees that skirt the margin are birch,
ash, oak, hazel, but there are no beeches. It is a
deep crystal pool, and has a "firm margin" of (arti-
ficially placed) stones. It is a short way below
some fine specimens of ice-worn rocks, which are
to the right of the stream as you ascend it, and
above these rocks is a well-marked moraine. The
spot referred to in the poem may be either the

above, or another (perhaps more likely) within the grounds of the Hall. It is a sequestered nook, beside the third waterfall—which is itself a treble fall. Seen two or three days after rain, when the stream is full enough to break over the whole face of the rock in showers of snowy brightness, yet low enough to show the rock behind its transparent veil, it is inexpressibly lovely. Trees change so much in eighty years, that the absence of "beeches" now would not make this site impossible. Of the circular pool beneath this triple fall it may be said, as Wordsworth describes it,

> . . . Both flocks and herds might drink
> On its firm margin, even as from a well;

and a "small slip of lawn" might easily have existed there in his time. I cannot be confident of the locality, however. Dr. Cradock writes: "As to Mary Hutchinson's pool, I think that it was not on the beck anywhere, but some detached little pool, far up the hill, to the eastwards of the Hall, in 'the woods.' The description does not well suit any part of Rydal beck; no spot thereon could long 'remain unknown,' as the brook was until lately much haunted by anglers." My difficulty as to a site "far up the hill" is that it must have been a pool of some size, if "both flocks and herds might drink" all round it; and there is no stream, scarce even a rill, that joins Rydal beck on the right, all the way up from its junction with the Rothay. Mr. Hull writes from Rydal Cottage: "Although closely acquainted with every nook about Rydal Park, I have never been able to discover any spot corresponding to that described in Wordsworth's lines to M. H. It is possible, however, that the 'small bed of water' may have been a temporary rain pool, such as sometimes lodges in the hollows on the mountain-slope after heavy rain." Mr. F. M.

Jones, the agent of the Rydal property, writes: " I
do not know of any pool of water in the upper
Rydal Park.   There are some pools up the river,
'Mirror Pool' among them; but I hardly think
there can ever have been 'beech trees' growing
near them."   There are many difficulties; and the
place may now be past identification.   Possibly
Wordsworth's wish may be fulfilled—

> The travellers know it not, and 'twill remain
> Unknown to them.

(See Preface, p. vi. etc.)
    The sixth poem is perhaps the most distinctive in
the series—

> When, to the attractions of the busy world
> Preferring studious leisure, I had chosen
> A habitation in this peaceful Vale,
> Sharp season followed of continual storm
> In deepest winter; and, from week to week,
> Pathway, and lane, and public road, were clogged
> With frequent showers of snow.   Upon a hill
> At a short distance from my cottage, stands
> A stately fir-grove, whither I was wont
> To hasten, for I found, beneath the roof
> Of that perennial shade, a cloistral place
> Of refuge, with an unincumbered floor.
> Here, in safe covert, on the shallow snow,
> And, sometimes, on a speck of visible earth,
> The redbreast near me hopped; nor was I loth
> To sympathise with vulgar coppice birds,
> That, for protection from the nipping blast,
> Hither repaired.   A single beech-tree grew
> Within this grove of firs! and, on the fork
> Of that one beech, appeared a thrush's nest;
> A last year's nest, conspicuously built
> At such small elevation from the ground
> As gave sure sign that they, who in that house

Of Nature and of love had made their home
Amid the fir-trees, all the summer long
Dwelt in a tranquil spot. And oftentimes,
A few sheep, stragglers from some mountain-flock,
Would watch my motions with suspicious stare,
From the remotest outskirts of the grove,—
Some nook where they had made their final stand,
Huddling together from two fears—the fear
Of me and of the storm. Full many an hour
Here did I lose. But in this grove the trees
Had been so thickly planted, and had thriven
In such perplexed and intricate array,
That vainly did I seek beneath their stems
A length of open space, where to and fro
My feet might move without concern or care;
And, baffled thus, though earth from day to day
Was fettered, and the air by storm disturbed,
I ceased the shelter to frequent,—and prized,
Less than I wished to prize, that calm recess.

The snows dissolved, and genial Spring returned
To clothe the fields with verdure. Other haunts
Meanwhile were mine; till, one bright April day,
By chance retiring from the glare of noon
To this forsaken covert, there I found
A hoary pathway traced between the trees,
And winding on with such an easy line
Along a natural opening, that I stood
Much wondering how I could have sought in vain
For what was now so obvious. To abide,
For an allotted interval of ease,
Under my cottage-roof, had gladly come
From the wild sea a cherished Visitant;
And with the sight of this same path—begun,
Begun and ended, in the shady grove,
Pleasant conviction flashed upon my mind
That, to this opportune recess allured,
He had surveyed it with a finer eye,

A heart more wakeful; and had worn the track
By pacing here, unwearied and alone,
In that habitual restlessness of foot,
That haunts the Sailor measuring o'er and o'er
His short domain upon the vessel's deck,
While she pursues her course through the dreary
    sea.

  When thou hadst quitted Esthwaite's pleasant
      shore,
And taken thy first leave of those green hills
And rocks that were the play-ground of thy youth,
Year followed year, my Brother! and we two,
Conversing not, knew little in what mould
Each other's mind was fashioned; and at length
When once again we met in Grasmere Vale,
Between us there was little other bond
Than common feelings of fraternal love.
But thou, a School-boy, to the sea hadst carried
Undying recollections; Nature there
Was with thee; she, who loved us both, she still
Was with thee; and even so didst thou become
A *silent* Poet; from the solitude
Of the vast sea didst bring a watchful heart
Still couchant, an inevitable ear,
And an eye practised like a blind man's touch.
—Back to the joyless Ocean thou art gone;
Nor from this vestige of thy musing hours
Could I withhold thy honoured name,—and now
I love the fir-grove with a perfect love.
Thither do I withdraw when cloudless suns
Shine hot, or wind blows troublesome and strong;
And there I sit at evening, when the steep
Of Silver-how, and Grasmere's peaceful lake,
And one green island, gleam between the stems
Of the dark firs, a visionary scene!
And, while I gaze upon the spectacle
Of clouded splendour, on this dream-like sight

Of solemn loveliness, I think on thee,
My Brother, and on all which thou hast lost.
Nor seldom, if I rightly guess, while Thou,
Muttering the verses which I muttered first
Among the mountains, through the midnight
          watch
Art pacing thoughtfully the vessel's deck
In some far region, here, while o'er my head,
At every impulse of the moving breeze,
The fir-grove murmurs with a sea-like sound,
Alone I tread this path;—for aught I know,
Timing my steps to thine: and, with a store
Of undistinguishable sympathies,
Mingling most earnest wishes for the day
When we, and others whom we love, shall meet
A second time, in Grasmere's happy Vale.

This fir-grove is between the Wishing-gate
and White Moss Common, and almost exactly
opposite the former.   Follow the old road from
Grasmere to Rydal to the point where the paths
diverge, one leading up to the common, the other
to the Gate; take the latter a short way, and turn
to the left by the first path leading along the
hillside by a wall, and the "fir-grove" will be seen
on the right; or, standing at the Wishing-gate and
looking eastward, the grove is to the left, not forty
yards from the gate.   Some of the firs (Scotch) are
still there, and several beech-trees, not "a *single*
beech-tree" as in the poem.   Dr. Cradock assures
me that Wordsworth pointed out the special beech-
tree, in which was the thrush's nest, "to Miss
Cookson, a few days before Dora Wordsworth's
death.   The wall was in a ruined plight, and the
party scrambled through it.   The tree is near the
upper wall, and from its shape tells its own tale."
"The plantation," Wordsworth remarks in his note
on this poem, "has been walled in, and is not so

accessible as when my brother John wore the path
in the manner here described.   The grove was a
favourite haunt with us all, while we lived at Town
End"[1] (I. F. MS.)   They used to call it John's
Grove.   It can be easily entered by a gate, about
a hundred yards beyond the Wishing-gate as one
goes towards Rydal.   The view from it, so exquisitely
described in the poem, is much interfered with by
larch plantations immediately below the firs.   In
the absence of definite testimony, I would have
supposed that the path which his brother trod faced
Silver-how, and the island of Grasmere; and that
the beech-tree was nearer the lower than the upper
wall, just above a cup-shaped depression in the
ground.   But Miss Cookson's statement is explicit.
Only fifteen firs survive at this part of the grove,
which is open and desolate.   Dr. Cradock remarks:
"As to there being more than one beech,
Wordsworth would not have hesitated to sacrifice
servile exactness to poetical effect.   He had a fancy
for 'one.'

> 'Fair as a star, when only one
>   Is shining in the sky.'

'*One* abode, no more.'   Grasmere's one green
island,' 'one green field.'   And again, the cattle,
'forty feeding like one.'"
    The following is the last of the *Poems on the
Naming of Places:*—

Forth from a jutting ridge, around whose base
Winds our deep Vale, two heath-clad Rocks ascend
In fellowship, the loftiest of the pair
Rising to no ambitious height; yet both,
O'er lake and stream, mountain and flowery mead,
Unfolding prospects fair as human eyes

---

[1] *Prose Works*, vol. iii. p. 30.

Ever beheld.   Up-led with mutual help,
To one or other brow of those twin Peaks
Were two adventurous Sisters wont to climb,
And took no note of the hour while thence they
        gazed,
The blooming heath their couch, gazed, side by
        side,
In speechless admiration.   I, a witness
And frequent sharer of their calm delight
With thankful heart, to either Eminence
Gave the baptismal name each Sister bore.
Now are they parted, far as Death's cold hand
Hath power to part the Spirits of those who love
As they did love.   Ye kindred Pinnacles—
That, while the generations of mankind
Follow each other to their hiding-place
In Time's abyss, are privileged to endure
Beautiful in yourselves, and richly graced
With like command of beauty—grant your aid
For MARY'S humble, SARAH'S silent, claim,
That their pure joy in Nature may survive
From age to age in blended memory.

These two rocks are near the "fir-grove," and
are easily identified.   They are "heath-clad" still.
They rise out of what is sometimes called the Bane
Riggs Wood ; so named, I understand, because
the shortest road from Ambleside to Grasmere
passes through it ; "bane" or "bain" signifying,
in the Westmoreland dialect, a short cut.   Dr.
Cradock says : "They are difficult of approach,
being enclosed in a wood, with dense undergrowth,
and surrounded by a high well-built wall.   They
can be well seen from the lower highroad, from a
spot close to the three-mile stone from Ambleside.
They are some fifty or sixty feet above the road,
about twenty yards apart, and separated by a
slight depression of say ten feet.   The view from

the easterly one is now much preferable, as it is less encumbered with shrubs ; and, for that reason also, is more heath-clad. The twin rocks are also well seen, though at a further distance, from the hill on White Moss Common, between the roads 'Old Corruption' and 'Bit-by-bit Reform.' Doubtless the rocks were far more easily approached fifty years ago, when walls, if any, were low and ill-built. It is probable, however, that even then they were enclosed and protected ;—for heath will not grow on the Grasmere hills in places much frequented by sheep." From the lower carriage road—Dr. Arnold's "Radical Reform".— they are best seen at a point two or three yards to the west of a large rock on the roadside near the milestone. The view of them from Loughrigg Terrace is also interesting.

In July 1806 Wordsworth wrote the following

To the Evening Star over Grasmere Water.

                    The Lake is thine ;
The mountains too are thine ; some clouds there are,
Some little feeble stars, but all is thine ;
Thou, thou art king, and sole proprietor.

In the same MS. paper the following jottings occur :—

A moon among her stars, a mighty vale,
Fresh as the freshest field, scooped out, and green
As is the greenest billow of the sea.

Again—

    The multitude of little rocky hills
    Rocky or green, that do like islands rise
    From the flat meadow lonely there.

The poems on *The Wishing-gate* and *The*

Wishing-gate Destroyed, are too well known to be quoted in full. But the opening stanzas of the first poem, with Wordsworth's prefatory note, are as follows :—

In the vale of Grasmere, by the side of the old highway leading to Ambleside, is a gate, which, time out of mind, has been called the Wishing-gate, from a belief that wishes formed or indulged there have a favourable issue.

Hope rules a land for ever green :
All powers that serve the bright-eyed Queen
    Are confident and gay ;
Clouds at her bidding disappear ;
Points she to aught ?—the bliss draws near,
    And fancy smoothes the way.

Not such the land of Wishes—there
Dwell fruitless day-dreams, lawless prayer,
    And thoughts with things at strife ;
Yet how forlorn, should *ye* depart,
Ye superstitions of the *heart*,
    How poor, were human life !

When magic lore abjured its might,
Ye did not forfeit one dear right,
    One tender claim abate ;
Witness this symbol of your sway,
Surviving near the public way,
    The rustic Wishing-gate !

Inquire not if the faery race
Shed kindly influence on the place,
    Ere northward they retired ;
If here a warrior left a spell,
Panting for glory as he fell ;
    Or here a saint expired.

Enough that all around is fair
Composed with Nature's finest care,
 And in her fondest love—
Peace to embosom and content—
To overawe the turbulent,
 The selfish to reprove.

Yea: even the Stranger from afar,
Reclining on this moss-grown bar,
 Unknowing, and unknown,
The infection of the ground partakes,
Longing for his Beloved—who makes
 All happiness her own.

The second poem begins thus:—

'Tis gone—with old belief and dream
That round it clung, and tempting scheme
 Released from fear and doubt;
And the bright landscape too must lie,
By this blank wall, from every eye,
 Relentlessly shut out.

Bear witness ye who seldom passed
That opening—but a look ye cast
 Upon the lake below,
What spirit-stirring power it gained
From faith which here was entertained,
 Though reason might say no.

Blest is that ground, where, o'er the springs
Of history, Glory claps her wings,
 Fame sheds the exulting tear;
Yet earth is wide, and many a nook
Unheard of is, like this, a book
 For modest meanings dear.

It was in sooth a happy thought
That grafted, on so fair a spot,
   So confident a token
Of coming good ;—the charm is fled ;
Indulgent centuries spun a thread,
   Which one harsh day has broken.

A gate, though not the "moss-grown bar" of
Wordsworth's time, still stands at the old place,
where he tells us one had stood " time out of mind."
Long may it stand, defying wind and weather.

The poem which follows this one, in the series
entitled *Poems of the Imagination*, is so characteristic that I insert it in full. It is called *The
Primrose of the Rock*. "This Rock," says Wordsworth, "stands on the right hand, a little way
leading up the vale from Rydal to Grasmere"
(I. F. MS.). "We have been in the habit of calling
it the Glow-worm Rock, from the number of glow-
worms we have often seen hanging on it as
described. The tuft of primroses has, I fear, been
washed away by heavy rains."

A Rock there is whose homely front
   The passing traveller slights :
Yet there the glow-worms hang their lamps,
   Like stars at various heights ; [1]
And one coy Primrose to that Rock
   The vernal breeze invites.

What hideous warfare hath been waged,
   What kingdoms overthrown,
Since first I spied that Primrose-tuft
   And marked it for my own ;
A lasting link in Nature's chain
   From highest heaven let down !

[1] Compare the reference to the glow-worms in the
second stanza of *The Waggoner*.

The flowers, still faithful to the stems,
　　Their fellowship renew ;
The stems are faithful to the root,
　　That worketh out of view :
And to the rock the root adheres
　　In every fibre true.

Close clings to earth the living rock,
　　Though threatening still to fall ;
The earth is constant to her sphere :
　　And God upholds them all :
So blooms this lonely Plant, nor dreads
　　Her annual funeral.

　　.　　　.　　　.　　　.　　　.　　　.

Here closed the meditative strain ;
　　But air breathed soft that day,
The hoary mountain-heights were cheered,
　　The sunny vale looked gay ;
And to the Primrose of the Rock
　　I gave this after-lay.

I sang—Let myriads of bright flowers,
　　Like Thee—in field and grove
Revive unenvied :—mightier far,
　　Than tremblings that reprove
Our vernal tendencies to hope,
　　Is God's redeeming love :

That love which changed— for wan disease,
　　For sorrow that had bent
O'er hopeless dust, for withered age—
　　Their moral element,
And turned the thistles of a curse
　　To types beneficent.

H

Sin-blighted though we are, we too,
   The reasoning Sons of Men,
From one oblivious winter called
   Shall rise, and breathe again;
And in eternal summer lose
   Our threescore years and ten.

To humbleness of heart descends
   This prescience from on high,
The faith that elevates the just,
   Before and when they die;
And makes each soul a separate heaven,
   A court for Deity.

The primrose has disappeared, and the glow-worms have, since 1860, deserted the place, but the rock is unmistakable; and it is one of the most interesting of the verifiable reminiscences of Wordsworth. The poem is perhaps the most profoundly imaginative in the series.

The poem, which was known in the Wordsworth household as *The Glow-worm*, which refers to his sister, and was written in 1802, but only published in the 1807 edition of the poems, should here find a place. It was often repeated aloud in the Grasmere orchard, although composed near Barnard Castle.

Among all lovely things my Love had been;
   Had noted well the stars; all flowers that grew
About her home; but she had never seen
   A glow-worm, never one, and this I knew.

While riding near her home one starry night,
   A single glow-worm did I chance to espy:
I gave a fervent welcome to the sight,
   And from my horse I leapt, great joy had I.

Upon a leaf the glow-worm did I lay,
　To bear it with me through the starry night:
And, as before, it shone without dismay;
　Albeit putting forth a fainter light.

When to the dwelling of my Love I came,
　I went into the orchard quietly;
And left the glow-worm, blessing it by name,
　Laid safely by itself, beneath a tree.

The whole next day I hoped, and hoped with fear;
　At night the glow-worm shone beneath the tree:
I led my Lucy to the spot, " Look here!"
　Oh! joy it was for her, and joy for me!

An interesting parallel and contrast may be traced between Wordsworth's primrose, which bloomed, and did not dread " her annual funeral," and Keble's reference to the "decaying life" of Nature, and the "vernal raptures" of the coming year, in his hymn for the Twenty-third Sunday after Trinity.

It was at the quarry, hard by "the primrose rock," that Wordsworth met *The Beggars*, on whom he wrote two poems; in the second of which (composed many years afterwards) the following lines occur :—

　They met me in a genial hour,
When universal nature breathed
As with the breath of one sweet flower,—
A time to overrule the power
Of discontent, and check the birth
Of thoughts with better thoughts at strife,
The most familiar bane of life
Since parting Innocence bequeathed
Mortality to Earth!
Soft clouds, the whitest of the year,

Sailed through the sky—the brooks ran clear;
The lambs from rock to rock were bounding;
With songs the budded groves resounding;
And to my heart are still endeared
The thoughts with which it then was cheered.

Returning from Rydal Lake to Grasmere by
either road, almost every turn brings up some
fresh suggestion of the poet.   It was near the
Wishing-gate that he met *The Sailor's Mother*.

Majestic in her person, tall and straight;
And like a Roman matron's was her mien and
      gait.
The ancient spirit is not dead;
Old times, thought I, are breathing there;
Proud was I that my country bred
Such strength, a dignity so fair:
She begged an alms, like one in poor estate.

The Vale of Grasmere is, as De Quincey remarked,
" solitary, yet sowed, as it were, with a thin diffusion
of humble dwellings—here a scattering, and there
a clustering, as in the starry heavens."[1] A few
hundred yards from Dove cottage Wordsworth
met the old leech-gatherer, immortalised in the
poem *Resolution and Independence*.   The " pool
bare to the eye of heaven," on the margin of
which

Motionless as a cloud the old man stood,
That heareth not the loud winds when they call,
And moveth altogether if it move at all,

must have been the pool on White Moss Common.
   On the way down from this pool to the side of the

---

[1] *Recollections of the Lakes,* p. 124.

lake, there used to be a grove on its north-eastern margin—in great measure destroyed by the new highroad along the side of the water—in which Wordsworth composed two poems, *The Brothers* and *Michael*. The character of Leonard in the former poem is in large part drawn from that of his brother John (who also supplied him with some material for *The Character of the Happy Warrior*). The story arose out of a fact mentioned to him at Ennerdale, that a shepherd had fallen asleep at the top of *The Pillar*, and perished by falling over the rock.

I will relate a tale for those who love
.To lie beside the lonely mountain brooks,
And hear the voices of the winds and flowers.
   .   .   .   .   It befell,
At the first falling of the autumnal snows,
Old Michael and his son one day went forth
In search of a stray sheep.   It was the time
When from the heights our shepherds drive their
    flocks
To gather all their mountain family
Into the homestalls, ere they send them back
There to defend themselves the winter long.
Old Michael for this purpose had driven down
His flock into the vale, but as it chanced,
A single sheep was wanting.   They had sought
The straggler during all the previous day
All over their own pastures, and beyond.
And now at sunrise, sallying forth again,
Far did they go that morning: with their search
Beginning towards the south, where from Dove
    Crag
(Ill home for bird so gentle), they looked down
On Deep-dale-head, and Brother's Water (named
From those two Brothers that were drowned
    therein);

Thence northward did they pass by Arthur's seat,
And Fairfield's highest summit, on the right
Leaving St. Sunday's Crag, to Grisdale tarn
They shot, and over that cloud-loving hill,
Seat-Sandal, a fond lover of the clouds;
Thence up Helvellyn, a superior mount,
With prospect underneath of striding edge,
And Grisdale's houseless vale, along the brink
Of Sheep-cot-cove, and those two other coves,
Huge skeletons of crags which from the coast
Of old Helvellyn spread their arms abroad
And make a stormy harbour for the winds.
Far went these shepherds in their devious quest,
From mountain ridges peeping as they passed
Down into every nook;   .   .   .   .
.   .   .   .   and many a sheep
On height or bottom[1] did they see, in flocks
Or single.   And although it needs must seem
Hard to believe, yet could they well discern,
Even at the utmost distance of two miles,
(Such strength of vision to the shepherd's eye
Doth practice give), that neither in the flocks
Nor in the single sheep was what they sought.
So to Helvellyn's eastern side they went,
Down looking on that hollow, where the pool
Of Thirlmere flashes like a warrior's shield,
His light high up among the gloomy rocks,
With sight of now and then a straggling gleam
On Armath's[2] pleasant fields.   And now they came
To that high spring which bears no human name,
As one unknown by others, aptly called
The Fountain of the Mists.   The father stooped
To drink of the clear water, laid himself
Flat on the ground, even as a boy might do,
To drink of the cold well.   When in like sort

[1] Bottom is a common Cumbrian word for valley.
[2] Armboth, on the western side of Thirlmere.

His son had drunk, the old man said to him
That now he might be proud, for he that day
Had slaked his thirst out of a famous well,
The highest fountain known on British land.
Thence, journeying on a second time, they passed
Those small flat stones, which, ranged by traveller's
    hands
In cyphers on Helvellyn's highest ridge,
Lie loose on the bare turf, some half o'ergrown
By the grey moss, but not a single stone
Unsettled by a wanton blow from foot
Of shepherd, man or boy.   They have respect
For strangers who have travelled far, perhaps ;
For men who in such places, feeling there
The grandeur of the earth, have left inscribed
Their epitaph, which rain and snow
And the strong wind have reverenced.

   •   •   •   •   •   •   •

• Though often thus industriously they passed
Whole hours with but small interchange of speech,
Yet were there times in which they did not want
Discourse both wise and pleasant, shrewd remarks
Of moral prudence, clothed in images
Lively and beautiful, in rural forms,
That made their conversation fresh and fair
As is a landscape; and the shepherd oft
Would draw out of his heart the mysteries
And admirations that were there, of God
And of His works : or, yielding to the bent
Of his peculiar humour, would let loose
His tongue, and give it the wind's freedom ; then,
Discoursing in remote imaginations, strong
Conceits, devices, plans, and schemes,
Of alterations human hands might make
Among the mountains, fens which might be
    drained,
Mines opened, forests planted, and rocks split,
The fancies of a solitary man.

Of *Michael*, Wordsworth said to Miss Fenwick,
" The sheepfold remains, or rather the ruins of it.
The character and circumstances of Luke were
taken from a family to whom had belonged, many
years before, the house we lived in at Town-End.
The name of the Evening Star was not given to
this house, but to another on the same side of the
valley, more to the north" (I. F. MS.).[1]   There is a
sheepfold, when you first enter the common going
up Green-head Ghyll, which is now "finished,"
and is used when required.   There are remains
of walling much higher up the Ghyll, but they
are probably the work of miners who were engaged
there.

The poem begins thus—

    If from the public way you turn your step
Up the tumultuous brook of Green-head Ghyll
You will suppose that with an upright path
Your feet must struggle ; in such bold ascent
The pastoral mountains front you, face to face.
But, courage ! for around that boisterous brook
The mountains have all opened out themselves,
And made a hidden valley of their own.
No habitation can be seen ; but they
Who journey thither find themselves alone
With a few sheep, with rocks and stones, and kites
That overhead are sailing in the sky.
It is in truth an utter solitude ;
Nor should I have made mention of this Dell
But for one object which you might pass by,
Might see and notice not.   Beside the brook
Appears a straggling heap of unhewn stones ;
And to that simple object appertains
A story—unenriched with strange events,

---

[1] *Prose Works*, vol. iii. p. 27.

Yet not unfit, I deem, for the fireside,
Or for the summer shade.   It was the first
Of those domestic tales that spake to me
Of Shepherds, dwellers in the valleys, men
Whom I already loved ;—not verily
For their own sakes, but for the fields and hills
Where was their occupation and abode.

    .   .   .   .

   Upon the forest side in Grasmere Vale
There dwelt a Shepherd, Michael was his name ;
An old man, stout of heart, and strong of limb.
His bodily frame had been from youth to age
Of an unusual strength : his mind was keen,
Intense, and frugal, apt for all affairs,
And in his shepherd's calling he was prompt
And watchful more than ordinary men.
Hence had he learned the meaning of all winds,
Of blasts of every tone ; and, oftentimes,
When others heeded not, he heard the South
Make subterraneous music, like the noise
Of bagpipers on distant Highland hills,
The Shepherd at such warning, of his flock
Bethought him, and he to himself would say,
"The winds are now devising work for me !"
And, truly, at all times, the storm, that drives
The traveller to a shelter, summoned him
Up to the mountains : he had been alone
Amid the heart of many thousand mists,
That came to him, and left him, on the heights.
So lived he till his eightieth year was past.
And grossly that man errs, who should suppose
That the green valleys, and the streams and rocks,
Were things indifferent to the Shepherd's thoughts
Fields, where with cheerful spirits he had breathed
The common air ; hills, which with vigorous step
He had so often climbed ; which had impressed
So many incidents upon his mind
Of hardship, skill or courage, joy or fear ;

Which, like a book, preserved the memory
Of the dumb animals whom he had saved,
Had fed or sheltered, linking to such acts
The certainty of honourable gain ;
Those fields, those hills—what could they
    less?—had laid
Strong hold on his affections, were to him
A pleasurable feeling of blind love,
The pleasure which there is in life itself.

Michael's home is thus described—

Their cottage on a plot of rising ground
Stood single, with large prospect, north and
    south,
High into Easdale, up to Dunmail-Raise,
And westward to the village near the lake ;
And from this constant light, so regular
And so far seen, the House itself, by all
Who dwelt within the limits of the vale,
Both old and young, was named THE EVENING
    STAR.

This cottage was gone when the poem was
written in 1800. It stood where the coach-house
and stables of "The Hollins" now stand. It is
easy for any one visiting Green-head Ghyll to
realise Michael in his old age, as described in
that most pathetic of poems.

                        Among the rocks
He went, and still looked up to sun and cloud,
And listened to the wind ; and, as before,
Performed all kinds of labour for his sheep,
And for the land, his small inheritance.
And to that hollow dell from time to time
Did he repair, to build the Fold of which
His flock had need.

Of his cottage it is said—

> The ploughshare has been through the ground
> On which it stood ; great changes have been wrought
> In all the neighbourhood :—yet the oak is left
> That grew beside their door ; and the remains
> Of the unfinished Sheepfold may be seen
> Beside the boisterous brook of Green-head Ghyll.

The cottage formerly inhabited by the Lewthwaites, the parents of Barbara Lewthwaite, whose name survives in connection with *The Pet Lamb*, is much altered and modernised, but it may still be seen on the high road immediately below "The Hollins." It is now called "The Grove," or "Grove Cottage." It appears from Wordsworth's note, however, that he borrowed nothing from Barbara except her name and her beauty, and the locality does not possess a high interest in connection with the poem.

The island in Grasmere Lake is frequently referred to in the poems; notably in the series of *Inscriptions* in the fifth volume. Number five in that series was "written with a pencil upon a stone in the wall of the house (an outhouse) on the island of Grasmere."

> Thou seest a homely Pile, yet to these walls
> The heifer comes in the snow-storm, and here
> The new-dropped lamb finds shelter from the wind.
> And hither does one Poet sometimes row
> His pinnace, a small vagrant barge, up-piled
> With plenteous store of heath and withered fern,
> (A lading which he with his sickle cuts
> Among the mountains) and beneath this roof
> He makes his summer couch, and here at noon
> Spreads out his limbs, while, yet unshorn, the Sheep,
> Panting beneath the burthen of their wool,

Lie round him, even as if they were a part
Of his own Household: nor, while from his bed
He looks, through the open door-place, toward
        the lake
And to the stirring breezes, does he want
Creations lovely as the work of sleep—
Fair sights and visions of romantic joy!

On the western shore of the lake, Wyke Cottage
may be seen, where Sarah Mackereth lived—*The
Westmoreland Girl*— nine years of age, who
plunged into the torrent and rescued a lamb when
it was being swept into the lake, child and lamb
being carried together some distance by the flood,
and who was the heroine of a poem written by
Wordsworth for his grandchildren. She married a
man named Davis, and settled at Broughton, in
Furness, where she died in 1872. The beck—
Wyke Gill beck—is that which descends from the
centre of Silver How. This picturesque cottage, with
round chimney—a yew tree and Scotch fir behind
it—is on the western side of the road which leads
from Grasmere to Langdale by Red Bank. The
Mackereths are a well-known Westmoreland family.
They belong to the "gentry of the soil," and have
been parish clerks in Grasmere for generations.
One of them was the tenant of the Swan Inn,
referred to in *The Waggoner*, the "host" who
painted, with his own hand, "the famous swan"
used as a sign. They have been in the district, I
am informed, for several hundred years.

Allan Bank, the house in which Wordsworth
lived for nearly four years—from the spring of
1807, when he left Dove Cottage, till the spring of
1811, when he removed to the parsonage at
Grasmere—is chiefly interesting as the place where
most of *The Excursion* was composed. The
house has been much altered and added to since

the poet's time. He was its first occupant. The grounds command fine views of Loughrigg and Silver How, with the lake below, as well as of the valley northwards towards Dunmail-Raise; but somehow Allan Bank is not associated with Wordsworth, as Hawkhead, Dove Cottage, and Rydal are. He has written nothing which leads us to think of it as in any way interesting to himself.

Loughrigg Tarn, on the southern slope of Loughrigg Fell, is described in Wordsworth's Book on the Lakes, and also in his *Epistle to Sir George Beaumont*, written in the year 1811, which records the first part of a journey taken by the poet's household from Grasmere to Bootle by the Sea for the benefit of the children; a composition which Wordsworth thought very little of. He never sent it to Sir George, ranking it in merit along with his tragedy of *The Borderers*. Some portions of it, however, have a topographical interest.

> . . . From our own dear Vale we pass
> And soon approach Diana's Looking-glass!
> To Loughrigg-tarn, round clear and bright as heaven,
> Such name Italian fancy would have given,
> Ere on its banks the few grey cabins rose
> That yet disturb not its concealed repose
> More than the feeblest wind that idly blows.

> Ah, Beaumont! when an opening in the road
> Stopped me at once by charm of what it showed
> The encircling region vividly exprest
> Within the mirror's depth, a world at rest—
> Sky streaked with purple, grove and craggy *bield*,
> And the smooth green of many a pendent field,
> And, quieted and soothed, a torrent small,
> A little daring would-be waterfall,
> One chimney smoking and its azure wreath,
> Associate all in the calm Pool beneath,

With here and there a faint imperfect gleam
Of water-lilies veiled in misty steam—
What wonder at this hour of stillness deep,
A shadowy link 'tween wakefulness and sleep,
When Nature's self, amid such blending, seems
To render visible her own soft dreams,
If, mixed with what appeared of rock, lawn, wood,
Fondly embosomed in the tranquil flood,
A glimpse I caught of that Abode, by Thee
Designed to rise in humble privacy,
A lowly Dwelling, here to be outspread,
Like a small Hamlet, with its bashful head
Half hid in native trees.   Alas 'tis not,
Nor ever was; I sighed, and left the spot
Unconscious of its own untoward lot,
And thought in silence, with regret too keen,
Of unexperienced joys that might have been;
Of neighbourhood and intermingling arts,
And golden summer days uniting cheerful hearts.
But time, irrevocable time, is flown,
And let us utter thanks for blessings sown
And reaped—what hath been, and what is, our own.

The reference in the concluding lines is to Sir
George Beaumont's purchase of the Tarn, with the
view of building a residence there.   What Wordsworth says of the subsequent sale of this property
may be quoted, because it led him to speak of the
yew-trees in Grasmere, one of which now shelters
his own grave.   The extracts are taken from the
I. F. MS.   "The project of building was given up,
Sir George retaining possession of the Tarn.   Many
years afterwards a Kendal tradesman, born upon
its banks, applied to me for the purchase of it, and
accordingly it was sold for the sum that had been
given for it, and the money laid out, under my
direction, upon a substantial oak fence for a certain
number of yew-trees to be planted in Grasmere

churchyard. Two were planted in each enclosure
(and principally, if not entirely, by my own hand)
with a view to remove, after a certain time, the one
which throve the least.   After several years, the
stouter plant being left, the others were taken up
and planted in other parts of the same churchyard,
and were adequately fenced.   The whole eight are
now thriving, and are an ornament to a place
which, during late years, has lost much of its
rustic simplicity by the introduction of iron
palisades to fence off family burying-grounds, and
by numerous ornaments, some of them in very bad
taste, from which this place of burial was in my
memory quite free; see the lines in the sixth
book of *The Excursion* beginning 'Green is the
churchyard'" (I. F. MS.).   " May the trees be taken
care of hereafter, when we are all gone; and some
of them will, perhaps, at some far distant time, rival
the majesty of the yew of Lorton, and those which
I have described as growing at Borrowdale, where
they are still to be seen in grand assemblage."[1]

The note appended to the sequel of this poem,
composed thirty years afterwards, is to the following effect: "Loughrigg Tarn, alluded to in the
foregoing epistle, resembles, though much smaller
in compass, the Lake Nemi, or *Speculum Dianæ*, as
it is often called, not only in its clear waters and
circular form, and the beauty immediately surrounding it, but also as being overlooked by the
eminence of Langdale Pikes, as Lake Nemi is by
that of Monte Calvo.   Since this epistle was
written, Loughrigg Tarn has lost much of its beauty
by the felling of many natural clumps of wood,
relics of the old forest, particularly upon the farm
called 'The Oaks,' from the abundance of that tree

[1] *Memoirs*, vol. i. p. 376: also *Prose Works*, vol.
iii. pp. 177, 202.

which grew there. It is to be regretted, upon
public grounds, that Sir George Beaumont did not
carry into effect his intention of constructing here
a Summer Retreat, in the style I have described,
as his taste would have set an example *how buildings with all the accommodations modern society
requires might be introduced even into the most
secluded parts of the country without injuring their
native character.*" There are few persons of or-
dinarily cultivated taste will not share this regret,
when they see the many modern erections at Grasmere and Ambleside, which, by the hardness of
their lines, and their general obtrusiveness, interfere
with the seclusion of these places, and jar with the
whole spirit of the district.

In July 1844, Wordsworth walked round by Rydal
and Grasmere to Loughrigg Tarn with Sir William
Rowan Hamilton, Charles Julius Hare, Archer
Butler of Dublin, the Rev. Percival Graves, etc.
Mr. Graves, now of Dublin, but then at Windermere,
writes of it thus : "The day was memorable as
giving birth to an interesting minor poem of Mr.
Wordsworth's. When we reached the side of
Loughrigg Tarn (which, you may remember, he
notes for its similarity, in the peculiar character of
its beauty, to the Lago di Nemi, *Dianæ Speculum*),
the loveliness of the scene arrested our steps and
fixed our gaze. The splendour of a July noon
surrounded us and lit up the landscape, with the
Langdale Pikes soaring above, and the bright Tarn
shining beneath; and when the poet's eyes were
satisfied with their feast on the beauties familiar to
them, they sought relief in the search, to them a
happy vital habit, for new beauty in the flower-
enamelled turf at his feet. There his attention was
arrested by a fair smooth stone, of the size of an
ostrich's egg, seeming to imbed at its centre, and
at the same time to display a dark, star-shaped

fossil of most distinct outline. Upon closer inspection, this proved to be the shadow of a daisy projected upon it with extraordinary precision by the intense light of an almost vertical sun. The poet drew the attention of the rest of the party to the minute but beautiful phenomenon, and gave expression at the time to thoughts suggested by it, which so interested our friend, Professor Butler, that he plucked the tiny flower, and saying that ' it should be not only the theme but the memorial of the thought they had heard,' bestowed it somewhere carefully for preservation." The little poem, in which some of these thoughts were crystallized, is as follows—

So fair, so sweet, withal so sensitive:
Would that the little flowers wère born to live
Conscious of half the pleasure which they give;

That to this mountain-daisy's self were known
The beauty of its star-shaped shadow, thrown
On the smooth surface of this naked stone!

And what if hence a bold desire should mount
High as the Sun, that he could take account
Of all that issues from his glorious fount!

So might he ken how by his sovereign aid
These delicate companionships are made;
And how he rules the pomp of light and shade;

And were the sister-power that shines by night
So privileged, what a countenance of delight
Would through the clouds break forth on human
        sight!

Fond fancies! wheresoe'er shall turn thine eye
On earth, air, ocean, or the starry sky,
Converse with Nature in pure sympathy;

All vain desires, all lawless wishes quelled
Be thou to love and praise alike impelled,
Whatever boon is granted or withheld.

I

The reference to the yew-trees leads us naturally
back to Grasmere and its churchyard.

The "Church" in *The Excursion*, Wordsworth
himself tells us, is that of Grasmere. Several of
its features are, however, taken from other places,
such as Bowness, and (perhaps?) Hawkshead. The
"Churchyard among the Mountains" is mainly that
of Grasmere, though some of the graves described
are elsewhere—*e.g.*, that of the "gentle dalesman,"
who was deaf.

> He grew up
> From year to year in loneliness of soul,
> And this deep mountain-valley was to him
> Soundless, with all its streams.

His grave is in the churchyard at Hawes Water.

In his account of the scenes and characters in
The Excursion (see Fenwick MS.), Wordsworth
refers to the house at Hackett, which he imaginatively converted into the parsonage, and proceeds:
"At the same time, and as by the waving of a
magic wand, I turn the comparatively confined vale
of Langdale into the stately and comparatively
spacious vale of Grasmere, and its ancient parish
church."[1]

> —So we descend: and winding round a rock
> Attain a point that showed the valley—stretched
> In length before us; and, not distant far,
> Upon a rising-ground a grey church tower,
> Whose battlements were screened by tufted trees.
> And towards a crystal Mere, that lay beyond
> Among steep hills and woods embosomed, flowed
> A copious stream with boldly-winding course;
> Here traceable, there hidden—there again
> To sight restored, and glittering in the sun.

[1] *Prose Works*, vol. iii. p. 199.

On the stream's bank, and everywhere appeared
Fair dwellings, single, or in social knots;
Some scattered o'er the level, others perched
On the hill sides, a cheerful, quiet scene,
Now in its morning purity arrayed.[1]

" The interior of the church has been improved
lately by underdrawing the roof and raising the
floor ; but the rude and antique majesty of its
former appearance has been impaired by painting
the rafters ; and the oak benches, with a simple
rail at the back dividing them from each other,
have given way to seats that have more the appearance of pews."[2]

Oft pausing, we pursued our way;
Nor reached the village churchyard till the sun,
Travelling at steadier pace than ours, had risen
Above the summits of the highest hills,
And round our path darted oppressive beams.

As chanced, the portals of the sacred Pile
Stood open ; and we entered.   On my frame,
At such transition from the fervid air,
A grateful coolness fell, that seemed to strike
The heart, in concert with that temperate awe
And natural reverence with the place inspired.
Not raised in nice proportions was the pile,
But large and massy ; for duration built ;
With pillars crowded, and the roof upheld
By naked rafters intricately crossed,
Like leafless underboughs, in some thick wood,
All withered by the depth of shade above.

[1] *Excursion*, book v.
[2] *Prose Works*, vol. iii. p. 201

Admonitory texts inscribed the walls,
Each in its ornamental scroll inclosed;
Each also crowned with winged heads—a pair
Of rudely-painted Cherubim.   The floor
Of nave and aisle, in unpretending guise,
Was occupied by oaken benches ranged
In seemly rows; the chancel only showed
Some vain distinctions, marks of earthly state
By immemorial privilege allowed;
Though with the Encincture's special sanctity
But ill according.   An heraldic shield,
Varying its tincture with the changeful light,
Imbued the altar-window; fixed aloft
A faded hatchment hung, and one by time
Yet undiscoloured.   A capacious pew
Of sculptured oak stood here, with drapery
    lined;
And marble monuments were here displayed
Thronging the walls; and on the floor beneath
Sepulchral stones appeared, with emblems
    graven
And foot-worn epitaphs.[1]

All these are in Grasmere church as described, the
"naked rafters intricately crossed," the "admonitory texts" "each in its ornamental scroll enclosed," the "oaken benches," the "heraldic shield"
in the "altar window," the "faded hatchment," the
"marble monuments," and "sepulchral stones, with
foot-worn epitaphs."   The Wanderer, the Solitary,
and Wordsworth withdraw from the church to

                                        a spot
Where sun and shade were intermixed; for there
A broad oak, stretching forth its leafy arms
From an adjoining pasture, overhung

[1] *Excursion*, book v.   *Poetical Works*, vol. v. p. 142.

Small space of that green churchyard with a light
And pleasant awning.   On the moss-grown wall
My ancient Friend and I together took
Our seats.[1]

An oak now grows in the field, a little to the east
of the churchyard wall, which cannot, however, be
that to which Wordsworth refers.   Probably an
oak then grew beside the wall above the Rothay.
While the three are seated together on that wall,
the village pastor is represented as joining them.
The character of the pastor is gathered, Wordsworth tells us, from that of several individuals:
notably from the Rev. Mr. Walker of Seathwaite,
" the wonderful Walker."

The dramatic structure of *The Excursion* is so
defective, that it is extremely difficult to follow the
changes of place ; and, for the main purpose which
Wordsworth had in view, this is unnecessary.
Nevertheless, there is more order in the develop-
ment of the narrative than is sometimes supposed.
The group of meditative talkers are first supposed
to be seated on the moss-grown wall to the *east* of
the churchyard, facing Silver How.   This I infer
from the reference to Wray Ghyll beck (*infra*,
p. 103), and from the way in which the pastor
describes the graves in the churchyard if seen in
April, after snow had fallen, and if approached
from the north.   I quote this passage, though it is
more prosaic than the rest, as a clue to the identification of places :—

.   .   .   .   .   . Human life
Is either fair and tempting, a soft scene
Grateful to sight, refreshing to the soul,
Or a forbidden track of cheerless view,

[1] *Excursion*, book v.

Even as the same is looked at, or approached.
Thus, when in changeful April fields are white
With new-fallen snow, if from the sullen north
Your walk conduct you hither, ere the sun
Hath gained his noontide height, this church-
    yard, filled
With mounds transversely lying side by side
From east to west, before you will appear
An unillumined, blank, and dreary plain,
With more than wintry cheerlessness and gloom
Saddening the heart. Go forward, and look back ;
Look, from the quarter whence the lord of light,
Of life, of love, and gladness doth dispense
His beams ; which, unexcluded in their fall,
Upon the southern side of every grave
Have gently exercised a melting power ;
Then will a vernal prospect greet your eye,
All fresh and beautiful, and green and bright,
Hopeful and cheerful :—vanished is the pall
That overspread and chilled the sacred turf,
Vanished or hidden ; and the whole domain,
To some, too lightly minded, might appear
A meadow carpet for the dancing hours.[1]

From the next quotation it will be seen that
Wordsworth's description of the place is wonderfully true to Grasmere and its surroundings. Thus
the pastor is represented as saying to the group
seated on the wall—

                    You behold,
High on the breast of yon dark mountain, dark
With stony barrenness, a shining speck
Bright as a sunbeam sleeping till a shower
Brush it away, or cloud pass over it ;
And such it might be deemed—a sleeping sun-
    beam ;

[1] *Excursion*, book v. p. 153.

But 'tis a plot of cultivated ground,
Cut off, an island in the dusky waste ;
And that attractive brightness is its own.
The lofty side, by Nature framed to tempt
Amid a wilderness of rocks and stones
The tiller's hand, a hermit might have chosen,
For opportunity presented thence
Far forth to send his wandering eye o'er land
And ocean, and look down upon the works,
The habitations, and the ways of men,
Himself unseen !   But no tradition tells
That ever hermit dipped his maple dish
In the sweet spring that lurks 'mid yon green
     fields ;
And no such visionary views belong
To those who occupy and till the ground,
High on that mountain where they long have
     dwelt
A wedded pair in childless solitude.
A house of stones collected on the spot,
By rude hands built, with rocky knolls in front,
Backed also by a ledge of rock, whose crest
Of birch trees waves over the chimney top.[1]

The mountain is Lingmoor, and Hackett may be the house described ; although it is impossible to say where was the " house of stones collected on the spot," or " the spring," or the shining plot of cultivated ground, " the sleeping sunbeam." They may have been real, or they may have been merely ideal creations.   The I. F. notes contain no hint.   But one of the next references to locality occurring in *The Excursion* is an unmistakable allusion to the Wray Ghyll Force, which descends between Silver How and Easdale—

[1] *Excursion*, book v.

> The soft voice
> Of yon white torrent falling down the rock,
> Speaks less distinctly to the same effect.[1]

No other white torrent falling down rocks is visible
from the churchyard of Grasmere. This one is
distinctly seen when looking towards Silver How
to the west.

The group who carry on high argument on the
deep questions raised in *The Excursion*, are afterwards supposed to leave the "moss-grown-wall—

> The vicar paused, and toward a seat advanced,
> A long stone seat, fixed in the churchyard wall ;
> Part shaded by cool sycamore, and part
> Offering a sunny resting place.   .   .   .
> Beneath the shade we all sat down.[2]   .   .   .

This "long stone seat" was fixed to the wall on
the left of the south entrance-gate into the churchyard ; and not, as might be supposed, on the
opposite wall, which runs down from the poet's
grave towards the bridge. The wall was rebuilt,
and the stone seat omitted from it by the late
rector.

Of the "decorated pillar," with the "dial," in the
churchyard, mentioned in the same book,[3] there is
no trace or tradition at Grasmere. There is, however, a pillar in Bowness churchyard on which a
dial used to stand.

The clergyman described in the seventh book is
the Rev. Joseph Sympson of Wytheburn, whose
household were for many years the principal associates of the Wordsworth family in Grasmere. The
I. F. MS. tell us that all that is said of them in the

---

[1] *Excursion*, book vi.   [2] *Ibid.* book vi.
[3] *Ibid.* book vi.

poem is "as faithful to the truth as words can make it."[1]

The vicar is addressing the others in the group, and he says—

—Once more look forth, and follow with your
    sight
The length of road that from yon mountain's base
Through bare enclosures stretches, 'till its line
Is lost within a little tuft of trees;
Then, reappearing in a moment, quits
The cultured fields: and up the heathy waste,
Mounts, as you see, in mazes serpentine,
Led towards an easy outlet of the vale.
That little shady spot, that sylvan tuft,
By which the road is hidden, also hides
A cottage from our view; though I discern
(Ye scarcely can) amid its sheltering trees
The smokeless chimney-top.—

                    All unembowered
And naked stood that lowly Parsonage
(For such in truth it is, and appertains
To a small Chapel in the vale beyond)
When hither came its last Inhabitant.
Rough and forbidding were the choicest roads
By which our northern wilds could then be
    crossed:
And into most of these secluded vales
Was no access for wain, heavy or light.[2]

The road "up the heathy waste," mounting "in mazes serpentine," is the Keswick road over Dunmail-Raise, the "easy outlet of the vale." The cottage in which the parson of Wytheburn then lived still stands on the right or eastern side of the

[1] *Prose Works*, vol. iii. p. 207.
[2] *Excursion*, book vii.

road as you ascend the Raise, beyond the Swan
Inn.   It abuts on the public road about 300 yards
beyond the bridge over Tongue Ghyll beck.

<blockquote>

                  Bleak and bare
They found the cottage, their allotted home;
Naked without, and rude within; a spot
With which the Cure not long had been endowed;
And far remote the chapel stood,—remote,
And, from his Dwelling, unapproachable,
Save through a gap high in the hills, an opening
Shadeless and shelterless, by driving showers
Frequented, and beset with howling winds.[1]

  .   .   .   .   .

                  So days and years
Passed on:—the inside of that rugged house
Was trimmed and brightened by the Matron's care,
And gradually enriched with things of price,
Which might be lacked for use or ornament.
What, though no soft and costly sofa there
Insidiously stretched out its lazy length,
And no vain mirror glittered upon the walls,
Yet were the windows of the low abode
By shutters weather-fended, which at once
Repelled the storm and deadened its loud roar.
There snow-white curtains hung in decent folds;
Tough moss, and long-enduring mountain plants
That creep along the ground with sinuous trail,
Were nicely braided; and composed a work
Like Indian mats, that with appropriate grace
Lay at the threshold and the inner doors;
And a fair carpet, woven of homespun wool
But tinctured daintily with florid hues,
For seemliness and warmth, on festal days,
Covered the smooth blue slabs of mountain stone
With which the parlour-floor, in simplest guise
Of pastoral homesteads, had been long inlaid.[2]
</blockquote>

[1] *Excursion*, book vii.   [2] *Ibid.* vii.

The Pastor continues—
When wishes, formed

In youth, and sanctioned by the riper mind,
Restored me to my native valley, here
To end my days; well pleased was I to see
The once-bare cottage, on the mountain-side,
Screen'd from assault of every bitter blast;
While the dark shadows of the summer leaves
Danced in the breeze, chequering its mossy roof.

   .   .   .   .   .   .

   Our very first in eminence of years
This old Man stood, the patriarch of the Vale!
And, to his unmolested mansion, death
Had never come, through space of forty years;
Sparing both old and young in that abode.
Suddenly then they disappeared; not twice
Had summer scorched the fields; nor twice had
    fallen,
On those high peaks, the first autumnal snow,
Before the greedy visiting was closed,
And the long privileged house left empty—swept
As by a plague.   Yet no rapacious plague
Had been among them; all was gentle death,
One after one, with intervals of peace.
A happy consummation! an accord
Sweet, perfect, to be wished for! save that here
Was something which to mortal sense might
    sound
Like harshness,—that the old grey-headed Sire,
The oldest, he was taken last, survived
When the meek Partner of his age, his Son,
His Daughter, and that late and high-prized gift,
His little smiling Grandchild, were no more.

   "All gone, all vanished! he deprived and bare,
How will he face the remnant of his life?
What will become of him?" we said, and mused
In sad conjectures—"Shall we meet him now

Haunting with rod and line the craggy brooks?
Or shall we overhear him, as we pass,
Striving to entertain the lonely hours
With music!" (for he had not ceased to touch
The harp or viol which himself had framed,
For their sweet purposes, with perfect skill).
"What titles will he keep? will he remain
Musician, gardener, builder, mechanist,
A planter, and a rearer from the seed?
A man of hope and forward-looking mind
Even to the last!"—Such was he, unsubdued.
But Heaven was gracious; yet a little while,
And this Survivor, with his cheerful throng
Of open projects, and his inward hoard
Of unsunned griefs, too many and too keen,
Was overcome by unexpected sleep,
In one blest moment.   Like a shadow thrown
Softly and lightly from a passing cloud,
Death fell upon him, while reclined he lay
For noontide solace on the summer grass,
The warm lap of his mother earth: and so,
Their lenient term of separation past,
That family (whose graves you there behold)
By yet a higher privilege once more
Were gathered to each other.[1]

In 1807, in his ninety-second year, old Mr.
Sympson was found dead in his garden on the
opposite side of the road from the cottage, just as
described above. There is now a new door into the
garden, but the posts are old enough to have been
there in Sympson's time. The house is one of the
most easily identified of all the places mentioned
in *The Excursion*. The "blue slabs of mountain
stone," which are common to all old houses in the
vale, are there, just as they were while the old

---

[1] *Excursion,* book vii.

pastor lived, and Wordsworth was his frequent
guest.   The windows too "by shutters weather-
fended," are described with curiously minute
fidelity.   The details as to the fiddle and the love
of planting, which I have not quoted, are from life;
so are the references to the fruit trees in his garden,
and to the interval between his wife's death and his
own.   She was twelve years his junior,

> She, far behind him in the vale of years,

and she predeceased him by a year and a half,

> Not twice had summer, etc.

I mention these details to show how faithful to fact
Wordsworth usually was; and to justify, to any
who may think otherwise, the probability of equal
faithfulness in his allusion to other things and
places.   The "little tuft of trees" (sycamores) still
shelters the old dwelling on the north.   Though no
longer its parsonage, the house still belongs to
Wytheburn church.

The Sympsons are buried in Grasmere.   Their
gravestone stands about ten yards north-west from
that of their poet, not far from the monument
erected in memory of Arthur Hugh Clough.   There
is only one stone, a low one, with a pointed top.

The following is the inscription on it:—"Here
lie the remains of the Reverend Jos. Sympson,
Minister of Wytheburn for more than 50 years.
He died June 27, 1807, aged 92; also of Mary, his
wife, who died Jan. 24, 1806, aged 81; also of Eliz.
Jane, their youngest D^r, who died Sep. 11, 1801,
aged 37."

Their graves are thus described—

> These grassy heaps lie amicably close,
> . . .   Like surges heaving in the wind

Along the surface of a mountain pool :
Five graves, and only five, that rise together
Unsociably sequestered, and encroaching
On the smooth playground of the village school.[1]

For the same reason as that already mentioned,
this very exact reference to the playground of the
village school should be noted. It is described as
"smooth" because it had no graves in it at that
time. "The school," says Dr. Cradock, "was then
and long afterwards held in the house abutting the
Lich-gate, and the children had no playground
except the churchyard. The portion of the ground
nearest the school was not used for burial until
the want of room made it necessary to 'encroach'
on it. The oldest tombstone bears the date 1777."
Wordsworth thus describes the churchyard—

Green is the Churchyard, beautiful and green,
Ridge rising gently by the side of ridge,
A heaving surface, almost wholly free
From interruption of sepulchral stones,
And mantled o'er with aboriginal turf
And everlasting flowers. These Dalesmen trust
The lingering gleam of their departed lives
To oral record, and the silent heart;
Depositories faithful and more kind
Than fondest epitaph.[2]

That it was "almost wholly free from interruption
of sepulchral stones," was literally true in Wordsworth's time. Dr. Cradock says, "I cannot count
more than two or three gravestones of earlier date
than 1800. Most of the others are of a much more
recent date."

[1] *Excursion*, book vii.
[2] *Ibid.* book vi.

On the passage in Book VII. of *The Excursion*, beginning

" Now from the living pass we once again," [1]

he remarks—

"This portion relates to the Greens, a very ancient Grasmere family, settled for generations at Pavement End, which, with a considerable tract of land, is still their property.   The poet describes them as dwelling at Goldrill side, and I had been told that the name was a pure invention to avoid the realism of 'Grasmere' or 'Pavement End.' Such, however, is not exactly the case.   On inquiry from Mr. Fleming Green, one of the family, now residing elsewhere in Grasmere, I find that a small stream, to which Wordsworth himself, from some fancy of his own, had given the name of Goldrill, ran formerly by the roadside, and then turned by the side of the farm at Pavement End towards the lake.   When the road was reconstructed the rill was covered, and can no more be seen there; but it issues freely from a culvert at the back of the premises, and runs by the hedgeside to the lake. Mr. Fleming Green remembers the rill as it was, and pointed out its course to me.   He is a son of one of the 'seven [2] lusty sons' mentioned in the poem.   He said, 'We stuck to the old house till we could no longer stand up in it.'   He is one of a race well termed 'lusty.'   The 'hoary grandsire' and many of his descendants lie buried in a long row a little to the left of the path leading from the church to the lichgate at the north.   Among them is little Margaret (her name and age not unrecorded), but her 'daisied hillock three spans long' is now

[1] *Excursion*, book vii.
[2] Mr. Fleming Green would read "six."

merged in the larger graves of her more aged kindred."

In a corner of this churchyard Wordsworth himself is buried. One who visited the place in 1877 wrote: "To lie under the mound on which the shadow of that grey tower falls, seems scarcely like a banishment from life, only a deeper sleep, in a home quieter but not less lovely than those which surround the margin of the lake. Voices of children come up from the village street, with the hum of rustic life. From sunny heights the lowing of cattle is heard, and the bleat of the sheep that pasture on the hillsides. And by day and night unceasingly, the Rotha, hurrying past the churchyard wall, mingles the babble of its waters with the soft *susurrus* of the breeze, that plays among the sheltering sycamores and yews."—(M. C. T.) The daisy, of which he wrote so much, has its "place upon its poet's grave;" seeming there, if anywhere, to have a "function apostolical."

> Time may restore us in his course
> Goethe's sage mind, and Byron's force;
> But when will Europe's latter hour
> Again find Wordsworth's healing power?
>
> Keep fresh the grass upon his grave
> O Rotha, with thy living wave,
> Sing him thy best! for few or none
> Hear thy voice right, now he is gone.[1]
>
> *Matthew Arnold.*

William Wordsworth and Mary Hutchinson, Dorothy Wordsworth, their daughter Dora (Mrs. Quillinan), and their children who died in infancy, lie together under the shade of one of the yew-trees

---

[1] *Memorial Verses. Poems,* vol. ii. p. 224. Ed. 1877.

which the poet planted. Earth contains few spots
more peaceful or more sacred. It is a fitter resting-
place for the dust of William Wordsworth, than a
corner in Westminster Abbey would have been.

There is another poem associated in a significant way with the vale of Grasmere. It is entitled
(expressively, if cumbrously), *Lines composed at
Grasmere one evening, after a stormy day, the
author having just read in a newspaper that the
dissolution of Mr. Fox was hourly expected.*

> Loud is the Vale ! the Voice is up
> With which she speaks when storms are gone ;
> A mighty unison of streams !
> Of all her Voices, One !
>
> Loud is the Vale ;—this inland Depth
> In peace is roaring like the Sea ;
> Yon star upon the mountain-top
> Is listening quietly.
>
> .   .   .   .   .
>
> A Power is passing from the earth
> To breathless Nature's dark abyss ;
> But when the great and good depart
> What is it more than this—
>
> That Man, who is from God sent forth,
> Doth yet again to God return?—
> Such ebb and flow must ever be,
> Then wherefore should we mourn?

The southern side of Grasmere suggests the last
book of *The Excursion,* entitled the " Discourse of
the Wanderer, and an Evening Visit to the Lake." In

K

the eighth book, entitled "The Parsonage," Wordsworth leaves Grasmere, and imaginatively goes
back to Langdale. He tells us, in the I. F. notes,
that towards the head of Little Langdale "stands
embowered, or partly shaded by yews and other
trees, something between a cottage and a mansion
or gentleman's house, such as they once were in
this country. This I convert into the Parsonage
. . . and upon the side of Loughrigg Fell, at
the foot of Grasmere Lake, and looking down upon
it and the whole Vale, with its accompanying mountains, the 'Pastor' is supposed by me to stand,
when at sunset he addresses his companions."[1]
Again, "The point fixed in my imagination is half-
way up the northern side of Loughrigg Fell."[2]

Dr. Cradock says : " The lake is, of course, in the
main, that of Grasmere, 'the grassy mountain's open
side' being avowedly Loughrigg terrace. But,
according to Wordsworth's habit, he has drawn his
imagery from various other places—*e.g.*, the island
of Grasmere is not 'with birch trees fringed.' (This
may well refer to Rydal.) Again, I know of no 'lilies
of the vale' at Grasmere, but they are found, I
believe, on one of the islands of Windermere,
certainly in woods near the river Leven, below that
lake. Again, the vicar refers to 'two islands' on
the lake, Grasmere having only one. I never saw
a goat 'browsing by dashing waterfalls,' still less
'spotted deer,' on or near Grasmere. The latter
may be seen at Ullswater."

It is impossible to trace an order in the combinations, or to separate and detach the local
elements combined, in the last book of *The Excursion*. The discourse is first carried on in the house of
the vicar, the parsonage of Langdale ; and, though
it is a momentary digression, I may remark that,

---

[1] *Prose Works*, vol. iii. p. 199.   [2] *Ibid.* p. 210.

in the noble passage in which Age is likened to "a
final Eminence," the "high peaks that bound the
vale where now we are," seem much more appropriate to Langdale than to Grasmere.

       Rightly it is said
That man descends into the VALE of years;
Yet have I thought that we might also speak,
And not presumptuously, I trust, of Age,
As of a final EMINENCE ; though bare
In aspect and forbidding, yet a point
On which 'tis not impossible to sit
In awful sovereignty; a place of power,
A throne, that may be likened unto his
Who, in some placid day of summer, looks
Down from a mountain-top,—say one of those
High peaks that bound the Vale where now
  we are.
Faint, and diminished to the gazing eye,
Forest and field, and hill and dale appear,
With all the shapes over their surface spread :
But, while the gross and visible frame of
  things
Relinquishes its hold upon the sense,
Yea almost on the Mind herself, and seems
All unsubstantialised,—how loud the voice
Of waters, with invigorated peal
From the full river in the vale below,
Ascending! For on that superior height
Who sits is disencumbered from the press
Of near obstructions, and is privileged
To breathe in solitude, above the host
Of ever-humming insects, 'mid thin air
That suits not them. The murmur of the
  leaves
Many and idle, visits not his ear:
This he is freed from, and from thousand
  notes

(Not less unceasing, not less vain than these),
By which the finer passages of sense
Are occupied; and the Soul, that would incline
To listen, is prevented or deterred.[1]

But after leaving the parsonage (whence they
can see beyond "the silvery lake" "streaked with
placid blue,"

As if preparing for the peace of evening),

they descend along a streamlet to a bridge where
they see a ram reflected in the water; then they go
into a boat, and sail to "the rocky isle with birch
trees fringed." This cannot be near Langdale, nor
is it Grasmere. It might be Rydal, and all that
follows would suit Rydal Mere, even to the "dashing waterfall" (with or without the "goats!") which
might very well be a cascade on the beck that
descends between Whitmoss Common and Nab
Scar; and the party might ascend Loughrigg
terrace later on, and proceed to a point whence
they could view Grasmere Vale. But after the discourse of the Wanderer they all return to the vicar's
house in Langdale, whence the "Solitary" makes
his way up to Blea Tarn, and his cell. This adds
to the difficulty of localisation. It is evidently a
picture, formed out of many elements, some real
and some ideal, which we need not attempt to
particularise. It will suffice to quote a few descriptive passages—

Forth we went,
And down the vale along the streamlet's edge
Pursued our way, a broken company,
Mute or conversing, single or in pairs.
Thus having reached a bridge, that overarched

[1] *Excursion*, book ix.

The hasty rivulet where it lay becalmed
In a deep pool, by happy chance we saw
A two-fold image; on a grassy bank
A snow-white ram, and in the crystal flood
Another and the same! Most beautiful,
On the green turf, with his imperial front
Shaggy and bold, and wreathèd horns superb,
The breathing creature stood; as beautiful
Beneath him, showed his shadowy counterpart.
Each had his glowing mountains, each his sky,
And each seemed centre of his own fair world:
Antipodes unconscious of each other,
Yet, in partition, with their several spheres,
Blended in perfect stillness, to our sight![1]

"Turn where we may," said I, "we cannot err
In this delicious region."—Cultured slopes,
Wild tracts of forest-ground, and scattered
        groves,
And mountains bare, or clothed with ancient
        woods,
Surrounded us; and, as we held our way
Along the level of the glassy flood,
They ceased not to surround us; change of
        place,
From kindred features diversely combined,
Producing change of beauty ever new.[2]
    Alert to follow as the Pastor led,
We clomb a green hill's side; and, as we clomb,
The Valley, opening out her bosom, gave
Fair prospect, intercepted less and less,
O'er the flat meadows and indented coast
Of the smooth lake, in compass seen:—far off,
And yet conspicuous, stood the old Church-
        tower,
In majesty presiding over fields

---

[1] *Excursion*, book ix.   [2] *Ibid.*

And habitations seemingly preserved
From all intrusion of the restless world
By rocks impassable and mountains huge.

   Soft heath this elevated spot supplied,
And choice of moss-clad stones, whereon we
    couched
Or sate reclined; admiring quietly
The general aspect of the scene; but each
Not seldom over anxious to make known
His own discoveries; or to favourite points
Directing notice, merely from a wish
To impart a joy, imperfect while unshared.
That rapturous moment ne'er shall I forget
When these particular interests were effaced
From every mind!—Already had the sun,
Sinking with less than ordinary state,
Attained his western bound; but rays of light—
Now suddenly diverging from the orb
Retired behind the mountain tops or veiled
By the dense air—shot upwards to the crown
Of the blue firmament—aloft, and wide:
And multitudes of little floating clouds,
Through their ethereal texture pierced—ere we,
Who saw, of change were conscious—had be-
    come
Vivid as fire; clouds separately poised,—
Innumerable multitude of forms
Scattered through half the circle of the sky;
And giving back, and shedding each on each,
With prodigal communion, the bright hues
Which from the unapparent fount of glory
They had imbibed, and ceased not to receive.
That which the heavens displayed, the liquid
    deep
Repeated; but with unity sublime!
   While from the grassy mountain's open side
We gazed, in silence hushed, with eyes intent

On the refulgent spectacle, diffused
Through earth, sky, water, and all visible space,
The Priest in holy transport thus exclaimed.[1]

(Then follows the concluding apostrophe, etc.)

As the seventh of the *Evening Voluntaries*
refers to Grasmere, a stanza from it may also be
quoted. The "oak-crowned hill" may be a peak
in the Easdale direction, or it may be Hammer-
scar. It is to the Silver How group that he is
referring.

The leaves that rustled on this oak-crowned hill,
And sky that danced among those leaves, are still;
Rest smooths the way for sleep; in field and bower
Soft shades and dews have shed their blended
    power
On drooping eyelid and the closing flower;
Sound is there none at which the faintest heart
Might leap, the weakest nerve of superstition start;
Save when the Owlet's unexpected scream
Pierces the ethereal vault; and ('mid the gleam
Of unsubstantial imagery, the dream,
From the hushed vale's realities, transferred
To the still lake) the imaginative Bird
Seems, 'mid inverted mountains, not unheard.

I have already remarked that Easdale valley is
associated with the freshest and most productive
period of Wordsworth's genius. It would be hard
to say whether the terrace walk at Lancrigg, or the
upper road from Grasmere to Rydal, is more closely
identified with him. Walking with Lady Richardson on that terrace in December 1843, he said:
"This is a striking anniversary to me, for this day
forty-four years ago my sister and I took up our
abode at Grasmere, and three days after we found

---

[1] *Excursion*, book ix.

out this walk, which long remained our favourite
haunt."[1]   Lady Richardson adds: "It was their
custom to spend the fine days of summer in the
open air, chiefly in the valley of Easdale. *The
Prelude* was chiefly composed in a green mountain
terrace on the Easdale side of Helm Crag, known
by the name of Under Lancrigg, a place which he
used to say he 'knew by heart.' The ladies sat at
their work on the hill-side while he walked to and
fro, on the smooth green mountain turf, humming
out his verses to himself, and then repeating them
to his sympathising and ready scribes, to be noted
down on the spot, and transcribed at home."[2]

This small mountain farm of Lancrigg belonged
at that time to an old statesman, Rowlandson by
name.   He was afterwards obliged to part with it,
in consequence of the imprudence of his son, and
in 1840 he sold it to Mrs. Fletcher, the mother of
the present proprietor, Lady Richardson.   The
poet Wordsworth acted as agent in the transaction,
his daughter Dora being the clerk who transcribed
the legal documents.   It is now one of the loveliest
spots in the Lake District.   Lady Richardson,
when on a visit at Fox How in 1839, made the
following allusion to Lancrigg:—"On consulting
Mr. Wordsworth about the beautiful little farm of
Lancrigg (now for sale), in Easdale, he entered into
the subject most kindly, and offered to find out for
me its real value.   He described the tangled copse,
and a natural terrace under the crag, a very favourite resort of his and his sister's in bygone days, and
said of the little 'Rocky Well,' 'I know it by

---

[1] *Memoirs*, vol. ii. p. 439.

[2] *William Wordsworth*, by Lady Richardson, from
Sharpe's London Magazine, 1851, p. 8.   One of the best
reviews of the *Memoirs*, and one of the most discrimi-
nating estimates of the poet that has ever been written.

heart.' He then asked Mrs. Wordsworth to look
at his *Miscellaneous Sonnets* and read the one
suggested to him by the likeness of a rock to a
sepulchral stone in that hazel copse. This she
did with much expression."[1] This well, of purest
and coolest water, is at the base of a Rock, in
delicious shade, where in May time the sorrel and
the primrose are of the largest size and the most
brilliant green. It is a spring more beautiful than
the "Nab Well" at Rydal, cooler than Brownrigg
on Helvellyn. The path leading westwards from
it, shaded by rich and varied underwood, is the
"natural terrace" where Wordsworth used to spend
these long summer days with his household, in
fellowship with Nature, and in the pure delights of
poetic labour. No one who has understood *The
Prelude*, with its profound vision of the Universe
and of Human Life, will walk for the first time
along this terrace, where it was chiefly composed,
without emotion. Midway is that moss-grown
stone described in the sonnet, to which Lady
Richardson refers.

> Mark the concentred hazels that enclose
> Yon old grey Stone, protected from the ray
> Of noontide suns :—and even the beams that
>   play
> And glance, while wantonly the rough wind
>   blows,
> Are seldom free to touch the moss that grows
> Upon that roof, amid embowering gloom,
> The very image framing of a tomb,
> In which some ancient Chieftain finds repose
> Among the lonely mountains.—Live, ye
>   trees!

[1] *Autobiography of Mrs. Fletcher*, p. 224. Third
Edition. Edinburgh : 1876.

And thou, grey Stone, the pensive likeness
   keep
Of a dark chamber where the Mighty sleep:
For more than Fancy to the influence bends
When solitary Nature condescends
To mimic Time's forlorn humanities.

Of this sonnet, Wordsworth said to Miss Fenwick,
"suggested in the wild hazel wood at the foot of
Helm Crag, where the stone still lies, with others
of like form and character, though much of the
wood that veiled it from the glare of day has
been felled."[1]   A few paces further west on this
walk, where the path opens, is the spot alluded to
above; where Dorothy Wordsworth used to sit
with her tablets, while her brother paced up and
down composing his verses, and then dictating
them to his devoted amanuensis, while Mrs.
Wordsworth read, and the children played around.

Referring to a visit of Wordsworth's to Lancrigg
in 1840, Lady Richardson says:[2] "We all walked
over the intack part of Lancrigg to our boundary
wall, and to the point the poet especially admires,
as commanding the wild mountain view into Far
Easdale on one side, and the more cultivated part
in the vale of Grasmere on the other, with the
church-tower, the lake, and the end of Loughrigg
as the boundary, which is a kind of sundial from
that point of view. We went through the West
Copse, which led us to Far Easdale, and back to
Thorney How, by the flat part of the valley which
goes by the name of Boothwaite, a favourite evening
stroll of the poet."   In a note—June 1878—she
adds: "The view was much better then (in 1840)
than now, as, owing to the growth of the trees,

---

[1] *Prose Works*, vol. iii. p. 57.
[2] *Autobiography*, p. 248.

much is taken from that point, and the character
of the sundial lost.   He liked the contrast of view,
the wildness of Far Easdale on the one side, and
the church-tower and village scene on the other."

Still more interesting is the record of a visit
made by the poet to Lancrigg in 1841.   "We took
a walk on the terrace, and he went as usual to his
favourite points.   On our return he was struck with
the berries on the holly-tree, and said, 'Why should
not you and I go and pull some berries from the
other side of the tree, which is not seen from the
window? and then we can go and plant them in
the rocky ground behind the house.'   We pulled
the berries, and set forth with our tools : I made
the holes, and the poet put in the berries.   He was
as earnest and eager about it, as if it had been a
matter of importance ; and as he put the seeds
in, he every now and then muttered, in his low
solemn tone, that beautiful verse from Burns's
Vision:—

> 'And wear thou this, she solemn said,
>   And bound the holly round my head,
>   The polished leaves and berries red
>   Did rustling play;
>   And like a passing thought, she fled
>   In light away.'

"He clambered to the highest rocks in the 'Tom
Intak,' and put in the berries in such situations as
Nature sometimes does, with such true and beautiful effect.   He said, 'I like to do this for posterity.
Some people are selfish enough to say, What has
posterity done for me?   But the past has done
much for us.'"[1]

---

[1] *Memoirs*, vol. ii. p. 438 : or *Prose Works*, vol. iii.
p. 436.

Lady Richardson pointed out these hollies to me
in 1878.   They are in various places along the
terrace.   May they live "for posterity."   Wordsworth asked her to preserve this terrace path in its
natural state, as it was in his day ; and she has
done so.   She pointed out a small group of oak-
trees in the flat of Easdale, like an island in the
green meadow, to which Wordsworth had often
called her attention.   "Watch your shrubs well,"
he said, "that they may not prevent the sight of
that clump of oaks ; for they give a great character
to the view."

CHAPTER V.

HELVELLYN, ULLSWATER, ETC.

In tracing out the places mentioned by Wordsworth, it seems a natural course, after leaving Grasmere, to go over to Patterdale by the Grisdale Hawes, and to return to Rydal by Kirkstone.

The places in the Ullswater district associated with the poet are best approached by the road from Grasmere to Helvellyn, leading past Grisdale Tarn. This path, up Tongue Ghyll, so often taken by Wordsworth and his friends, is, on many grounds, the most interesting of the routes to Helvellyn. The way in which the mountains open up, and the valleys seem to deepen as you ascend, is striking : and the view to the west and south, from the rocks on the side of Seat Sandal, just above the Tongue Ghyll waterfall, is specially fine. Ascending Tongue Ghyll to Grisdale Hawes, the passage at the beginning of the eighth book of *The Prelude* will occur to many—

> What sounds are those, Helvellyn, that are heard
> Up to thy summit, through the depth of air
> Ascending, as if distance had the power
> To make the sounds more audible? What crowd
> Covers, or sprinkles o'er, yon village green?
>
> .   .   .   .   .   .
>
> They hold a rustic fair—a festival,

125

Such as, on this side now, and now on that,
Repeated through his tributary vales,
Helvellyn, in the silence of his rest,
Sees annually, if clouds towards either ocean
Blown from their favourite resting-place, or mists
Dissolved, have left him an unshrouded head.[1]

Few of the tarns in the Lake District are more
impressive than Grisdale, in its loneliness and
seclusion. The following stanza in reference to it
is by another poet, and a man of rare endowments
(the late Frederick Faber), of whom Wordsworth
said, " He had not only as good an eye for Nature
as I have, but a better one, and sometimes pointed
out to me effects on the mountains which I had
never detected." [2]

Father Faber says that if he wished "to build
himself a hermitage,"

In yon pale hollow would I dwell
    Where waveless Grisdale meekly lies,
And the three clefts of grassy fell
    Let in the blueness of the skies;
And lowland sounds come travelling up
To echo in that mountain cup.

Where from the tarn the shallow brook
    By rough Helvellyn shapes its way, ·
The window of my cell should look
    Eastward upon the birth of day, etc.[3]

This is the exact spot where the parting took
place between the brothers William and John

---

[1] *The Prelude*, book viii.

[2] See *Recollections of Wordsworth*, by Aubrey de Vere.
Prose Works, vol. iii. p. 488.

[3] *Poems*, lxxxviii. p. 250. Ed. 1857.

Wordsworth, and where the poet afterwards composed the following elegiac stanzas.

[I have the less scruple in quoting the above lines, as with all their excellence, they heighten by contrast the effect of the stanzas which follow. The work of such a man as Faber, compared with Wordsworth's, shows how rare it is, in interpreting Nature, to reach the point where perfect simplicity and supreme insight go hand in hand.]

ELEGIAC VERSES,

IN MEMORY OF MY BROTHER, JOHN WORDSWORTH, COMMANDER OF THE E. I. COMPANY'S SHIP THE EARL OF ABERGAVENNY, IN WHICH HE PERISHED BY CALAMITOUS SHIPWRECK, FEB. 6TH, 1805.

Composed near the Mountain track, that leads from Grasmere through Grisdale Hawes, where it descends towards Patterdale.

1805.

I.

The Sheep-boy whistled loud, and lo!
That instant, startled by the shock,
The Buzzard mounted from the rock
Deliberate and slow :
Lord of the air, he took his flight ;
Oh! could he on that woeful night
Have lent his wing, my brother dear,
For one poor moment's space to Thee,
And all who struggled with the Sea,
When safety was so near.

II.

Thus in the weakness of my heart
I spoke (but let that pang be still)
When rising from the rock at will,
I saw the Bird depart.

And let me calmly bless the Power
That meets me in this unknown Flower,
Affecting type of him I mourn!
With calmness suffer and believe,
And grieve, and know that I must grieve,
Not cheerless, though forlorn.

III.

Here did we stop; and here looked round
While each into himself descends,
For that last thought of parting Friends
That is not to be found.
Hidden was Grasmere Vale from sight,
Our home and his, his heart's delight,
His quiet heart's selected home.
But time before him melts away,
And he hath feeling of a day
Of blessedness to come.

IV.

Full soon in sorrow did I weep,
Taught that the mutual hope was dust,
In sorrow, but for higher trust,
How miserably deep!
All vanished in a single word,
A breath a sound, and scarcely heard.
Sea—Ship—drowned—Shipwreck—so it came;
The meek, the brave, the good, was gone;
He who had been our living John
Was nothing but a name.

V.

That was indeed a parting! oh,
Glad am I, glad that it is past;
For there were some on whom it cast
Unutterable woe.
But they as well as I have gains;—
And grieve, and know that I must grieve,

From many a humble source, to pains
Like these, there comes a mild release;
Even here I feel it, even this Plant
Is in its beauty ministrant
To comfort and to peace.

VI.

He would have loved thy modest grace,
Meek Flower!   To Him I would have said
" It grows upon its native bed
Beside our Parting-place;
There, cleaving to the ground it lies
With multitude of purple eyes,
Spangling a cushion green like moss; [1]
But we will see it, joyful tide!
Some day, to see it in its pride,
The mountain will we cross."

VII.

--Brother and friend, if verse of mine
Have power to make thy virtues known,
Here let a monumental Stone
Stand—sacred as a Shrine;
And to the few who pass this way,
Traveller or Shepherd, let it say,
Long as these mighty rocks endure,—
Oh do not thou too fondly brood,
Although deserving of all good,
On any earthly hope, however pure!

Wordsworth's note to the poem is to the following
effect:---

[1] The plant alluded to is the Moss Campion (*Silene acaulis* of Linnæus).
See among the *Poems on the Naming of Places*, No. vi.

" *Moss Campion (Silene acaulis).*"

This most beautiful plant is scarce in England, though it is found in great abundance upon the mountains of Scotland. The first specimen I ever saw of it, in its native bed, was singularly fine, the tuft or cushion being at least eight inches in diameter, and the root proportionably thick. I have only met with it in two places among our mountains, in both of which I have since sought for it in vain.

Botanists will not, I hope, take it ill, if I caution them against carrying off, inconsiderately, rare and beautiful plants. This has often been done, particularly from Ingleborough and other mountains in Yorkshire, till the species have totally disappeared, to the great regret of lovers of Nature living near the places where they grew.

Dr. Cradock writes thus of the poem: "The parting place of the brothers William and John, at the foot of Grisdale Tarn, is marked with unusual precision in the poet's note on these verses. It is exactly where the Helvellyn path diverges from the old packhorse track to Patterdale, and is passed by hundreds of tourists. I have found the moss campion in times past within a few yards of the spot, but I do not think that it can now be seen within 200 yards of it. It goes out of flower before the main influx of tourists, and may thus escape entire destruction. The time of its flowering shows that Wordsworth's visit must have been in the spring or very early summer [of 1805], and therefore while his grief was fresh. His burst of feeling on seeing the buzzard rise from the crags of Dollywagon is most true to Nature. It is marvellous with what perverse ingenuity recent sorrow assimilates every object to itself. The far-fetched connection between the bird's flight and the shipwreck might possibly have occurred to any one under the same circumstances. But the comfort which Wordsworth found in the little flower is all his own. In order to understand it, it is necessary to understand *him*."

The buzzard may still be seen wheeling over the crags of Doli-wagen Pike; and the moss campion still grows not far from the coolest of springs. With Wordsworth's note before me, I shall not particularise the spot, as the plant is doubtless less abundant than it used to be.

Is it too much to expect of tourists and travellers that they should learn to admire the loveliest things in Nature, without snatching them from their birthplace, and destroying them? Can they not rejoice in the presence of Beauty, and let the memory of what they have seen remain a possession and a joy for ever, without adding the secondary gratification of plucking it, and carrying it a few miles, to wither in their hands, or those of others? It is surely sacrilege to uproot such memorials as the moss campion of Grisdale Tarn, or the daffodils and the Christmas roses at Dove Cottage.

Some years ago, at the suggestion of the Rev. H. D. Rawnsley, Vicar of Crosthwaite, the Wordsworth Society placed a small memorial at this parting place of the brothers. About a hundred yards from where the stream turns from the Tarn, on the left hand of the road descending to Patterdale, a panel has been cut in the native rock, on which an inscription has been graven, taken from the *Elegiac Stanzas*.

The poem most directly associated with Helvellyn is *Fidelity*. It commemorates the devotion of a dog to its master, who was killed by falling over the rocks at Red Tarn. The two stanzas which

describe and enshrine the spirit of the place are as
follows :—

> It was a cove, a huge recess,
> That keeps, till June, December's snow ;
> A lofty precipice in front,
> A silent tarn below !
> Far in the bosom of Helvellyn,
> Remote from public road or dwelling,
> Pathway, or cultivated land ;
> From trace of human foot or hand.
>
> There sometimes doth a leaping fish
> Send through the tarn a lonely cheer ;
> The crags repeat the raven's croak,
> In symphony austere ;
> Thither the rainbow comes—the cloud –
> And mists that spread the flying shroud ;
> And sunbeams : and the sounding blast,
> That, if it could, would hurry past ;
> But that enormous barrier holds it fast.

Thomas Wilkinson refers to this incident at
some length, in his poem, *Grasmere Vale*. A
reference to it will be found in Lockhart's *Life of
Scott*, and also in a letter from Mr. Luff, of
Patterdale, to his wife, July 23, 1805, published in
The Prose Works of Wordsworth, vol. ii. p.172.

The mountain group of Helvellyn and her sister
hills, which Wordsworth ascended so often, suggests another of his poems, addressed to Miss
Blackett—who was living at Fox Ghyll—*To* ———,
On her first ascent to the summit of Helvellyn.

> Inmate of a mountain-dwelling,
> Thou hast clomb aloft, and gazed

From the watch-towers of Helvellyn;
Awed, delighted, and amazed!

Potent was the spell that bound thee,
Not unwilling to obey;
For blue Ether's arms, flung round thee,
Stilled the pantings of dismay.

Lo! the dwindled woods and meadows;
What a vast abyss is there!
Lo! the clouds, the solemn shadows,
And the glistenings—heavenly fair!

And a record of commotion
Which a thousand ridges yield;
Ridge, and gulf, and distant ocean
Gleaming like a silver shield!

Maiden! now take flight;—inherit
Alps or Andes—they are thine!
With the morning's roseate Spirit,
Sweep their length of snowy line;

Or survey their bright dominions
In the gorgeous colours drest
Flung from off the purple pinions,
Evening spreads throughout the west!

.   .   .   .

For the power of hills is on thee
As was witnessed through thine eye
Then when old Helvellyn won thee
To confess their majesty!

Amongst the memorials of the Italian tour, which
Wordsworth took with Henry Crabb Robinson,
there is one entitled *Musings near Aquapendente*,

also associated with Helvellyn. The sight of the
broom, growing amongst the Appennines in the
month of April, at once suggests his own Westmoreland hills and vales. His spirit flies homeward, and he thinks how it is faring with the place
he loved so well.

> What! with this broom in flower
> Close at my side! She bids me fly to greet
> Her sisters, soon like her to be attired
> With golden blossoms opening at the feet
> Of my own Fairfield. The glad greeting given,
> Given with a voice and by a look returned
> Of old companionship, Time counts not minutes
> Ere, from accustomed paths, familiar fields,
> The local Genius hurries me aloft,
> Transported over that cloud-wooing hill,
> Seat Sandal, a fond suitor of the clouds,
> With dream-like smoothness, to Helvellyn's
>   top,
> There to alight upon crisp moss, and range
> Obtaining ampler boon, at every step,
> Of visual sovereignty—hills multitudinous,
> (Not Apennine can boast of fairer) hills
> Pride of two nations, wood and lake and plains,
> And prospect right below of deep coves shaped
> By skeleton arms, that from the mountain's
>   trunk
> Extended, clasp the winds, with mutual moan
> Struggling for liberty, while undismayed
> The shepherd struggles with them. Onward
>   thence
> And downward by the skirt of Greenside fell
> And by Glenridding-screes, and low Glencoign,
> Places forsaken now, though loving still
> The muses, as they loved them in the days
> Of the old minstrels and the border bards.—
> But here am I fast bound; and let it pass,

The simple rapture ;—who that travels far
To feed his mind with watchful eyes could
    share
Or wish to share it?— One there surely was,
" The Wizard of the North," with anxious hope
Brought to this genial climate, when disease
Preyed upon body and mind, yet not the less
Had his sunk eye kindled at those dear words
That spake of bards and minstrels ; and his spirit
Had flown with mine to old Helvellyn's brow
Where once together, in his day of strength,
We stood rejoicing, as if earth were free
From sorrow, like the sky above our heads.

In the Grasmere Journal of Dorothy Wordsworth
there are numerous fragments of verses, evidently
dictated by the brother to the sister, but left in an
unfinished state.   One of these refers to the old
Westmoreland shepherd Michael, immortalized in
the poem, over which Wordsworth spent so much
time and labour, and were originally meant to form
part of that poem.
The following lines occur in it—

There is a shapeless crowd of unhewn stones
That lie together, some in heaps, and some
In lines, that seem to keep themselves alive
In the last dotage of a dying form.
At least so seems it to a man who stands
In such a lonely place, ...

Shall he who gives his days to low pursuits
Amid the undistinguishable crowd
Of cities, 'mid the same eternal flow
Of the same objects, melted and reduced
To one identity, by differences
That have no law, no meaning, and no end,
Shall he feel yearning to these lifeless forms

And shall we think that Nature is less kind
To those who all day long, through a long life,
Have walked within her sight?   It cannot be.

Descending to the Patterdale valley, there are
two poems referring to the district of Ullswater,
both so perfect in their way, that, however well
known, a book such as this would be incomplete
without them.   The one is entitled *Airey Force
Valley*, the other is the poem on *The Daffodils*.
The first is an admirable specimen of what I may
call idealised realism.   It is faithful to the place
in its minutest detail, while the whole scene is
perfectly transfigured.   You see the brook as it
flows, and are instantly carried in imagination to
its birthplace, and to its origin, coeval with the
hills.   Its voice does not lessen, but rather deepens
the calm of the valley.   The breeze just entering
the grove, by the oak unfelt, but moving the
lighter leaves of the ash, and making

A soft eye-music of slow-waving boughs,

is one of the happiest in the whole range of
Wordsworth's imagery; the appeal which Nature
makes through one of the senses being heightened
by its being expressed in terms of another sense.

————Not a breath of air
Ruffles the bosom of this leafy glen.
From the brook's margin, wide around, the trees
Are steadfast as the rocks; the brook itself,
Old as the hills that feed it from afar,
Doth rather deepen than disturb the calm
Where all things else are still and motionless
And yet, even now, a little breeze, perchance
Escaped from boisterous winds that rage
    without,

Has entered, by the sturdy oaks unfelt,
But to its gentle touch how sensitive
Is the light ash! that, pendent from the brow
Of yon dim cave, in seeming silence makes
A soft eye-music of slow-waving boughs
Powerful almost as vocal harmony
To stay the wanderer's steps and soothe his
    thoughts.

"The Light Ash" is still "pendent" from the
rocks at Aira Force. Within a short distance of it,
and near Ullswater, are the ruins of Lyulph's
Tower, in connection with which Wordsworth's
poem, *The Somnambulist*, will be remembered, of
which the first and last stanzas are as follows—

List, ye who pass by Lyulph's Tower
    At eve; how softly then
Doth Aira-force, that torrent hoarse
    Speak from the woody glen!
Fit music for a solemn vale!
    And holier seems the ground
To him who catches on the gale
The spirit of a mournful tale,
    Embodied in the sound.

Wild stream of Aira, hold thy course,
    Nor fear memorial lays,
Where clouds that spread in solemn
        shade,
    Are edged with golden rays!
Dear art thou to the light of heaven,
    Though minister of sorrow;
Sweet is thy voice at pensive even;
And thou, in lovers' hearts forgiven,
    Shalt take thy place with Yarrow!

Not far from Lyulph's Tower is Gowbarrow Park, for ever associated with the poem on *The Daffodils*, two lines of which, in the last stanza—the finest in the poem—were added by Mrs. Wordsworth; in reference to which the poet truly remarks, "If thoroughly felt, they would annihilate nine-tenths of the reviews of the kingdom; as they would find no readers." He refers to the style of literary criticism then current. The daffodils still grow in abundance on the shore of the lake below Gowbarrow Park. Mrs. Wordsworth's lines are printed in italics.

> I wandered lonely as a cloud
> That floats on high o'er vales and hills,
> When all at once I saw a crowd,
> A host, of golden daffodils;
> Beside the lake, beneath the trees,
> Fluttering and dancing in the breeze.
>
> Continuous as the stars that shine
> And twinkle on the milky way,
> They stretched in never-ending line
> Along the margin of a bay;
> Ten thousand saw I at a glance,
> Tossing their heads in sprightly dance.
>
> The waves beside them danced; but they
> Out-did the sparkling waves in glee:
> A poet could not but be gay,
> In such a jocund company:
> I gazed—and gazed— but little thought
> What wealth the show to me had brought:
>
> For oft, when on my couch I lie
> In vacant or in pensive mood,

They flash upon that inward eye
Which is the bliss of solitude;
And then my heart with pleasure fills,
And dances with the daffodils.

In Dorothy Wordsworth's Journal the following occurs, under date April 15, 1802—

" It was a threatening misty morning, but mild. We set off after dinner from Eusmere. Mr. Clarkson went a short way with us, but turned back. The wind was furious, and we thought we must have returned. We first rested in the large boat-house, then under a furze bush opposite Mr. Clarkson's. Saw the plough going in the field. The wind seized our breath. The lake was rough. There was a boat by itself, floating in the middle of the bay below Water Millock. We rested again in the Water Millock Lane. The hawthorns, black and green; the birches here and there greenish, but there is yet more of purple to be seen on the twigs. . . . A few primroses by the roadside . . . wood-sorrel flower, the ane-mone, scentless violets, strawberries, and that starry yellow flower which Mr. C. calls pilewort. When we were in the woods beyond Gowbarrow Park, we saw a few daffodils close to the water side. We fancied that the sea had floated the seeds ashore, and that the little colony had so sprung up. But as we went along there were more, and yet more; and, at last, under the boughs of the trees, we saw that there was a long belt of them along the shore, about the breadth of a country turnpike road. I never saw daffodills so beautiful. They grew among the mossy stones, about and above them; some rested their heads upon these stones, as on a pillow, for weariness; and the rest tossed and reeled and danced, and

seemed as if they verily laughed with the wind that
blew upon them over the lake. They looked so
gay, ever glancing, ever changing. This wind
blew directly over the lake to them. There was
here and there a little knot, and a few stragglers
higher up; but they were so few as not to disturb
the simplicity, unity, and life of that one busy
highway. We rested again and again. The bays
were stormy, and we heard the waves at different
distances, and in the middle of the water, like the
sea. . . . "

The day after *The Daffodils* was composed, he
wrote the following, while resting at the foot of
Brother's Water—

> The Cock is crowing,
> The stream is flowing,
> The small birds twitter,
> The lake doth glitter,
> The green field sleeps in the sun;
> The oldest and youngest
> Are at work with the strongest;
> The cattle are grazing,
> Their heads never raising;
> There are forty feeding like one!
>
> Like an army defeated
> The snow hath retreated,
> And now doth fare ill
> On the top of the bare hill;
> The Ploughboy is whooping—anon—anon:
> There's joy in the mountains;
> There's life in the fountains;
> Small clouds are sailing,
> Blue sky prevailing;
> The rain is over and gone!

To the right of Brother's Water, as you look
towards Kirkstone, is the secluded ravine of

Hartsope, at the foot of Dovedale.   It was near
to this, "above Hartsope Hall," that Wordsworth
saw the grand atmospheric effect "above and
among the mountains," described in the second
book of *The Excursion*.

Through the dull mist, a step,
A single step, that freed me from the skirts
Of the blind vapour, opened to my view
Glory beyond all glory ever seen
By waking sense or by the dreaming soul!
The appearance, instantaneously disclosed,
Was of a mighty city—boldly say
A wilderness of building, sinking far
And self-withdrawn into a boundless depth
Far sinking into splendour—without end!
Fabric it seemed of diamond and of gold,
With alabaster domes, and silver spires,
And blazing terrace upon terrace, high
Uplifted: here, serene pavilions bright,
In avenues disposed; there, towers begirt
With battlements, that on their restless fronts
Bore stars—illumination of all gems!
By earthly nature had the effect been wrought
Upon the dark materials of the storm
Now pacified: on them, and on the coves
And mountain-steeps and summits, whereunto
The vapours had receded, taking there
Their station under a cerulean sky.
Oh, 'twas an unimaginable sight!
Clouds, mists, streams, watery rocks and emerald
    turf,
Clouds of all tincture, rocks and sapphire sky
Confused, commingled, mutually inflamed,
Molten together, and composing thus,
Each lost in each, that marvellous array
Of temple, palace, citadel, and huge
Fantastic pomp of structure without name,

In fleecy folds voluminous enwrapped.
Right in the midst, where interspace appeared
Of open court, an object like a throne
Under a shining canopy of state
Stood fixed; and fixed resemblances were seen
To implements of ordinary use.
But vast in size, in substance glorified;
Such as by Hebrew prophets were beheld
In vision—forms uncouth of mightiest power
For admiration and mysterious awe.[1]

Mention of Patterdale recalls the fact that a cottage under Place Fell at one time very nearly became the poet's home. Had it done so, Ullswater would have been immortalised as Rydal has been. The crags of Place Fell and Hallin Fell would have been described as Nab Scar and Loughrigg have been; all the rocky promontories and natural terraces of Ullswater, the streams and groves of Patterdale, would have been made familiar to posterity by his genius. The following is the account of the transaction supplied in the *Memoirs*.

A small cottage and a little estate, under the magnificent hill called Place Fell, attracted his attention in 1805; and, hearing that it might be purchased, he made an offer of £800 for it. The owner would not part with it for less than £1000. This Wordsworth did not think it prudent to give. But Lord Lonsdale, desirous of presenting the small property to Wordsworth, paid £800 to his account, under the impression that the ground was to be sold for that amount. Wordsworth, however, would only accept of £200, which he thought was the amount the proprietor had asked in excess of its real value.[2]

---

[1] *Excursion*, book ii.   [2] *Memoirs*, vol. i. p. 319.

From Brother's Water one naturally ascends the
Pass of Kirkstone.

It is thus that Dorothy Wordsworth recorded her
walk with her brother on the 16th of April, 1800, the
day after the poem on *The Daffodils* was written:
"The sun shone, the wind had passed away, the
hills looked cheerful.   The river was very bright,
as it flowed into the lake.   The church rises up
behind a little knot of rocks, the steeple not so high
as an ordinary three-storey house; trees in a row
in the garden under the wall.   We set forward.
The valley is at first broken by little rocky, woody
knolls, that make retiring places, fairy valleys in
the vale.   The river winds along under these hills,
travelling not in a bustle, but not slowly, to the
lake.   We saw a fisherman in the flat meadow on
the other side of the water.   He came towards us,
and threw his line over the two-arched bridge.   It
is a bridge of a heavy construction, almost bending
inwards in the middle; but it is grey, and there is
a look of ancientry in the architecture of it that
pleased me.   As we go on, the vale opens out more
into one vale, with somewhat of a cradle bed.
Cottages, with groups of trees on the side of the
hills.   We passed a pair of twin children, two years
old; sat on the next bridge which we crossed, a
single arch.   We rested again upon the turf, and
looked at the same bridge.   We observed arches
in the water, occasioned by the large stones
sending it down in two streams.   A sheep came
plunging through the river, stumbled up the bank,
and passed close to us.   It had been frightened
by an insignificant looking dog on the other side.
It's fleece dropped a glittering shower under its
belly.   Primroses by the roadside; pilewor. that
shone like stars of gold in the sun; violets, strawberries retired and half-buried in the grass.   When
we came to the foot of Brother's Water, I left

William sitting on the bridge, and went along the path on the right side of the lake through the wood. I was delighted with what I saw: the water under the boughs of the bare old trees, the simplicity of the mountains, and the exquisite beauty of the path. There was one grey cottage. I repeated the *Glowworm* as I walked along. I hung over the gate, and thought I could have stayed for ever. When I returned I found William writing a poem descriptive of the sights and sounds we saw and heard. There was the gentle flowing of the stream, the glittering lively lake, green fields, without a living creature to be seen on them; behind us, a flat pasture, with forty-two cattle feeding; to our left, the road leading to the hamlet. No smoke there; the sun shone on the bare roofs. The people were at work, ploughing harrowing and sowing; lassies working; a dog barking now and then; cocks crowing, birds twittering; the snow in patches at the top of the highest hills; yellow palms, purple and green twigs on the birches, ashes with their glittering stems quite bare. The hawthorn, a bright green, with black stems under the oak. The moss of the oaks glossy. . . . As we went up the vale of Brother's Water, more and more cattle feeding; a hundred of them. William finished his poem before we got to the foot of Kirkstone."

Again: "The walk up Kirkstone was very interesting. The becks among the rocks were all alive. William showed me the little mossy streamlet, which he had before loved when he saw its bright green track in the snow. The view above Ambleside very beautiful. There we sat, and looked down on the green vale. We watched the crows at a little distance from us become white as silver, as they flew in the sunshine, and when they went still farther they looked like shapes of water passing over the green fields."

Of his poem called *The Pass of Kirkstone*, Wordsworth said it embodied "Thoughts and feelings of many walks in all weathers, by day and night, over this pass, alone, and with beloved friends."[1]

I.

Within the mind strong fancies work,
A deep delight the bosom thrills,
Oft as I pass along the fork
Of these fraternal hills:
Where, save the rugged road, we find
No appanage of human kind,
Nor hint of man; if stone or rock
Seem not his handy-work to mock
By something cognisably shaped;
Mockery—or model roughly hewn,
And left as if by earthquake strewn,
Or from the Flood escaped:
Altars for Druid service fit;
(But where no fire was ever lit,
Unless the glow-worm to the skies
Thence offer nightly sacrifice)
Wrinkled Egyptian monument;
Green moss-grown tower; or hoary tent;
Tents of a camp that never shall be razed—
On which four thousand years have gazed!

II.

Ye plough-shares sparkling on the slopes!
Ye snow-white lambs that trip
Imprisoned 'mid the formal props
Of restless ownership!
Ye trees, that may to-morrow fall
To feed the insatiate Prodigal!
Lawns, houses, chattels, groves and fields,
And all the fertile valley shields;

[1] I. F. MS.

M

Wages of folly--baits of crime,
Of life's uneasy game the stake,
Playthings that keep the eyes awake
Of drowsy, dotard Time ;—
O care ! O guilt !—O vales and plains,
Here, 'mid his own unvexed domains,
A Genius dwells, that can subdue
At once all memory of You,—
Most potent when mists veil the sky,
Mists that distort and magnify ;
While the coarse rushes, to the sweeping
      breeze,
Sigh forth their ancient melodies !

III.

List to those shriller notes !—*that* march
Perchance was on the blast,
When, through this Height's inverted arch,
Rome's earliest legion passed !
—They saw adventurously impelled,
And older eyes than theirs beheld,
This block—and yon, whose church-like
      frame
Gives to this savage Pass its name.
Aspiring Road ! that lov'st to hide
Thy daring in a vapoury bourn,
Not seldom may the hour return
When thou shalt be my guide :
And I (as all men may find cause,
When life is at a weary pause,
And they have panted up the hill
Of duty with reluctant will)
Be thankful, even though tired and faint,
For the rich bounties of constraint ;
Whence oft invigorating transports flow
That choice lacked courage to bestow !

IV.

My Soul was grateful for delight
That wore a threatening brow ;
A veil is lifted—can she slight
The scene that opens now ?
Though habitation none appear,
The greenness tells, man must be there :
The shelter—that the perspective
Is of the clime in which we live :
Where Toil pursues his daily round :
Where Pity sheds sweet tears—and Love,
In woodbine bower or birchen grove,
Inflicts his tender wound.
—Who comes not hither ne'er shall know
How beautiful the world below ;
Nor can he guess how lightly leaps
The brook adown the rocky steeps.
Farewell, thou desolate Domain !
Hope, pointing to the cultured plain,
Carols like a shepherd-boy :
And who is she ?—Can that be Joy !
Who, with a sunbeam for her guide,
Smoothly skims the meadows wide :
While Faith, from yonder opening cloud,
To vale and hill proclaims aloud,
"Whate'er the weak may dread, the wicked
      dare,
Thy lot, O man, is good, thy portion fair !"

CHAPTER VI.

AMBLESIDE, LANGDALE, BLEA TARN, ETC.

DESCENDING to Ambleside by Stock Ghyll, the mountain in front, across the valley, is Wansfell; thus addressed by Wordsworth, as it is seen from Rydal Mount—

> Wansfell! this Household has a favoured lot,
> Living with liberty on thee to gaze,
> To watch while Morn first crowns thee with her
>   rays,
> Or when along thy breast serenely float
> Evening's angelic clouds.   Yet ne'er a note
> Hath sounded (shame upon the Bard!) thy praise
> For all that thou, as if from Heaven, hast brought
> Of glory lavished on our quiet days.
> Bountiful Son of Earth! when we are gone
> From every object dear to mortal sight,
> As soon we shall be, may these words attest
> How oft, to elevate our spirits, shone
> Thy visionary majesties of light,
> How in thy pensive glooms our hearts found rest,

To this may be added the sonnet which follows it, referring to Ambleside—

> While beams of orient light shoot wide and high,
> Deep in the vale a little rural Town
> Breathes forth a cloud-like creature of its own,
> That mounts not toward the radiant morning sky,

But, with a less ambitious sympathy,
Hangs o'er its Parent waking to the cares,
Troubles, and toils that every day prepares.
So Fancy, to the musing Poet's eye,
Endears that Lingerer.   And how blest her sway
(Like influence never may my soul reject)
If the calm Heaven, now to its zenith decked
With glorious forms in numberless array,
To the lone shepherd on the hills disclose
Gleams from a world in which the saints repose.

The forty-fifth sonnet in the third section of the
same series (the *Miscellaneous Sonnets*) is not inappropriate here.

ON THE PROJECTED KENDAL AND WINDERMERE RAILWAY.

Is then no nook of English ground secure
From rash assault !   Schemes of retirement sown
In youth, and 'mid the busy world kept pure
As when their earliest flowers of hope were blown,
Must perish ;—how can they this blight endure?
And must he too the ruthless change bemoan
Who scorns a false utilitarian lure
'Mid his paternal fields at random thrown ?
Baffle the threat, bright Scene, from Orrest-head
Given to the pausing traveller's rapturous glance :
Plead for thy peace, thou beautiful romance
Of Nature ; and, if human hearts be dead,
Speak, passing winds ; ye torrents, with your
        strong
And constant voice, protest against the wrong.

After reading this sonnet one naturally wonders
what its author would have thought of the appro-
priation of Thirlmere by Manchester.

Wordsworth appends the following note : " The
degree and kind of attachment which many of the
yeomanry feel to their small inheritances can

scarcely be overrated. Near the house of one of them stands a magnificent tree, which a neighbour of the owner advised him to fell for profit's sake. 'Fell it!' exclaimed the owner, 'I had rather fall on my knees and worship it.'" Dr. Cradock says: "The yeoman was, I believe, Mr. Birkett, owner of a farm which lies a few fields back on the left of the road, between Waterhead and Troutbeck Bridge. My informant was the Reverend Mr. Jefferies of Grasmere, who was living in the country at the time of the occurrence which provoked the sonnet. I am told that the tree (an oak) is still standing, but I have not seen it."

Another sonnet, number six of the first series, refers to a spot in this part of the district, which is, I suspect, very little known. The following "note" upon it occurs in the I. F. MS. "This rill trickles down the hill-side into Windermere near Low Wood. My sister and I, on our first visit together to this part of the country, walked from Kendal, and we rested to refresh ourselves by the side of the lake where the streamlet falls into it. This sonnet was written some years after, in recollection of that happy ramble, that most happy day and hour." [1]

There is a little unpretending Rill
Of limpid water, humbler far than aught
That ever among Men or Naiads sought
Notice or name!—It quivers down the hill,
Furrowing its shallow way with dubious will:
Yet to my mind this scanty stream is brought
Ofter than Ganges or the Nile; a thought
Of private recollection sweet and still!
Months perish with their moons; year treads
    on year:

[1] *Prose Works*, vol. iii. p. 53.

But, faithful Emma ! thou with me canst say
That, while ten thousand pleasures disappear,
And flies their memory fast almost as they ;
The immortal Spirit of one happy day
Lingers beside that Rill, in vision clear.

Dr. Cradock writes : " There can surely be no
doubt as to the identity of the 'little unpretending
rill.'   It runs into the lake about 100 yards south-
wards from Low Wood Hotel garden, at the point
where Wordsworth and his sister, walking from
Kendal, first came upon the lake.   It comes down
from High Skelgill, and crosses the road, very near
its junction with the lane leading to Troutbeck."

Dr. Cradock's opinion on this point has been
doubted by several.   The Rev. R. Percival Graves of
Dublin writes that when he left the parsonage at Bowness, while at Dovenest in 1843, he called at Rydal
Mount, and " was told, both by Mr. and Mrs. Wordsworth, as a fact in which I should take a special
interest, that the 'little unpretending rill,' associated
by the poet with the 'immortal spirit of one happy
day,' was the rill which, rising near High Skelgill,
at the back of Wansfell, descends steeply down the
hill-side, from behind the house at Dovenest, and
crossing beneath the road, enters the lake near the
gate of the drive which leads up to Dovenest."

Ascending the valley of Langdale, and following
the windings of the Brathay, another of the
descriptive sonnets is our best guide to the spirit of
the place.   It was suggested on the banks of that
stream, by the sight of those ubiquitous Pikes,
which are visible from so many remote points in
the district—the twin Langdales, as seen in the
late autumn.   The sonnet is entitled *November 1st.*

How clear, how keen, how marvellously bright
The effluence from yon distant mountain's head,

Which, strown with snow smooth as the sky
    can shed,
Shines like another sun—on mortal sight
Uprisen as if to check approaching Night,
And all her twinkling stars.   Who now would
    tread,
If so he might, yon mountain's glittering head—
Terrestrial, but a surface, by the flight
Of sad mortality's earth-sullying wing,
Unswept, unstained ?   Nor shall the aërial
    Powers
Dissolve that beauty, destined to endure,
White, radiant, spotless, exquisitely pure.
Through all vicissitudes, till genial Spring
Has filled the laughing vales with welcome
    flowers.

Proceeding up the valley we reach the small
village of Chapel Stile, where is the grave of the
Rev. Owen Lloyd, on whose headstone is carved
Wordsworth's commemorative epitaph beginning

> By playful smiles (alas ! too oft
> A sad heart's sunshine).

And, as the spot is not far distant, this is the most
fitting place to quote the pastoral on *The Idle
Shepherd-Boys ; or, Dungeon-Ghyll Force.*

> The valley rings with mirth and joy ;
> Among the hills the echoes play
> A never never ending song,
> To welcome in the May.
> The magpie chatters with delight ;
> The mountain raven's youngling brood
> Have left the mother and the nest ;
> And they go rambling east and west
> In search of their own food ;
> Or through the glittering vapours dart
> In very wantonness of heart.

Beneath a rock upon the grass,
Two boys are sitting in the sun:
Their work, if any work they have,
Is out of mind—or done.
On pipes of sycamore they play
The fragments of a Christmas hymn;
Or with that plant which in our dale
We call staghorn, or fox's tail,
Their rusty hats they trim:
And thus, as happy as the day,
Those shepherds wear the time away.

Along the river's stony marge
The sand-lark chants a joyous song;
The thrush is busy in the wood,
And carols loud and strong.
A thousand lambs are on the rocks,
All newly born! both earth and sky
Keep jubilee, and more than all,
Those boys with their green coronal;
They never hear the cry,
That plaintive cry! which up the hill
Comes from the depth of Dungeon-Ghyll.

.   .   .   .   .   .

It was a spot which you may see
If ever you to Langdale go;
Into a chasm a mighty block
Hath fallen, and made a bridge of rock:
The gulf is deep below;
And, in a basin black and small,
Receives a lofty waterfall.

Of this poem Wordsworth said, with pardonable
egoism: "When Coleridge and Southey were
walking together upon the Fells, Southey observed
that if I wished to be considered a faithful painter
of rural manners, I ought not to have said that my
shepherd-boys trimmed their rustic hats, as de-

scribed in the poem. Just as the words had passed his lips, two boys appeared, with the very plant entwined round their hats."

With Hackett, "the craggy ridge that rises between the two Langdales and looks towards Windermere," is associated the *Epistle to Sir George Beaumont*, already referred to, which describes the cottage—

> High on the sunny hill,
> Luminous region, fair as if the prime
> Were tempting all astir to look aloft and climb.

Here, too, he listened to the flute-playing of the Rev. Samuel Tilbrook of Peterhouse, Cambridge (who had purchased Ivy Cottage, below Rydal Mount), which suggested the sonnet beginning

> The fairest, brightest, hues of ether fade,
> The sweetest notes must terminate and die;

and concluding thus—

> Yet sacred is to me this mountain's head
> Whence I have risen, uplifted on the breeze
> Of harmony above all earthly care.

Hackett cottage is also described in *The Excursion*, and it is more especially with the view of identifying the places referred to in that poem that we may now imaginatively wander up the Langdale valley.

Of *The Excursion*, Wordsworth said to Miss Fenwick: "In the poem I suppose that the pedlar and I ascended from a plain country up the vale of Langdale, and struck off a good way above the chapel to the western side of the vale. We ascended the hill, and thence looked down upon

the circular recess in which lies Blea Tarn, chosen
by the Solitary for his retreat."[1]   This is more
indefinite than appears at first sight.   They
"ascended the hill"—which, of course, is Lingmoor—but by what route? by the cleft which
divides Lingmoor from Side Pike, almost opposite
Millbeck and Dungeon Ghyll in Great Langdale?
or past Oak How and up the higher part of Lingmoor to its tarn, descending by Blea Tarn Ghyll?
The question is, as we shall see, important, as its
answer will determine the site of that recess in the
Blea Tarn Valley, which the Solitary describes so
minutely.   This is his description of their walk
through lower Langdale, past Elter Water and
Chapel Stile—

> He led me towards the hills
> Up through an ample vale, with higher hills
> Before us, mountains stern and desolate;
> But, in the majesty of distance, now
> Set off, and to our ken appearing fair
> Of aspect, with aërial softness clad,
> And beautified with morning's purple beams.[2]

He contrasts the joy of those who walk in these
mountain regions, with that of those who ride or
drive—

> How faint
> Compared with ours! who, pacing side by side,
> Could, with an eye of leisure, look on all
> That we beheld; and lend the listening sense
> To every grateful sound of earth and air;
> Pausing at will—our spirits braced, our thoughts
> Pleasant as roses in the thickets blown,
> And pure as dew bathing their crimson leaves.[3]

[1] I. F. MS.   [2] *Excursion*, book ii.   [3] *Ibid.*

The "throng of people" engaged at their "annual wake" next described must have been the villagers of Langdale. The Wanderer points to the "craggy summits"[1] on the left, and

> as if their quest had been
> Some secret of the mountains, cavern, fall
> Of water, or some lofty eminence,
> Renowned for splendid prospect far and wide.

We are told how they diverged, and

> Scaled, without a track to ease our steps,
> A steep ascent; and reached a dreary plain,
> With a tumultuous waste of huge hill-tops
> Before us; savage region! which I paced
> Dispirited.[2]

This refers unmistakably to the summit of Ling-moor, the "tumultuous waste of huge hill-tops" being an apt description of Great End, Bowfell, Shelter Crags, and Pike o' Blisco, straight before them, the Langdales to the north on the right, Wrynose, Wetherlam, and the Coniston mountains to the south-west. They walked along the summit of Lingmoor,

> When, all at once, behold!
> Beneath our feet, a little lowly vale,
> A lowly vale, and yet uplifted high
> Among the mountains; even as if the spot
> Had been from eldest time by wish of theirs
> So placed, to be shut out from all the world!
> Urn-like it was in shape, deep as an urn;
> With rocks encompassed, save that to the south
> Was one small opening, where a heath-clad ridge
> Supplied a boundary less abrupt and close;
> A quiet treeless nook, with two green fields,
> A liquid pool that glittered in the sun,
> And one bare dwelling; one abode, no more!

[1] *Excursion*, vol. vi.   [2] *Ibid.*

It seemed the home of poverty and toil,
Though not of want; the little fields made green
By husbandry of many thrifty years,
Paid cheerful tribute to the moorland house.
—There crows the cock, single in his domain :
The small birds find in spring no thicket there
To shroud them ; only from the neighbouring vales
The cuckoo, straggling up to the hill tops,
Shouteth faint tidings of some gladder place.[1]

The "little lowly vale" is, of course, the head of
Little Langdale, with Blea Tarn in the centre, as
seen from the top of Lingmoor, the only point
(except the summit of Blake Rigg) from which it
seems "urnlike." The "small opening"—"where
a heath-clad ridge supplied a boundary"—is that
which leads down into Little Langdale by Fell
Foot and Busk. The "nook" is not now "treeless," but the fir-wood on the western side enhances
the solitude, and deepens the sense of seclusion.
The "liquid pool that glittered in the sun," is, of
course, Blea Tarn. The "one abode, no more," is
the cottage, still solitary, now called Blea Tarn
House, which is passed on the left under Side Pike.
It is still true that up to this nook, "from neighbouring vales," the cuckoo

Shouteth faint tidings of some gladder place.

The thoughts and feelings of the poet, when they
first caught sight of this green recess from the top
of Lingmoor, are thus expressed—

Ah ! what a sweet Recess, thought I, is here !
Instantly throwing down my limbs at ease
Upon a bed of heath :—full many a spot
Of hidden beauty have I chanced to espy
Among the mountains ; never one like this ;

[1] *Excursion*, book ii.

So lonesome, and so perfectly secure ;
Not melancholy—no, for it is green,
And bright, and fertile, furnished in itself
With the few needful things that life requires.
—In rugged arms how softly does it lie,
How tenderly protected !   Far and near
We have an image of the pristine earth,
The planet in its nakedness : were this
Man's only dwelling, sole appointed seat,
First, last, and single, in the breathing world,
It could not be more quiet : peace is here
Or nowhere ; days unruffled by the gale
Of public news or private ; years that pass
Forgetfully ; uncalled upon to pay
The common penalties of mortal life,
Sickness, or accident, or grief, or pain.[1]

Before they descend from the top of the mountain
they hear a funeral dirge—

We listened, looking down upon the hut
But seeing no one ;

and then the funeral procession, issuing from the
cottage, winds away to the south, down the ridge
into Little Langdale.   Thereafter they descend.

So, to a steep and difficult descent
Trusting ourselves, we wound from crag to crag,
Where passage could be won ; and, as the last
Of the mute train, behind the heathy top
Of that off-sloping outlet, disappeared,
I, more impatient in my downward course,
Had landed upon easy ground ; and there
Stood waiting for my Comrade.   When behold
An object that enticed my steps aside !
A narrow, winding, entry opened out

[1] *Excursion*, book ii.

Into a platform—that lay, sheepfold-wise,
Enclosed between an upright mass of rock
And one old moss-grown wall ;—a cool recess,
And fanciful !   For where the rock and wall
Met in an angle, hung a penthouse,
Framed by thrusting two rude staves into the wall
And overlaying them with mountain sods ;
To weather-fend a little turf-built seat
Whereon a full-grown man might rest, nor dread
The burning sunshine, or a transient shower ;
But the whole plainly wrought by children's
        hands !
Whose skill had thronged the floor with a
        proud show
Of baby houses, curiously arranged ;
Nor wanting ornament of walks between,
With mimic trees inserted in the turf,
And gardens interposed.[1]

This is the recess in which Voltaire's novel was
supposed to be found.   It was, I think, at a point
about 200 yards above the house, in a narrow gorge
below a waterfall, where a "moss-grown wall" still
approaches close to the rock on the other side of
the stream, and where a "penthouse" might easily
be made by children.

The question will have occurred to many a
reader of *The Excursion*, Did Wordsworth mean
this to be a literal description of what he saw in his
mountain rambles ? or, since the characters are in
part ideal, and framed out of elements supplied by
different individuals, is not the scene also idealised ?
I do not think that it is so to any considerable
extent.   While the actual meeting with an individual
called the "Solitary," living at Blea Tarn, and the
finding of a copy of Voltaire in a penthouse, belong

---

[1] *Excursion*, book ii.

to the embellishment or drapery of the poem, it
would be a total misreading of the genius of Wordsworth to suppose that he idealised the scenery ; or
that he would describe it at all, without a broad
basis of fact.   Inaccuracies there are, as well as
idealisations, in his description of the locality (as we
shall see); but Wordsworth's mind was too firmly
anchored to reality, nay, it was too topographical,
to permit of his building up a wholly ideal picture,
especially since he meant it to serve as the vehicle
of ethical and religious teaching.

He tells us (I. F. MS.)—speaking of the picture
given by the Wanderer of the living—"in this
nothing is introduced but what was taken from
Nature and real life."   But he goes on to say, " The
cottage was called Hackett, and stands, *as described*, on the southern extremity of the ridge which
separates the two Langdales."   A house in that
situation could not, of course, be the Blea Tarn
Cottage.   On the other hand, the cottage in which
the Solitary lived *must* have been at Blea Tarn.
Wordsworth probably meant by his Fenwick note
merely to indicate that his description of Blea Tarn
Cottage was borrowed from Hackett.

If we suppose the "penthouse," etc., to have
been, as I think it was, in Blea Tarn Ghyll, it is very
easy to realise the two men descending from it to
the place where the Wanderer

> made a sudden stand ;
> For full in view, approaching through a gate
> That opened from the enclosure of green fields,
> Into the rough uncultivated ground
> Behold the man, etc.[1]

This of course refers to the flat ground on the more
level part of the valley, near the cottage, along the
side of which the present road passes.

[1] *Excursion*, book ii.

Then, after their greeting and conversation on the

> Many precious rites
> And customs of our rural ancestry, etc.,

they proceed all together to the cottage.

> Homely was the spot;
> And, to my feeling, ere we reached the door,
> Had almost a forbidding nakedness;
> Less fair, I grant, even painfully less fair,
> Than it appeared when from the beetling rock
> We had looked down upon it.   All within,
> As left by the departed company,
> Was silent; save the solitary clock
> That on mine ear ticked with a mournful
>   sound.
> Following our Guide, we clomb the cottage-
>   stairs
> And reached a small apartment dark and low,
> Which was no sooner entered than our Host
> Said gaily, "This is my domain, my cell,
> My hermitage, my cabin, what you will"—

>   .   .   . Scattered was the floor,
> And, in like sort, chair, window-seat, and shelf,
> With books, maps, fossils, withered plants, and
>   flowers,
> And tufts of mountain moss.   Mechanic tools
> Lay intermixed with scraps of paper, some
> Scribbled with verse: a broken angling-rod
> And shattered telescope, together linked
> By cobwebs, stood within a dusky nook;
> And instruments of music, some half-made,
> Some in disgrace, hung dangling from the walls.[1]

In this little room, "dark and low," in the upper

[1] *Excursion*, book ii.

N

flat of the cottage, they sat down to a homely rustic
meal. (I fancy that the "solitary clock," the "cottage
stairs," and the "apartment dark and low," are all
reminiscences of Hackett); and Wordsworth goes
on to describe, in a noble passage, how

> While at our pastoral banquet thus we sate
> Fronting the window of that little cell,
> I could not, ever and anon, forbear
> To glance an upward look on two huge Peaks,
> That from some other vale peered into this.
> "Those lusty twins," exclaimed our host, "if here
> It were your lot to dwell, would soon become
> Your prized companions.   Many are the notes
> Which, in his tuneful course, the wind draws
>   forth
> From rocks, woods, caverns, heaths, and dashing
>   shores ;
> And well those lofty brethren bear their part
> In the wild concert—chiefly when the storm
> Rides high; then all the upper air they fill
> With roaring sound, that ceases not to flow,
> Like smoke, along the level of the blast,
> In mighty current; theirs, too, is the song
> Of stream and headlong flood that seldom fails;
> And, in the grim and breathless hour of noon,
> Methinks that I have heard them echo back
> The thunder's greeting. Nor have Nature's laws
> Left them ungifted with a power to yield
> Music of finer tone; a harmony,
> So do I call it, though it be the hand
> Of silence, though there be no voice ;—the
>   clouds,
> The mist, the shadows, light of golden suns,
> Motions of moonlight, all come thither—touch,
> And have an answer—thither come, and shape
> A language not unwelcome to sick hearts
> And idle spirits :—there the sun himself,

At the calm close of summer's longest day,
Rests his substantial orb ;—between those heights
And on the top of either pinnacle,
More keenly than elsewhere in night's blue vault,
Sparkle the stars, as of their station proud.
Thoughts are not busier in the mind of man
Than the mute agents stirring there :—alone
Here do I sit and watch." [1]

I cannot resist quoting what Mr. Stopford Brooke
says of this passage: " Mark how the wind rejoices
in these peaks, and they give back its wild pleasure:
how all the things which touch and haunt them get
their reply; how they are loved and love; how busy
are the mute agents there; how proud the stars to
shine on them." [2]
It is usually supposed that the

two huge peaks
That from some other vale peer into this,
Those lusty twins .   .   .

refer to the Langdales, for no other reason, I suspect, than that the Langdales are twins.   But, if
the three men were seated, as described, in the
upper room of the cottage (which has one small
window looking towards the Pikes), they could not
possibly see them.   Side Pike and Pike o' Blisco
alone could be seen.   Either then, *these* are the
peaks referred to, or, what is much more likely, the
realism of the narrative here gives way, and the
finer Pikes of Langdale are introduced, though
they are not visible from the house, because they
belong to the district, and can be seen from so
many points around.
On the whole, I think that Wordsworth referred to
the Langdale Pikes.   Let any one, as he approaches

[1] *Excursion*, book ii.
[2] *Theology in the English Poets*, p. 108.

Blea Tarn from Little Langdale, see them slowly rising and peering alone over the depression or haws, which divides the Langdales, and he will not doubt that they are the "lusty twins." Let the haws be in shadow, and the Pikes in sunlight (or the reverse), and the effect is one of the most striking in the whole district of the Lakes.

Blea Tarn House is a humble cottage, resembling Ann Tyson's house at Hawkshead, in which Wordsworth boarded when at school. On the ground-floor are a parlour, kitchen, and dairy. Ascending by nine stone steps to the upper flat, there are four small rooms, and one of these looks, as I have said, northwards in the direction of the Langdale Pikes. There are what seem the foundations of an older house a little lower down, say twenty yards nearer the tarn, beside a pollard ash; and there are two cherry trees still farther down, one of considerable age. But I believe the present house was standing at the beginning of this century. It seems quite as old as the house at Grasmere, in which the incumbent of Wytheburn—the clergyman described at the beginning of the seventh book of *The Excursion*—lived. There are two large poplars to the north of the cottage, and a sycamore near them. I cannot believe that the place was *entirely* "treeless" in Wordsworth's time.

The description of the ruined chapel, which follows, towards the end of the second book of *The Excursion*, is not taken from Langdale, but avowedly from the ruins on the ridge which separates Patterdale from Boardale and Martindale, near which Wordsworth saw the grand atmospheric effect recorded in page 141.

But it is in reference to the places described at the beginning of the third book of *The Excursion*, entitled *Despondency*, that the identification of

details is most satisfactory.   This book commences
thus—

A humming bee—a little tinkling rill—
A pair of falcons wheeling on the wing,
In clamorous agitation, round the crest
Of a tall rock, their airy citadel—
By each and all of these the pensive ear
Was greeted, in the silence that ensued,
When through the cottage-threshold we had
    passed.
And, deep within that lonesome valley, stood
Once more beneath the concave of a blue
And cloudless sky—Anon exclaimed our Host,

  .   .   .   .   .

But which way shall I lead you?—how contrive,
In spot so parsimoniously endowed,
That the brief hours, which yet remain, may reap
Some recompense of knowledge or delight?"
So saying, round he looked, as if perplexed ;
And, to remove those doubts, my grey-haired
    Friend
Said—" Shall we take this pathway for our
    guide?—
Upward it winds, as if, in summer heats,
Its line had first been fashioned by the flock
Seeking a place of refuge at the root
Of yon black Yew-tree, whose protruded boughs
Darken the silver bosom of the crag,
From which she draws her meagre sustenance.
There in commodious shelter may we rest.
Or let us trace this streamlet to its source ;
Feebly it tinkles with an earthy sound,
And a few steps may bring us to the spot
Where, haply, crowned with flow'rets and green
    herbs,
The mountain infant to the sun comes forth,
Like human life from darkness."—A quick turn

Through a straight passage of encumbered ground,
Proved that such hope was vain ; for now we
        stood
Shut out from prospect of the open vale,
And saw the water, that composed this rill,
Descending, disembodied, and diffused
O'er the smooth surface of an ample crag,
Lofty and steep, and naked as a tower.
All further progress here was barred ;—And who,
Thought I, if master of a vacant hour,
Here would not linger, willingly detained?
Whether to such wild objects he were led
When copious rains have magnified the stream
Into a loud and white-robed waterfall
Or introduced at this more quiet time.[1]

There is still a single "yew-tree" high up the
eastern side of the valley, in the face of Lingmoor
Fell, "darkening the silver bosom of the crag."
The three men are supposed to be standing on the
west of the tarn, and just a little to the north of the
fir-wood which overshadows it,

> Deep within the lonesome valley.

I think that the place can be identified even by
the streamlet, which the Solitary proposes they
should trace to its source.   But the identification
becomes complete to the letter, in the light of what
follows.

Upon a semicirque of turf-clad ground,
The hidden nook discovered to our view
A mass of rock, resembling, as it lay
Right at the foot of that moist precipice,
A stranded ship, with keel upturned, that rests

[1] *Excursion*, book iii.

Fearless of winds and waves.   Three several
    stones
Stood near, of smaller size, and not unlike
To monumental pillars: and, from these
Some little space disjoined, a pair were seen,
That with united shoulders bore aloft
A fragment, like an altar, flat and smooth:
Barren the tablet, yet thereon appeared
A tall and shining holly, that had found
A hospitable chink, and stood upright,
As if inserted by some human hand
In mockery, to wither in the sun,
Or lay its beauty flat before a breeze,
The first that entered.   But no breeze did now
Find entrance ;—high or low appeared no trace
Of motion, save the water that descended,
Diffused adown that barrier of steep rock,
And softly creeping, like a breath of air,
Such as is sometimes seen, and hardly seen,
To brush the still breast of a crystal lake.[1]

The "barrier of steep rock" is the low perpendicular crag to the west of the tarn, immediately
behind the fir-wood, and the "semicirque of turf-
clad ground" is apparent at a glance, whether seen
from below the rock or from above.   Not only will
no other place answer to the description, but this
corresponds to it with remarkable fidelity.   There
are many "perched blocks" high up the flank of
Blake Rigg to the west, and on the slope of Lingmoor to the east, which might at first sight be
mistaken for the stone like "a stranded ship with
keel upturned," or the "fragment like an altar;"
but though many large fragments of ice-borne rock
lie about in curious positions, there is no "secluded"
spot on the hill slopes.   The "semicirque" is the

---

[1] *Excursion*, book iii.

cup-shaped recess between the fir-wood and the
cliff; and on entering it the rock resembling the
"ship with keel upturned" is obvious.   It lies
north-west to south-east, and is not an ice-borne
block, but a fragment fallen from the crag above.
It is now broken into three fragments by the
weathering of many years.   A sycamore of average
size is growing at its side; its root being in the
cleft, where the stone is broken.

Holly grows luxuriantly all along the face of the
crag above, so that the bush found in the stone
resembling a "Druid altar" is easily explained.
The brook is a short one, flowing through the
meadow pasture of the wood; and is, after 100
yards, lost in the turfy slope, but is seen again upon
the face of the "moist precipice," "softly creeping,"
precisely as described.   The "three several stones"
that "stand near" are, I think, the one to the front,
in a line with the keel of the ship; and the other
two, to the right and left respectively.   The "pair"
with the "fragment like an altar, flat and smooth,"
are to the left, and close at hand.

> " Behold a cabinet for sages built,
> Which kings might envy !"—Praise to this effect
> Broke from the happy old Man's reverend lip;
> Who to the Solitary turned, and said,
> " In sooth, with love's familiar privilege,
> You have decried the wealth which is your own.
> Among these rocks and stones, methinks, I see
> More than the heedless impress that belongs
> To lonely Nature's casual work : they bear
> A semblance strange of power intelligent,
> And of design not wholly worn away.
> Boldest of plants that ever faced the wind.
> How gracefully that slender shrub looks forth
> From its fantastic birth-place !   And I own,
> Some shadowy intimations haunt me here.

That in these shows a chronicle survives
Of purposes akin to those of Man,
But wrought with mightier arm than now
    prevails.
—Voiceless the stream descends into a gulf
With timid lapse :—and lo ! while in this strait
I stand—the chasm of sky above my head
Is heaven's profoundest azure ; no domain
For fickle, short-lived clouds to occupy,
Or to pass through ; but rather an abyss
In which the everlasting stars abide ;
And whose soft gloom, and boundless depth,
    might tempt
The curious eye to look for them by day.[1]

.   .   .   .   .   .

  A pause ensued ; and with minuter care
We scanned the various features of the scene :
And soon the Tenant of that lonely vale
With courteous voice thus spake—
               " I should have grieved
Hereafter, not escaping self-reproach,
If from my poor retirement ye had gone
Leaving this nook unvisited : but, in sooth,
Your unexpected presence had so roused
My spirits, that they were bent on enterprise ;
And, like an ardent hunter, I forgot,
Or, shall I say?—disdained, the game that lurks
At my own door. The shapes before our eyes
And their arrangement doubtless must be
    deemed
The sport of Nature, aided by blind Chance,
Rudely to mock the works of toiling Man.
And hence, this upright shaft of unhewn stone,
From Fancy, willing to set off her stores
By sounding titles, hath acquired the name
Of Pompey's pillar ; that I gravely style

        [1] *Excursion,* book iii.

My Theban obelisk; and, there, behold
A Druid cromlech!—thus I entertain
The antiquarian humour, and am pleased
To skim along the surfaces of things,
Beguiling harmlessly the listless hours.
But if the spirit be oppressed by sense
Of instability, revolt, decay,
And change, and emptiness, these freaks of
        Nature
And her blind helper Chance, do *then* suffice
To quicken, and to aggravate—to feed
Pity and scorn, and melancholy pride,
Not less than that huge Pile (from some abyss
Of mortal power unquestionably sprung)
Whose hoary diadem of pendent rocks
Confines the shrill-voiced whirlwind, round
        and round
Eddying within its vast circumference,
On Sarum's naked plain—than pyramid
Of Egypt, unsubverted, undissolved—
Or Syria's marble ruins towering high
Above the sandy desert, in the light
Of sun or moon.[1]

"Voiceless the stream descends, with timid lapse," is a perfect description of this tiniest and gentlest of rills, flowing through the meadow grass; while the "chasm of sky above," of which the Wanderer speaks, though an exaggeration, is more appropriate to this spot than to any other in the "lonely dell." Further, it must be remembered that the Solitary speaks of this place as "at his own door." The spot is not a quarter of a mile from the cottage.

There was "a slope of mossy turf, defended from the sun," on which the Solitary invited Wordsworth

[1] *Excursion*, book. iii.

and the Wanderer to rest, and on which they sat
down.   It was in a "covert nook," [1] a "hollow
dell," [2] a "deep hollow;" [3] and from it, the path
leading out of the glen and over into Little Langdale, along which the funeral train had passed, was
visible. [4]   All these things point to the one spot I
have indicated, on the west of the tarn.   No one
who knows the *Excursion* well can visit the locality
without being struck by the singularly minute
fidelity of Wordsworth's allusions to place—his
descriptive accuracy—while he does not attempt
to take a verbal photograph of the scene.   In
addition, all that is said of the scenery is introduced
casually, and serves as the mere setting or frame-
work for a moral discourse of the loftiest order.

There are some passages in the discourse of the
Wanderer in the next, and finest, chapter of *The
Excursion*—entitled *Despondency Corrected*—which
derive at least a portion of their significance from
the place and the circumstances in which they are
supposed to be spoken.   For example—

> Then, as we issued from that covert nook,
> He thus continued, lifting up his eyes
> To heaven :—" How beautiful this dome of sky;
> And the vast hills, in fluctuation fixed
> At thy command, how awful!   Shall the soul
> Human and rational, report of Thee
> Even less than these !—Be mute who will, who
>   can,
> Yet I will praise Thee with impassioned voice :
> My lips, that may forget Thee in the crowd,
> Cannot forget Thee here ; where Thou hast built,
> For Thy own glory, in the wilderness !
> Me didst Thou constitute a priest of Thine
> In such a temple as we now behold

[1] *Excursion*, p. 100.   [2] *Ibid.* p. 134.
[3] *Ibid.* p. 112.   [4] *Ibid.* p. 134.

Reared for thy presence : therefore, am I bound
To worship here, and everywhere—as one
Not doomed to ignorance, though forced to tread,
From childhood up, the ways of poverty.
From unreflecting ignorance preserved,
And from debasement rescued.   By thy grace
The particle divine remained unquenched ;
And 'mid the wild weeds of a rugged soil,
Thy bounty caused to flourish deathless flowers,
From paradise transplanted : wintry age
Impends ; the frost will gather round my heart ;
If the flowers wither, I am worse than dead !
  –Come, labour, when the worn-out frame
        requires
Perpetual sabbath : come, disease and want :
And sad exclusion through decay of sense ;
But leave me unabated trust in thee—
And let thy favour, to the end of life,
Inspire me with ability to seek
Repose and hope among eternal things—
Father of heaven and earth ! and I am rich,
And will possess my portion in content !

    And what are things eternal?—powers depart,"
The grey-haired Wanderer steadfastly replied,
Answering the question which himself had asked,
" Possessions vanish, and opinions change,
And passions hold a fluctuating seat :
But, by the storms of circumstance unshaken,
And subject neither to eclipse nor wane,
Duty exists ;– immutably survive,
For our support, the measures and the forms,
Which an abstract intelligence supplies ;
Whose kingdom is where time and space are not.
Of other converse which mind, soul, and heart,
Do, with united urgency, require,
What more that may not perish?—Thou, dread
        source,

Prime, self-existing cause and end of all
That in the scale of being fill their place ;
Above our human region, or below,
Set and sustained ;—Thou, who didst wrap the
        cloud
Of infancy around us, that thyself,
Therein, with our simplicity awhile
Might'st hold, on earth, communion undisturbed ;
Who from the anarchy of dreaming sleep,
Or from its death-like void, with punctual care,
And touch as gentle as the morning light,
Restor'st us, daily, to the powers of sense
And reason's steadfast rule—thou, thou alone
Art everlasting, and the blessèd Spirits,
Which thou includest, as the sea her waves :
For adoration thou endur'st ; endure
For consciousness the motions of thy will ;
For apprehension those transcendent truths
Of the pure intellect, that stand as laws,
(Submission constituting strength and power)
Even to thy Being's infinite majesty !
This universe shall pass away—a work
Glorious ! because the shadow of thy might,
A step or link, for intercourse with thee.
Ah ! if the time must come, in which my feet
No more shall stray where meditation leads,
By flowing stream, through wood, or craggy wild,
Loved haunts like these ; the unimprisoned Mind
May yet have scope to range among her own,
Her thoughts, her images, her high desires.
If the dear faculty of sight should fail,
Still, it may be allowed me to remember
What visionary powers of eye and soul
In youth were mine ; when, stationed on the top
Of some huge hill—expectant, I beheld
The sun rise up, from distant climes returned
Darkness to chase and sleep ; and bring the day
His bounteous gift ! or saw him toward the deep

Sink, with a retinue of flaming clouds
Attended ; then, my spirit was entranced
With joy exalted to beatitude ;
The measure of my soul was filled with bliss,
And holiest love ; as earth, sea, air, with light,
With pomp, with glory, with magnificence ![1]

Again—

'Tis, by comparison, an easy task
Earth to despise ; but, to converse with heaven
This is not easy :—to relinquish all
We have, or hope, of happiness and joy,
And stand in freedom loosened from this world,
I deem not arduous : but must needs confess
That 'tis a thing impossible to frame
Conceptions equal to the soul's desires ;
And the most difficult of tasks to *keep*
Heights which the soul is competent to gain.
—Man is of dust : ethereal hopes are his,
Which, when they should sustain themselves aloft,
Want due consistence ; like a pillar of smoke,
That with majestic energy from earth
Rises ; but, having reached the thinner air,
Melts, and dissolves, and is no longer seen.[2]

The group are supposed to leave the recess at the
foot of the crag, and to wander back towards the
cottage.

While, in this strain, the venerable Sage
Poured forth his aspirations, and announced
His judgments, near that lonely house we paced
A plot of green-sward, seemingly preserved
By Nature's care from wreck of scattered stones
And from encroachment of encircling heath :
Small space ! but, for reiterated steps,

[1] *Excursion*, book iv.   [2] *Ibid.*

Smooth and commodious; as a stately deck
Which to and fro the mariner is used
To tread for pastime, talking with his mates,
Or haply thinking of far-distant friends,
While the ship glides before a steady breeze.
Stillness prevailed around us ; and the voice
That spake was capable to lift the soul
Toward regions yet more tranquil.[1]

Resuming his discourse, the Wanderer says—

                              "Ambition reigns
In the waste wilderness ; the Soul ascends
Drawn towards her native firmament of heaven,
When the fresh eagle, in the month of May,
Upborne, at evening, on replenished wing,
This shaded valley leaves ; and leaves the dark
Empurpled hills, conspicuously renewing
A proud communication with the sun
Low sunk beneath the horizon !—List !—I heard,
From yon huge breast of rock, a voice sent forth
As if the visible mountain made the cry.
Again !"—The effect upon the soul was such
As he expressed : from out the mountain's heart
The solemn voice appeared to issue, startling
The blank air—for the region all around
Stood empty of all shape of life, and silent
Save for that single cry, the unanswer'd bleat
Of a poor lamb—left somewhere to itself,
The plaintive spirit of the solitude !
He paused, as if unwilling to proceed,
Through consciousness that silence in such place
Was best, the most affecting eloquence.
But soon his thoughts returned upon themselves,
And, in soft tone of speech, thus he resumed.[2]

---

[1] *Excursion*, book iv.   [2] *Ibid.*

And the Solitary is again addressed by the Wanderer in the following strain—

These craggy regions, these chaotic wilds,
Does that benignity pervade that warms
The mole contented with her darksome walk
In the cold ground ; and to the emmet gives
Her foresight, and intelligence that makes
The tiny creatures strong by social league ;
Supports the generations, multiplies
Their tribes, till we behold a spacious plain
Or grassy bottom, all, with little hills—
Their labour, covered, as a lake with waves ;
Thousands of cities, in the desert place
Built up of life, and food, and means of life !
Nor wanting here, to entertain the thought,
Creatures that in communities exist,
Less, as might seem, for general guardianship
Or through dependence upon mutual aid,
Than by participation of delight
And a strict love of fellowship, combined.
What other spirit can it be that prompts
The gilded summer flies to mix and weave
Their sports together in the solar beam,
Or in the gloom of twilight hum their joy?
More obviously the self-same influence rules
The feathered kinds; the fieldfare's pensive flock,
The cawing rooks, and sea-mews from afar,
Hovering above these inland solitudes,
By the rough wind unscattered, at whose call
Up through the trenches of the long-drawn vales
Their voyage was begun : nor is its power
Unfelt among the sedentary fowl
That seek yon pool, and there prolong their stay
In silent congress ; or together roused
Take flight; while with their clang the air
    resounds.
And over all, in that ethereal vault

Is the mute company of changeful clouds;
Bright apparition, suddenly put forth,
The rainbow smiling on the faded storm;
The mild assemblages of the starry heavens;
And the great Sun, earth's universal lord![1]

  .   .   .   .   .   .

Take courage, and withdraw yourself from ways
That run not parallel to Nature's course.
Rise with the lark! your matins shall obtain
Grace, be their composition what it may,
If but with hers performed; climb once again,
Climb every day, those ramparts; meet the
  breeze
Upon their tops, adventurous as a bee
That from your garden thither soars to feed
On new-blown heath; let yon commanding rock
Be your frequented watch-tower; roll the stone
In thunder down the mountains; with all your
  might
Chase the wild goat; and if the bold red deer
Fly to those harbours, driven by hound and horn
Loud echoing, add your speed to the pursuit;
So, wearied to your hut shall you return,
And sink at evening into sound repose.[2]

And, by the poet, thus —

        How divine,
The liberty, for frail, for mortal, man
To roam at large among unpeopled glens
And mountainous retirements, only trod
By devious footsteps; regions consecrate
To oldest times! and, reckless of the storm
That keeps the raven quiet in her nest,
Be as a presence or a motion—one
Among the many there; and while the mists

[1] *Excursion*, book iv.   [2] *Ibid.*

Flying, and rainy vapours, call out shapes
And phantoms from the crags and solid earth
As fast as a musician scatters sounds
Out of an instrument; and while the streams
(As at a first creation and in haste
To exercise their untried faculties)
Descending from the region of the clouds,
And starting from the hollows of the earth
More multitudinous every moment, rend
Their way before them—what a joy to roam
An equal among mightiest energies;
And haply sometimes with articulate voice,
Amid the deafening tumult, scarcely heard
By him that utters it, exclaim aloud,
" Rage on, ye elements! let moon and stars
Their aspects lend, and mingle in their turn
With this commotion (ruinous though it be)
From day to night, from night to day, pro-
    longed!"[1]

Again, the "grey haired Wanderer" addresses him—

                    A consciousness is yours
How feelingly religion may be learned
In smoky cabins, from a mother's tongue—
Heard while the dwelling vibrates to the din
Of the contiguous torrent, gathering strength
At every moment, and, with strength, increase
Of fury; or, while snow is at the door,
Assaulting and defending, and the wind,
A sightless labourer, whistles at his work—
Fearful; but resignation tempers fear,
And piety is sweet to infant minds.
—The Shepherd-lad, that in the sunshine carves,
On the green turf, a dial, to divide
The silent hours; and who to that report

        [1] *Excursion*, book iv.

Can portion out his pleasures, and adapt,
Throughout a long and lonely summer's day
His round of pastoral duties, is not left
With less intelligence for *moral* things
Of gravest import.   Early he perceives,
Within himself, a measure and a rule,
Which to the sun of truth he can apply,
That shines for him, and shines for all mankind.
Experience daily fixing his regards
On Nature's wants, he knows how few they are,
And where they lie, how answered and appeased.
This knowledge ample recompense affords
For manifold privations; he refers
His notions to this standard; on this rock
Rests his desires; and hence, in after life,
Soul-strengthening patience, and sublime content.
Imagination—not permitted here
To waste her powers, as in the worldling's mind,
On fickle pleasures, and superfluous cares,
And trivial ostentation—is left free
And puissant to range the solemn walks
Of Time and Nature, girded by a zone
That, while it binds, invigorates and supports.
Acknowledge, then, that whether by the side
Of his poor hut, or on the mountain top,
Or in the cultured field, a Man so bred
(Take from him what you will upon the score
Of ignorance or illusion) lives and breathes
For noble purposes of mind: his heart
Beats to the heroic song of ancient days:
His eye distinguishes, his soul creates.[1]

And again—

                              Access for you
Is yet preserved to principles of truth,
Which the imaginative Will upholds

[1] *Excursion,* book iv.

In seats of wisdom, not to be approached
By the inferior Faculty that moulds,
With her minute and speculative pains,
Opinion, ever changing!
                              I have seen
A curious child, who dwelt upon a tract
Of inland ground, applying to his ear
The convolutions of a smooth-lipped shell;
To which, in silence hushed, his very soul
Listened intensely; and his countenance soon
Brightened with joy; for from within were heard
Murmurings, whereby the monitor expressed
Mysterious union with its native sea.
Even such a shell the universe itself
Is to the ear of Faith; and there are times,
I doubt not, when to you it doth impart
Authentic tidings of invisible things;
Of ebb and flow, and ever-during power;
And central peace, subsisting at the heart
Of endless agitation.   Here you stand,
Adore, and worship, when you know it not;
Pious beyond the intention of your thought;
Devout above the meaning of your will.
—Yes, you have felt, and may not cease to feel.
The estate of man would be indeed forlorn
If false conclusions of the reasoning power
Made the eye blind, and closed the passages
Through which the ear converses with the heart.
Has not the soul, the being of your life,
Received a shock of awful consciousness,
In some calm season, when these lofty rocks
At night's approach bring down the unclouded sky
To rest upon their circumambient walls;
A temple framing of dimensions vast,
And yet not too enormous for the sound
Of human anthems;—choral song, or burst
Sublime of instrumental harmony,
To glorify the Eternal?   What if these

Did never break the stillness that prevails
Here—if the solemn nightingale be mute,
And the soft woodlark here did never chant
Her vespers—Nature fails not to provide
Impulse and utterance.   The whispering air
Sends inspiration from the shadowy heights,
And blind recesses of the caverned rocks;
The little rills, and waters numberless,
Inaudible by daylight, blend their notes
With the loud streams: and often, at the hour
When issue forth the first pale stars, is heard,
Within the circuit of this fabric huge,
One voice—the solitary raven, flying
Athwart the concave of the dark blue dome,
Unseen, perchance above all power of sight—
An iron knell ! with echoes from afar
Faint—and still fainter—as the cry, with which
The wanderer accompanies her flight
Through the calm region, fades upon the ear,
Diminishing by distance till it seemed
To expire ; yet from the abyss is caught again,
And yet again recovered?[1]

No apology is needed for giving these long extracts
from the sublimer passages of *The Excursion*, which
relate to the abode of the Recluse in Langdale.   It
will be seen and felt by all who visit the place—
having first read and understood the poem—how
its solitude, its repose, with "the strength of the
hills" all around it, its silence broken only by the
voice of waters, or of sheep on the hill-side, or of
ravens far up in the corries of Blake Rigg, made
the neighbourhood of Blea Tarn perhaps the fittest
place in Westmoreland for these discourses of
the Wanderer.   Certain it is that some of the profoundest thoughts of philosophy, expressed in noblest

---

[1] *Excursion*, book iv.

numbers—thoughts which would have interested Heraclitus, and delighted Plato, which would have been hailed by Spinosa, and awakened a response in the soul of Immanuel Kant — such as those embodied in the last quotation — are for ever associated with this retreat of the Solitary at Blea Tarn.

CHAPTER VII.

RYDAL MOUNT, LAKE, ETC.

The Excursion was composed, for the most part, while the poet lived at Allan Bank. In the spring of 1811 he removed to the Grasmere parsonage, where he stayed two years; and early in 1813 he left Grasmere for Rydal Mount, which was his home for thirty-seven years, till his death in 1850.

The Mount has often been described, and it has undergone no very material alteration since his death, more than forty years ago. The house—which had in many places fallen to decay during the interval between Mrs. Wordsworth's death in 1859, and the year in which the present tenant entered on his lease—required a complete alteration within, to render it habitable. Those who find fault with the changes that have been made—the loss of the old picturesque frontage, with its ten windows, and the removal of the gravel terrace, with the ash tree near which was hung the "osier cage" of the doves—must remember that, as houses decay, they must be rebuilt—which usually implies some change on the old design—and that as shrubbery continues to grow, it must either be pruned or removed. It is natural to wish that the memorials of the poet in his old home should be preserved as unaltered as possible; and this has been done at Rydal Mount.

At the same time,

> The old order changeth, yielding place to new,
> Lest one good custom should corrupt the world.

If Rydal Mount—the house and part of the grounds—has succumbed, like everything else in the world, to the inevitable law by which changes are wrought in all "works of art and man's device," those who regret that it has not been kept up exactly as the poet left it, may remember that such preservation could not, in the nature of things, go on for ever; and further, that had our poet belonged to this generation, and entered on the possession of the Mount a dozen years ago, he would doubtless have set the example of introducing changes upon the old order that prevailed in his time. Nor, in conceding this, do I put a weapon—as I may perhaps be told—in the hands of those who contest the very object for which this little book is written. Here, too, as in things of graver moment than the preservation of houses and garden grounds, change is inevitable; but all change should be on the lines of the past; a new departure guided by the spirit of the past, and loyal to all that was best within it.

Returning from this digression, what Wordsworth wrote, when afraid of being obliged to quit the Mount, and when he purchased the small adjoining property below, which still belongs to the family, may be quoted in proof of the principle affirmed. He refers to the old Roman roads in the district around Ambleside, no trace of which survives; and then to the terrace constructed by himself, outside the Mount property to the west, and called in the household "The Far Terrace," leading to "Nab Well."

> The massy ways, carried across these heights
> By Roman perseverance, are destroyed,

Or hidden under ground, like sleeping worms.
How venture then to hope that Time will spare
This humble Walk? Yet on the mountain's side
A POET's hand first shaped it ; and the step
Of that same Bard—repeated to and fro
At morn, at noon, and under moonlight skies
Through the vicissitudes of many a year—
Forbade the weeds to creep o'er its gray line.
No longer scattering to the heedless winds
The vocal raptures of fresh poesy,
Shall he frequent those precincts ; locked no more
In earnest converse with beloved Friends,
Here will he gather stores of ready bliss,
As from the beds and borders of a garden
Choice flowers are gathered ! But, if power may
    spring
Out of a farewell yearning—favoured more
Than kindred wishes mated suitably
With vain regrets—the Exile would consign
This Walk, his loved possession, to the care
Of those pure Minds that reverence the Muse.

The following is part of the description of the
house and grounds, with which the poet's nephew
and biographer, the late Bishop of Lincoln, began
his uncle's *Memoirs*, written in 1850.   It is graphi-
cally told.   Perhaps no one could have told it so well.

"The house stands upon the sloping side of a
rocky hill, called Nab Scar.   It has a southern
aspect.   In front of it is a small semicircular area
of gray gravel, fringed with shrubs and flowers, the
house forming the diameter of a circle.   From this
area there is a descent by a few stone steps southward, and then a gentle ascent to a grassy mound.
Here let us rest a little.   At our back is the house ;
in front, rather to the left in the horizon is Wansfell,
on which the light of the evening sun rests.
Beneath it, the blue smoke shows the place of the

town of Ambleside. In front is the lake of Windermere shining in the sun; also in front, but more to
the right, are the fells of Loughrigg, one of which
throws up a massive solitary crag, on which the
poet's imagination pleased itself to plant an imperial
castle—

Aërial rock, whose solitary brow
From this low threshold daily meets the sight.

"Looking to the right, in the garden, is a beautiful glade, overhung with rhododendrons in most
luxuriant leaf and bloom. Near them is a tall ash
tree, in which a thrush has sung for hours together
during many years. Not far from it is a laburnum.
in which the osier cage of the doves was hung.
Below, to the west, is the vegetable garden, not
parted off from the rest, but blended with it by
parterres of flowers and shrubs.
"Returning to the platform of gray gravel before
the house, we pass under the shade of a fine
sycamore, and ascend to the westward by fourteen
steps of stones, about nine feet long, in the interstices of which grow the yellow flowering poppy
and the wild geranium or poor robin,

                                        gay
With his red stalks upon a sunny day;

a favourite with the poet, as his verses show. The
steps above mentioned lead to an upward-*sloping*
terrace, about 250 feet long. On the right side it
is shaded by laburnums, Portugal laurels, mountain
ash, and fine walnut trees and cherries; on the left
it is flanked by a low stone wall, coped with rude
slates, and covered with lichens, mosses, and wild
flowers. The fern waves on the wall, and at its

base grow the wild strawberry and foxglove.
Beneath this wall, and parallel to it, on the left, is a
level terrace, constructed by the poet, for the sake
of a friend most dear to him and his, who, for the
last twenty years of Mr. Wordsworth's life, was
often a visitor and inmate of Rydal Mount.[1] This
terrace was a favourite resort of the poet, being
more easy for pacing to and fro, when old age
began to make him feel the acclivity of the other
terrace to be toilsome. Both these terraces command beautiful views of the vale of the Rothay, and
the banks of the lake of Windermere.

"The *ascending* terrace leads to an arbour, lined
with fir cones, from which, passing onwards, on
opening the latch-door, we have a view of the lower
end of Rydal Lake, and of the long, wooded, and
rocky hill of Loughrigg, beyond and above it. Close
to this arbour door is a beautiful sycamore, with
five Scotch firs in the fore ground, and a deep bay
of wood, to the left and front, of oak, ash, holly,
hazel, fir, and birch. The terrace path here winds
gently off to the right, and becomes what was
called by the poet and his household the *Far*
Terrace, on the mountain side. . . . This terrace,
after winding along in a serpentine line for about
150 feet, ends in a little gate, beyond which is a
beautiful well of clear water, called the 'Nab Well,'
which was to the poet of Rydal—a professed
water-drinker—what the Bandusian fount was to
the Sabine bard.

"Returning to the arbour we descend, by a
narrow flight of stone steps, to the kitchen garden,
and passing through it southward we open a gate
and enter a field sloping down to the valley, and
called, from its owner's name, 'Dora's field.' Not

---

[1] He refers to Miss Fenwick, to whom we owe the
inestimable MS. notes on the poems.

far on the right on entering the field is the stone
bearing the inscription—

> In these fair vales hath many a Tree
>   At Wordsworth's suit been spared;
> And from the builder's hand this Stone,
> For some rude beauty of its own,
>   Was rescued by the Bard;
> So let it rest; and time will come
>   When here the tender-hearted
> May heave a gentle sigh for him,
>   As one of the departed.[1]

"Near the same gate we see a pollard oak, on the
top of whose trunk may yet be discerned some
traces of the primrose which sheltered the wren's
nest.

> .   .   .   She who planned the mossy lodge,
>   Mistrusting her evasive skill,
> Had to a primrose looked for aid,
>   Her wishes to fulfil.

"On the left of this gate we see another oak, and
beneath it a pool, to which the gold and silver fish,
once swimming in a vase in the library of the
house, were transported for the enjoyment of
greater freedom.

---

[1] To this poem the I. F.MS. appends the following
note: "Engraven during my absence in Italy upon a
brass plate inserted in the stone." *Prose Works*, vol. iii.
p. 183. The alarm felt about being "exiled" from
Rydal Mount was not wholly groundless. Some temporary misunderstanding had arisen between the inmates
of the Mount and those of the Hall. Wordsworth,
however, about this time, purchased the field below the
Mount, on which he might have built a house, if so
minded. The field is still in possession of his family"
(Dr. CRADOCK).

Removed in kindness from their glassy cell
To the fresh waters of a living well;
An elfin pool, so sheltered that its rest
No winds disturb.

"The house itself is a modest mansion of a sober
hue, tinged with weather stains, with two tiers of
five windows : on the right of these is a porch, and
above, and to the right, are two other windows;
the highest looks out of what was the poet's bed-
room.   The gable end at the east, that first seen
on entering the grounds from the road, presents on
the ground-floor the window of the old hall or
dining-room.   The house is mantled over here and
there with roses, and ivy, and jessamine, and
Virginia creeper.   We may pause on the threshold
of the porch at the hospitable ' *Salve* ' inscribed on
the pavement brought by a friend from Italy."[1]
In the grounds of Rydal Mount every walk—the
trees, the rocks, the terraces, the views on every
side, whatever appeals to eye or ear—all suggest,
in one way or another, the work and the personality
of Wordsworth, the life he lived there, and what
he has done for posterity.   The whole place seems
consecrate to genius, and to simple, elevated,
unworldly thought.   The special charm of the
Mount recalls the verses of an Indian poet, in
which he describes the retirement of the Yogi, or
ascetic recluses of his time.   The resemblance is,
of course, partial, but the fascination of the place
is strangely mingled with this Oriental picture,
which comes down to us from the times of Chaucer.

Where through the delight of its pleasantness,
Sitting down one hardly wills to rise again,
The feeling of unworldliness grows doubly strong
                When it is once beheld :

[1] *Memoirs*, vol. i. pp. 19-27.

A spot prepared by holy men,
Helpful to calm delight,
Exhilarating to the heart,
                    And reassuring ;

There studious thought leads on to studious
        thought,
Experience doth wed the heart ;
Such the exceeding power of its delightsomeness
                    Perpetually :

    .   .   .   .

It detains him who would not be detained,
The restless it compelleth to sit down,
Its soothing power arouseth
                    Unworldly thoughts.[1]

    .   .   .   .

In speaking of the Mount, Wordsworth himself
refers to the "beauty of the situation, its being
backed and flanked by lofty fells, which bring the
heavenly bodies to touch, as it were, the earth upon
the mountain tops, while the prospect in front lies
open to a length of level valley, the extended lake,
and a terminating ridge of low hills."[2]

In the Bishop of Lincoln's sketch the most
characteristic poems referring to Rydal are alluded
to. I may refer, in addition, to *The Lament of
Mary Queen of Scots on the Eve of a New Year*,
which arose, the poet tells us, out of "a flash of
moonlight that struck the ground when I was
approaching the steps that lead from the garden at
Rydal Mount to the front of the house."[3]   The
following is the first stanza—

        Smile of the Moon ! for so I name
        That silent greeting from above ;

[1] From *The Retirement of the Yogi*, by Dnyanoba.
Translated by the Rev. J. Murray Mitchell, D.D.
        [2] I. F. MS.   [3] *Ibid.*

A gentle flash of light that came
From her whom drooping captives love ;
Or art thou of still higher birth ?
Thou that didst part the clouds of earth,
My torpor to reprove !

The sonnet on the setting sun going down
behind Loughrigg Fell was suggested in front of
the Mount.

I watch, and long have watched, with calm regret
Yon slowly-sinking star—immortal Sire
(So might he seem) of all the glittering quire!
Blue ether still surrounds him—yet—and yet ;
But now the horizon's rocky parapet
Is reached, where forfeiting his bright attire,
He burns—transmuted to a dusky fire—
Then pays submissively the appointed debt
To the flying moments, and is seen no more.
Angels and gods!   We struggle with our fate,
While health, power, glory, from their height
        decline
Depressed! and then extinguished ; and our
        state,
In this, how different, lost Star, from thine,
That not to-morrow shall our beams restore!

With the summer-house, between the two terraces is associated the poem entitled, *Contrast : the
Parrot and the Wren.* The wren was one that
haunted this summer-house for many years.   I quote
three stanzas—

This moss-lined shed, green, soft, and dry,
Harbours a self-contented Wren,
Not shunning man's abode, though shy,
Almost as thought itself, of human ken.

Strange places, coverts, unendeared,
She never tried; the very nest
In which this Child of Spring was reared,
Is warmed, thro' winter, by her feathery breast.

To the bleak winds she sometimes gives
A slender unexpected strain;
Proof that the hermitess still lives,
Though she appear not, and be sought in vain.

Within the house itself, the place where *The Cuckoo clock*—the gift of Miss Fenwick—stood in the staircase, suggests the poem of that name.

Wouldst thou be taught, when sleep has taken
    flight,
By a sure voice that can most sweetly tell,
How far-off yet a glimpse of morning light,
And if to lure the truant back be well,

  .   .   .   .   .   .

Better provide thee with a Cuckoo-clock
For service hung behind thy chamber-door;
And in due time the soft spontaneous shock
The double note, as if with living power,
Will to composure lead—or make thee blithe as
    bird in bower.
List, Cuckoo—Cuckoo! oft tho' tempests howl,
Or nipping frost remind thee trees are bare,
How cattle pine, and droop the shivering fowl,
Thy spirits will seem to feed on balmy air;
I speak with knowledge— by that Voice beguiled
Thou wilt salute old memories as they throng
Into thy heart; and fancies, running wild
Through fresh green fields, and budding groves
    among,
Will make thee happy, happy as a child;
Of sunshine wilt thou think, and flowers, and song,
And breathe as in a world where nothing can go
    wrong

The room occupied by Miss Wordsworth, the poet's sister, recalls the lines on *The Redbreast*, suggested to him " in a Westmoreland cottage."

Part of Wordsworth's note to this poem is to the following effect: " My sister being confined to her room by sickness, a redbreast, without being caged, took up its abode with her, and at nights used to perch upon a nail from which a picture had hung. It used to sing and fan her face with its wings in a manner that was very touching."

> Heart-pleased we smile upon the Bird
> If seen, and with like pleasure stirred
> Commend him, when he's only heard
> But small and fugitive our gain
> Compared with *hers* who long hath lain,
> With languid limbs and patient head
> Reposing on a lone sick-bed ;
> Where now, she daily hears a strain
> That cheats her of too busy cares,
> Eases her pain, and helps her prayers.
> And who but this dear Bird beguiled
> The fever of that pale-faced Child ;
> Now cooling, with his passing wing,
> Her forehead, like a breeze of spring :
> Recalling now, with descant soft
> Shed round her pillow from aloft,
> Sweet thoughts of angels hovering nigh,
> And the invisible sympathy.
>
> .   .   .   .   .   .
>
> Thrice happy Creature ! in all lands
> Nurtured by hospitable hands.

As the biography tells us, the tall ash tree (in which the thrush used to sing) with the laburnum near (in which the osier cage with the doves was hung), grew on the west side of the Mount.   Both are gone.   The ash is represented in the vignette

sketch of the house, prefixed to the third chapter
of the *Memoirs*.   In " Dora's field " the fine oak-
tree, beneath which is the pool to which the gold
and silver fishes were transferred, still stands; and
in the other tree,

> In a green covert, where, from out
> The forehead of a pollard oak,
> The leafy antlers sprout,

where the "wren's nest" was built, wrens still
occasionally build; and primroses grow on the
ground beneath.   It is a curious link with the
past.   How many generations of wrens have there
broken the egg !   ·

> The hermit has no finer eye
> For *shadowy quietness.*

Of another poem, beginning,

> This lawn a carpet all alive
> With shadows flung from leaves, to strive
> In dance, amid a press
> Of sunshine, an apt emblem yields
> Of worldlings revelling in the fields
>   Of strenuous idleness,

Wordsworth tells us : " This lawn is the sloping one
adjoining the kitchen garden (at Rydal Mount),
and was made out of it.   Hundreds of times have
I here watched the dancing of shadows amid a
press of sunshine, and other beautiful appearances
of light and shade, flowers and shrubs;" and the
conclusion of his note expresses so profound a truth
so simply that it too may be quoted.   "Admiration
and love, to which all knowledge truly vital must
tend, are felt by men of real genius in proportion

as their discoveries in Natural Philosophy are enlarged; and the beauty in form of a plant or an animal is not made less but more apparent as a whole, by a more accurate insight into its constituent properties and powers. A savant who is not also a poet in soul, and a religionist in heart, is a feeble and unhappy creature."[1]   It is still a lawn.

The poem concludes—

> Yet, spite of all this eager strife,
> This ceaseless play, the genuine life
>   That serves the steadfast hours
> Is in the grass beneath, that grows
> Unheeded, and the mute repose
>   Of sweetly-breathing flowers.

The quatrain which Wordsworth wrote in the album of his god-daughter, Rotha Quillinan, was suggested by what he had often observed on the lawn of Rydal Mount.   Its two last lines are—

> The daisy, by the shadow that it casts,
> Protects the lingering dewdrop from the sun.

We cannot leave the slopes of Rydal without recalling the delightful lines addressed to the poet's daughter Dora, entitled *The Longest Day*, written in 1817, and suggested by the sight of her playing in front of the house.

> Let us quit the leafy arbour,
> And the torrent murmuring by ;
> For the sun is in his harbour,
> Weary of the open sky.

>   .   .   .   .   .   .

[1] I. F. MS.

Dora! sport, as now thou sportest,
On this platform, light and free ;
Take thy bliss, while longest, shortest,
Are indifferent to thee!

Who would check the happy feeling
That inspires the linnet's song?
Who would stop the swallow, wheeling
On her pinions swift and strong?

Summer ebbs ;—each day that follows
Is a reflux from on high,
Tending to the darksome hollows
Where the frosts of winter lie.

Now, even now, ere wrapt in slumber,
Fix thine eyes upon the sea
That absorbs time, space, and number ;
Look thou to Eternity!

Again, the seat on the Mount suggests the *Ode to Lycoris.* It was the sight of the "swanlike specks of mountain snow," reflected in Rydal Mere, and so "transferred," as Wordsworth says, "to the sub-aqueous sky," that reminded him "of the swans which the fancy of the ancient classic poets yoked to the car of Venus;"[1] We know not where the

Wild cave whose jagged brows were fringed
With flaccid threads of ivy,

was ; to which he refers in the second poem to Lycoris. But it was doubtless some one or other of the many "Rydalian" retreats. This is what he says of it—

Long as the heat shall rage, let that dim cave
Protect us, there deciphering as we may

[1] I. F. MS.

Diluvian records; or the sighs of Earth
Interpreting; or counting for old Time
His minutes by reiterated drops,
Audible tears from some invisible source
That deepens upon fancy—more and more
Drawn toward the centre whence those sighs
    creep forth
To awe the lightness of humanity.
Or, shutting up thyself within thyself,
There let me see thee sink into a mood
Of gentler thought, protracted till thine eye
Be calm as water when the winds are gone,
And no one can tell whither.   Dearest Friend !
We too have known such happy hours together
That, were power granted to replace them
    (fetched
From out the pensive shadows where they lie)
In the first warmth of their original sunshine,
Loth should I be to to use it ; passing sweet
Are the domains of tender memory !

Several of the poems refer to Rydal stream and
waterfall.   In the *Evening Walk*, written in his
eighteenth and nineteenth year, and addressed to
his sister, he tells us (in a a footnote to the poem)
that he is describing "features which characterise
the lower waterfall of Rydal."

Then while I wandered where the huddling rill
Brightens with water-breaks the hollow ghyll
As by enchantment, an obscure retreat
Opened at once, and stayed my devious feet.
While thick above the rill the branches close,
In rocky basin its wild waves repose,
Inverted shrubs, and moss of gloomy green,
Cling from the rocks, with pale wood weeds
    between ;
And its own twilight softens the whole scene,

Save where aloft the subtle sunbeams shine
On withered briers that o'er the crags recline;
Save where, with sparkling foam, a small cascade
Illumines, from within, the leafy shade;
Beyond, along the vista of the brook,
Where antique roots its bustling course o'erlook,
The eye reposes on a secret bridge
Half gray, half shagged with ivy to its ridge.

In the line I have italicised, an example of Wordsworth's subtle observation of Nature in his earliest
poetic efforts will be seen; and any one who has
looked up the glade from the summer-house below
this fall, or from the side of the brook, upon the
surroundings of the cascade, will find in this poem
—otherwise by no means remarkable—a good
illustration of how he kept close to Nature from the
very first, while he idealised everything he saw.
The record of actual fact, with a good deal of local
colour superadded, was necessary to give him at
once a solid hold of the realities of existence, and a
point of departure in his most imaginative flights.
  Of the poem beginning,

  " Lyre, though such power do in thy magic live,"

Wordsworth says, " The natural imagery of these
verses was suggested by frequent, I may say
intense, observation of the Rydal torrent."
  I quote the concluding portion of it—

  And on, or in, or near, the brook, espy
    Shade upon the sunshine lying
        Faint, and somewhat pensively;
    And downward Image gaily vying
        With its upright living tree
  Mid silver clouds, and openings of blue sky,
  As soft almost and deep as her cerulean eye.

Nor less the joy with many a glance
Cast up the Stream or down at her beseeching,
To mark its eddying foam-balls prettily distrest
By ever-changing shape and want of rest ;
      Or watch, with mutual teaching,
      The current as it plays
      In flashing leaps and stealthy creeps
      Adown a rocky maze ;
Or note (translucent summer's happiest chance!)
In the slope-channel floored with pebbles bright,
Stones of all hues, gem emulous of gem,
So vivid that they take from keenest sight
The liquid veil that seeks not to hide them.

The *Haunted Tree*, the "time-dismantled oak,"
was in the park of Rydal ; and there, too, was the
ancient elm, with ivy twining round it

    In grisly folds and strictures serpentine,

referred to in the Ecclesiastical Sonnets, Part I.,
No. XXI.   It was near the path to the upper waterfall.

No poem, however, connected with Rydal is so
fine as the ninth *Evening Voluntary*, "Composed
on an Evening of extraordinary Splendour and
Beauty," of which he says, "felt, and in a great
measure composed, upon the little Mount in front
of our abode at Rydal."[1]   In it, Wordsworth rises
almost to the level of his earlier *Ode on Immortality.*

             I.

Had this effulgence disappeared
With flying haste, I might have sent,
Among the speechless clouds, a look
Of blank astonishment ;

[1] I. F. MS.

But 'tis endued with power to stay,
And sanctify one closing day,
That frail Mortality may see—
What is?—ah no, but what *can* be!
Time was when field and watery cove
With modulated echoes rang,
While choirs of fervent Angels sang
Their vespers in the grove;
Or, crowning, star-like, each some sovereign
    height,
Warbled, for heaven above and earth below,
Strains suitable to both.—Such holy rite,
Methinks, if audibly repeated now
From hill or valley, could not move
Sublimer transport, purer love,
Than doth this silent spectacle—the gleam—
The shadow—and the peace supreme!

II.

No sound is uttered—but a deep
And solemn harmony pervades
The hollow vale from steep to steep,
And penetrates the glades.
Far-distant images draw nigh,
Called forth by wondrous potency
Of beamy radiance, that imbues
Whate'er it strikes with gem-like hues!
In vision exquisitely clear,
Herds range along the mountain side;
And glistening antlers are descried;
And gilded flocks appear.
Thine is the tranquil hour, purpureal Eve!
But long as godlike wish, or hope divine,
Informs my spirit, ne'er can I believe
That this magnificence is wholly thine!
—From worlds not quickened by the sun
A portion of the gift is won;

An intermingling of Heaven's pomp is spread
On ground which British shepherds tread!

III.

And, if there be whom broken ties
Afflict, or injuries assail,
Yon hazy ridges to their eyes
Present a glorious scale,
Climbing suffused with sunny air.
To stop—no record hath told where!
And tempting Fancy to ascend,
And with immortal Spirits blend!
—Wings at my shoulders seem to play;
But rooted here, I stand and gaze
On those bright steps that heavenward raise
Their practicable way.
Come forth, ye drooping old men, look abroad,
And see to what fair countries ye are bound!
And if some traveller, weary of his road,
Hath slept since noon-tide on the grassy
        ground,
Ye Genii! to his covert speed;
And wake him with such gentle heed
As may attune his soul to meet the dower
Bestowed on that transcendent hour!

IV.

Such hues from their celestial Urn
Were wont to stream before mine eye,
Where'er it wandered in the morn
Of blissful infancy.
This glimpse of glory, why renewed?
Nay, rather speak with gratitude;
For, if a vestige of those gleams
Survived, 'twas only in my dreams.
Dread Power! whom peace and calmness
        serve

No less than Nature's threatening voice,
If aught unworthy be my choice,
From THEE if I would swerve;
Oh, let thy grace remind me of the light
Full early lost, and fruitlessly deplored;
Which, at this moment, on my waking sight
Appears to shine, by miracle restored;
My soul, though yet confined to earth,
Rejoices in a second birth!
—'Tis past, the visionary splendour fades:
And night approaches with her shades.

The multiplication of mountain-ridges, described
at the commencement of the third stanza of this
Ode as a kind of Jacob's Ladder, leading to
Heaven, is produced either by watery vapours, or
sunny haze;—in the present instance by the latter
cause. Allusions to the thought which pervades
the ode, *Intimations of Immortality*, will be seen
in the last stanza of the poem.

The references to Rydal Mere are too numerous
to quote in full.

Like a fair sister of the sky,
Unruffled doth the blue lake lie,
The mountains looking on.

This occurs in one of the *Poems of Sentiment and
Reflection*. What he wrote, "on the same occasion,"
is exquisite in its allusion to the second summer,
with its tender spring-like feeling—

Departing summer hath assumed
An aspect tenderly illumed,
The gentlest look of spring;
That calls from yonder leafy shade
Unfaded, yet prepared to fade,
A timely carolling.

> No faint and hesitating trill.
> Such tribute as to winter chill
> The lonely redbreast pays!
> Clear, loud, and lively is the din,
> From social warblers gathering in
> Their harvest of sweet lays.

These two poems were composed on the Mount.

Amongst the *Evening Voluntaries*, we have two
"composed by the side of Rydal Mere." The
former begins thus—

> The linnet's warble sinking towards a close,
> Hints to the thrush 'tis time for their repose;
> The shrill-voiced thrush is heedless, and again
> The monitor revives his own sweet strain;
> But both will soon be mastered, and the copse
> Be left as silent as the mountain-tops,
> Ere some commanding star dismiss to rest
> The throng of rooks, that now, from twig or nest
> (After a steady flight on home-bound wings,
> And a last game of mazy hoverings
> Around their ancient grove), with cawing noise
> Disturb the liquid music's equipoise.

The latter is as follows—

> Soft as a cloud is yon blue Ridge—the Mere
> Seems firm as solid crystal, breathless, clear,
> And motionless; and, to the gazer's eye,
> Deeper than ocean, in the immensity
> Of its vague mountains and unreal sky!
> But, from the process in that still retreat,
> Turn to minuter changes at our feet;
> Observe how dewy Twilight has withdrawn
> The crowd of daises from the shaven lawn,
> And has restored to view its tender green,

That, while the sun rode high, was lost beneath
    their dazzling sheen.
—An emblem this of what the sober Hour
Can do for minds disposed to feel its power!
Thus oft, when we in vain have wish'd away
The petty pleasures of the garish day,
Meek eve shuts up the whole usurping host
(Unbashful dwarfs each glittering at his post)
And leaves the disencumbered spirit free
To reassume a staid simplicity.

    'Tis well—but what are helps of time and
        place,
When wisdom stands in need of Nature's
        grace:
Why do good thoughts, invoked or not,
    descend,
Like Angels from their bowers, our virtues to
    befriend;
If yet To-morrow, unbelied, may say,
"I come to open out, for fresh display
The elastic vanities of yesterday?"

The lines on the Mountain Echo were suggested
while Wordsworth was walking on the southern
side of Rydal Mere, opposite Nab Scar, whence
the echo proceeded—

    Yes, it was the mountain Echo,
    Solitary, clear, profound,
    Answering to the shouting Cuckoo,
    Giving to her sound for sound!

    Unsolicited reply
    To a babbling wanderer sent;
    Like her ordinary cry,
    Like—but oh, how different!

Have not *we* too?—yes, we have
Answers, and we know not whence;
Echoes from beyond the grave,
Recognised intelligence!

Such rebounds our inward ear
Catches sometimes from afar—
Listen, ponder, hold them dear;
For of God—of God they are.

The sonnet on *The Wild Duck's Nest,*

Words cannot paint the o'ershadowing yew-
    tree bough,
And dimly-gleaming nest,

was suggested by one which he observed on the
largest of the Rydal islands; the same island in
which he wrote an *Inscription upon a Stone, in a
Deserted Quarry.*

It was on the walk between Rydal and Grasmere
that the poem on *The Clouds* was composed;
"suggested while I was walking on the foot-road.
The clouds were driving over the top of Nab Scar
across the vale." [1]

Army of Clouds! ye wingèd Host in troops
Ascending from behind the motionless brow
Of that tall rock, as from a hidden world,
O whither with such eagerness of speed?
What seek ye, or what shun ye? of the gale
Companions, fear ye to be left behind,
Or racing o'er your blue ethereal field
Contend ye with each other? of the sea
Children, thus post ye over vale and height
To sink upon your mother's lap—and rest?

   .   .   .   .

[1] I. F. MS.

.   .   .   From a fount of life
Invisible, the long procession moves
Luminous or gloomy, welcome to the vale
Which they are entering, welcome to mine eye
That sees them, to my soul that owns in them,
And in the bosom of the firmament
O'er which they move, wherein they are con-
    tained,
A type of her capacious self and all
Her restless progeny.

.   .   .   .
                Our song is of the Clouds,
And the wind loves them ! and the gentle gales—
Which by their aid re-clothe the naked lawn
With annual verdure, and revive the woods,
And moisten the parched lips of thirsty flowers—
Love them; and every idle breeze of air
Bends to the favourite burthen.   Moon and stars
Keep their most solemn vigils when the Clouds
Watch also, shifting peaceably their place
Like bands of ministering Spirits, or when they
    lie,
As if some Protean art the change had wrought,
In listless quiet o'er the ethereal deep
Scattered, a Cyclades of various shapes
And all degrees of beauty.   O ye Lightnings !
Ye are their perilous offspring : and the sun—
Source inexhaustible of life and joy,

.   .   .   .
A blazing intellectual deity—
Loves his own glory in their looks, and showers
Upon that unsubstantial brotherhood
Visions with all but beatific light
Enriched—too transient were they not renewed.

Compare with this his remark on the clouds,
quoted in the preface to this volume (pp. x.-xi.)

No single road in the Lake District—not even

that in Easdale—is more associated with Wordsworth, than this old (upper) path between Rydal
and Grasmere, under Nab Scar. None is more
interesting to those who have felt the power of his
inspiration, and the truth of his insight.

>   A humble walk
> .   .   .   .   .   . this path,
> A little hoary line and faintly traced,
> Work, shall we call it, of the shepherd's foot
> Or of his flock?—joint vestige of them both.
> I pace it unrepining, for my thoughts
> Admit no bondage and my words have wings.

I have already remarked that Wordsworth
composed most of his poems out of doors;
"nine-tenths of my verses," he remarked, "have
been murmured out in the open air." As his servant
at the Mount said to a stranger, contrasting his
library with his study, "This is my master's library,
where he keeps his books; his study is out of
doors." Along this road under Nab Scar he
walked, in all weathers, composing his verses,
during his residence at Rydal Mount, just as he
had frequented the terrace at Lancrigg, or "the
Grove" of Grasmere, while he lived at Dove
Cottage.

It is now little used, and as a consequence is, in
many places, a grassy path—like the terraces on
the western side of Derwentwater, or those near
Howtown under Swarth Fell—with exquisite curves
and windings, and endless unexpected surprises,
every turn of the road revealing some new feature
or combination of features. Here and there small
brooks, heard but not seen, keep up "the voice of
many waters," and just serve to make the silence
audible. In the early weeks of May, when the
green is freshest, though the leaf is not fullest, and

the woods are clothed with sorrel and anemone,
and the "soft hyacinthine haze" is "dreaming round
the roots" of the trees, and the groves are vocal
with their earliest choirs, when the reflections of
the hills are visible in the lake, and the mountain
ridges are glorified against the sky, there is, I think,
no more delightful walk in England, or anywhere.
It is one of these easy paths along a mountain slope,
with numerous ups and downs, intersected by lines
of rock, in which every few yards reveal a fresh
grouping of mountain and valley, foreground and
horizon, such as is to be found nowhere out of
England, and, so far as I know, nowhere in such
perfection as in this district of the lakes.   The
views of Loughrigg and of Rydal Mere from this
terrace are exquisite.   The *Evening Walk*, composed in youth and dedicated to his sister,
should be read after one is familiar with this road.
The lines are not intended as a description of Rydal
exclusively; but they are as applicable to it as to
any other part of the district.   I extract the following, which is in harmony with the passage already
quoted from the same poem, referring to Rydal
waterfall.

Into a gradual calm the breezes sink,
A blue rim borders all the lake's still brink;
There doth the twinkling aspen's foliage sleep,
And insects clothe, like dust, the glassy deep:
And now, on every side, the surface breaks
Into blue spots, and slowly lengthening streaks;
Here, plots of sparkling water tremble bright
With thousand thousand twinkling points of light:
There, waves that, hardly weltering, die away,
Tip their smooth ridges with a softer ray;
And now the whole wide lake in deep repose
Is hushed, and like a burnished mirror glows,

.   .   .   .

In foamy breaks the rill, with merry song,
Dashed o'er the rough rock, lightly leaps along;
From lonesome chapel at the mountain's feet,
Three humble bells their rustic chime repeat;
Sounds from the waterside the hammered boat;
And *blasted* quarry thunders, heard remote;

Even here, amid the sweep of endless woods,
Blue pomp of lakes, high cliffs, and falling floods,
Not undelightful are the simplest charms,
Found by the grassy door of mountain-farms.

.   .   .   .

Now, while the solemn evening shadows sail,
On slowly-waving pinions, down the vale;
And, fronting the bright west, yon oak entwines
Its darkening boughs and leaves, in stronger
        lines;

.   .   .   .

The song of mountain-streams, unheard by
        day,
Now hardly heard, beguiles my homeward way.
Air listens, like the sleeping water still,
To catch the spiritual music of the hill,
Broke only by the slow clock tolling deep,
Or shout that wakes the ferryman from sleep,
The echoed hoof nearing the distant shore,
The boat's first motion—made with dashing oar;
Sound of closed gate across the water borne,
Hurrying the timid hare through rustling corn;
The sportive outcry of the mocking owl;
And at long intervals the mill-dog's howl;
The distant forge's swinging thump profound;
Or yell, in the deep woods, of lonely hound.

It is worth mentioning that Wordsworth says of
this poem, "There is not an image in it which I
have not observed; and now, in my seventy-third
Q

year, I recollect the time and place when most of them were noticed."[1]

The Pilgrim's Dream, or the Star and the Glow-worm, was suggested on this road. *The Oak and the Broom :* a pastoral, has a still closer connection with it. The spot is fixed within narrow limits by Wordsworth's own note : "The ponderous block of stone which is mentioned in the poem remains, I believe, to this day, a good way up Nab Scar; broom grows under it and in many places on the side of the precipice."[2] It is beyond doubt on the wooded part of Nab Scar through which the pathway leads. There is one huge block of stone high above the path which answers well to the description—

> I saw a crag, a lofty stone
> As ever tempest beat !
> Out of its head an Oak had grown,
> A Broom out of its feet.
> The time was March, a cheerful noon—
> The thaw-wind, with the breath of June,
> Breathed gently from the warm south-west.

The Waterfall and the Eglantine is another "poem of the fancy," of which, though the intrinsic interest is less, the locality referred to can be identified with perfect accuracy. The eglantine grew on the little brook that now runs under two cottages just above the path, which have been built since the poet's time, and marked Brockstone on the Ordnance map. "The plant itself, of course, has long disappeared; but in following up the rill through the copse, above the cottages, I found an unusually large eglantine growing by the side of the stream" (Dr. Cradock, in 1877). In the follow-

[1] I. F. MS.   [2] *Ibid.*

ing year I found it growing luxuriantly in two places.

The following is from Dorothy Wordsworth's Journal, April 23, 1802 :—

"It being a beautiful morning, we set off at 11 o'clock, intending to stay out of doors all the morning. We went towards Rydal, under Nab Scar. The sun shone, and we were lazy. Coleridge pitched upon several places to sit down upon, but we could not be all of one mind respecting sun and shade, so we pushed on to the foot of the Scar. It was very grand when we looked up, very stoney; here and there a budding tree. William observed that the umbrella yew-tree, that breasts the wind, had lost its character as a tree, and had become like solid wood. Coleridge and I pushed on before. We left William sitting on the stones, feasting with silence, and I sat down upon a rocky seat: a couch it might be, under the bower of William's *Eglantine, Andrew's Broom*. He was below us, and we could see him. He came to us, and repeated his poems, while we sat beside him. We lingered long, looking into the vales. Ambleside Vale, with the copses, the village under the hills, and the green fields ; Rydal, with a lake all alive and glittering, yet but little stirred by breezes ; and our own dear Grasmere, making a little round lake of Nature's own, with never a house, never a green field, but the copses and the bare hills enclosing it, and the river flowing out of it. Above rose Coniston Fells, in their own shape and colour . . . the sky, and the clouds, and a few wild creatures. Coleridge went to search for something new. We saw him climbing up towards a rock. He called us, and we found him in a bower—the sweetest that was ever seen. The rock on one side is very high, and all covered with ivy, which hung loosely about, and bore branches

of brown berries. On the other side, it was higher
than my head. We looked down on the Ambleside Vale that seemed to wind away from us, the
village lying under the hill. The fir-tree island
was reflected beautifully. . .· . About this
bower there is mountain ash, common ash, yew-
tree, ivy, holly, hawthorn, roses, flowers, and a
carpet of moss. Above, at the top of the rock,
there is another spot. It is scarce a bower, a little
parlour, not enclosed by walls, but shaped out for
a resting-place by the rocks, and the ground rising
above it.   It had a sweet moss carpet.   We
resolved to go and plant flowers in both these
places to-morrow."

Taking the lower road from Rydal to Grasmere
—after passing Nab Cottage, where De Quincey
and Hartley Coleridge used to live, and another
small cottage (Whitemoss), built by Wordsworth
for the use of the quarrymen at Rydal—we come
to two quarries. At the second a road ascends to
Whitemoss. Where this quarry now is, there was
in Wordsworth's time a smooth-faced, sloping rock,
doubtless polished by the glacier that once filled
the vales of Grasmere and Rydal. He "used to
call it Tadpole slope, from having frequently
observed there the water-bubbles gliding under
the ice exactly in the shape of that creature." [1]

Hast thou seen, with flash incessant,
Bubbles gliding under ice,
Bodied forth and evanescent,
No one knows by what device ?
Such are thoughts !—A wind-swept meadow
Mimicking a troubled sea,
Such is life ; and death a shadow
From the rock eternity !

[1] I. F. MS.

A little way past this place—where the quarry now is—the middle road to Grasmere ascends, that which goes past the " Glow-worm rock," and leads on to the " Wishing-gate," and the "stately Firgrove."   The Glow-worm or Primrose rock has been already referred to. It is easily identified, and is unmistakable. It was probably upon this same rock, and certainly on some one upon the right hand as you ascend the short slope, that Wordsworth saw the monument of ice, spoken of in the eleventh of the poems entitled *Inscriptions*—

> I saw this rock, while vernal air
> Blew softly o'er the russet heath,
> Uphold a monument as fair
> As church or abbey furnisheth.

CHAPTER VIII.

THE road from Rydal to Grasmere also suggests
the poem of *The Waggoner*, the opening stanzas
of which are perfect in their description of a June
evening in the district—

'Tis spent—this burning day of June !
Soft darkness o'er its latest gleams is stealing ;
The buzzing dor-hawk, round and round, is
    wheeling,—
That solitary bird
Is all that can be heard
In silence deeper far than that of deepest noon !

   Confiding Glow-worms, 'tis a night
Propitious to your earth-born light !
But where the scattered stars are seen
In hazy straits the clouds between,
Each, in his station twinkling not,
Seems changed into a pallid spot.

The mountains against heaven's grave weight
Rise up, and grow to wondrous height ;
The air, as in a lion's den,
Is close and hot ;—and now and then
Comes a tired and sultry breeze
With a haunting and a panting
Like the stifling of disease ;

But the dews allay the heat,
And the silence makes it sweet.

The waggoner ascends the middle road from
Rydal (the reference to the "glow-worms" will
show that he passes "the Glow-worm rock"), and
goes down to Dove Cottage, in Grasmere, where

At the bottom of the brow,
Where once the DOVE and OLIVE-BOUGH
Offered a greeting of good ale
To all who entered Grasmere Vale ;
And called on him who must depart
To leave it with a jovial heart ;
There, where the DOVE and OLIVE-BOUGH
Once hung, a Poet harbours now,
A simple water-drinking Bard.

He goes on through Grasmere, past the Swan Inn.

He knows it to his cost, good Man !
Who does not know the famous Swan !
Object uncouth! and yet our boast,
For it was painted by the Host ;
His own conceit the figure planned,
'Twas coloured all by his own hand ;
And that frail Child of thirsty clay,
Of whom I sing this rustic lay,
Could tell with self-dissatisfaction
Quaint stories of the bird's attraction !

.   .   .   .

And now the conqueror essays
The long ascent of Dunmail-raise.

As he proceeds a storm gathers, and he barely sees
the rocks at the summit of Helm Crag, where two
figures appear to sit, as two are also traced on the
Cobbler, near Arrochar, in Argyle—

The Astrologer, sage Sidrophel,
Where at his desk and book he sits,

Puzzling aloft his curious wits ;
He whose domain is held in common
With no one but the ANCIENT WOMAN,
Cowering beside her rifted cell,
As if intent on magic spell ;—
Dread pair, that, spite of wind and weather,˙
Still sit upon Helm-crag together !

At the crest of the ridge, he reaches the boundary
between the shires of Westmoreland and Cumberland—

That pile of stones,
Heaped over brave King Dunmails bones ;
He who had once supreme command,
Last king of rocky Cumberland ;

.   .   .   .   .   .

Green is the grass for beast to graze,
Around the stones of Dunmail-raise !

Descending from the top of the Raise, he passes

Wytheburn's modest House of prayer
As lowly as the lowliest dwelling

and, about half a mile farther on, reaches "the
Cherry Tree"—then a public-house, and still standing on the eastern side of the road—where

'Tis the village merry-night,

and the inhabitants of Wytheburn have met for a
rustic dance. After two hours' delay they "coast
the silent lake" of Thirlmere, and pass the "Rock
of Names."

As this rock is one of the most interesting memorials of Wordsworth and his friends, and is threatened with immersion under the waters of a reservoir,
I must quote the verses in *The Waggoner* referring
to it, which were omitted from the poem when first

published, but in the edition of 1836 were inserted
in a note.   The rock was the trysting-place of the
poets from Grasmere and Keswick, where they often
met ; it being nearly half-way between the two
places.

An upright mural block of stone,
Moist with pure water trickling down.

.   .   .   .   .   .

—A star, declining towards the west,
Upon the watery surface threw
Its image tremulously imprest,
That just marked out the object and withdrew :

.   .   .   .   .   .

ROCK OF NAMES!

Light is the strain, but not unjust
To Thee, and thy memorial-trust
That once seemed only to express
Love that was love in idleness ;
Tokens as year hath followed year
How changed, alas, in character !
For they were graven on thy smooth breast
By hands of those my soul loved best ;
Meek women, men as true and brave
As ever went to a hopeful grave :
Their hands and mine, when side by side,
With kindred zeal and mutual pride,
We worked until the Initials took
Shapes that defied a scornful look.—
Long as for us a genial feeling
Survives, or one in need of healing,
The power, dear Rock, around thee cast,
Thy monumental power, shall last
For me and mine !   O thought of pain,
That would impair it or profane !
And fail not Thou, loved Rock ! to keep
Thy charge when we are laid asleep.

Wordsworth came to reside in Grasmere in 1799. In 1800 Captain John Wordsworth lived with his brother for some time, but left him finally on September 29th, 1800: therefore their names must have been cut on the rock during that summer of 1800.

This rock is on the right hand of the road, a short way past Waterhead. On it were carved the letters—

W. W.

M. H.

D. W.

S. T. C.

J. W.

S. H.

which are the initials of William Wordsworth, Mary Hutchinson, Dorothy Wordsworth, Samuel Taylor Coleridge, John Wordsworth, and Sarah Hutchinson. It is too much to expect of British Philistia, that it will abstain from carving or scratching any other names alongside the initials of this group of poets, —for they were *all* poets! In 1878 the rock was wonderfully free from such; and its preservation was probably due to the dark olive-coloured moss, with which the "pure water trickling down" had covered the face of the "mural block," and thus secured it from observation, even on that highway. When the Manchester reservoir works were started, the rock suffered injury; and it was covered up by the pious efforts of Mr. Rawnsley, to preserve it from further desecration. I have been told that it has recently been cracked, and irreparably injured.

"The Muse" takes farewell of the Waggoner, as he is proceeding with the Sailor and his quaint model of the Vanguard, along the shining level of this lake. It "scents the morning air," and

> Quits the slow-paced waggon's side,
> To wander down yon hawthorn dell

With murmuring Greta for her guide.
—There doth she ken the awful form
Of Raven-crag—black as a storm—
Glimmering through the twilight pale;
And Ghimmer-crag, his tall twin brother,
Each peering forth to meet the other:—

Raven-crag is well known—a rock on the western
side of Thirlmere, where the Greta issues from the
lake. Ghimmer-crag—the crag of the ewe-lamb—
is not so obvious; but I am inclined to think that
it is the "Fisher-crag" of the Survey maps and
Guide-books. No other rock round Thirlmere can
with any accuracy be called the "tall twin brother"
of Raven-crag. Certainly not *Great How*, on the
eastern shore; while neither High Seat nor Bleaberry
Fell is visible from the road, and their height in no
sense resembles Raven-crag. If Fisher-crag is the
"twin brother," why was the name changed? and
why not now go back to Wordsworth's *Ghimmer-
crag*, a name, which, in his day, it had probably
borne time out of mind?

The closing lines of the following passage will
perhaps suggest the strain of the *Metrical Romances*
of Sir Walter Scott, with whom the poet of this district had many associations. The Muse proceeds—

And, while she roves through St. John's Vale,
Along the smooth unpathwayed plain,
By sheep-track or through cottage lane,
Where no disturbance comes to intrude
Upon the pensive solitude,
Her unsuspecting eye, perchance,
With the rude shepherd's favoured glance,
Behold the faeries in array,
Whose party-coloured garments gay
The silent company betray:
Red, green, and blue; a moment's sight!

For Skiddaw-top with rosy light
Is touched—and all the band take flight.
—Fly also, Muse! and from the dell
Mount to the ridge of Nathdale Fell;
Thence, look thou forth o'er wood and lawn
Hoar with the frost-like dews of dawn;
Across yon meadowy bottom look,
Where close fogs hide their parent brook;
And see, beyond that hamlet small,
The ruined towers of Threlkeld-hall,
Lurking in a double shade,
By trees and lingering twilight made!
There, at Blencathara's rugged feet,
Sir Lancelot gave a safe retreat
To noble Clifford: from annoy
Concealed the persecuted boy,
Well pleased in rustic garb to feed
His flock, and pipe on shepherd's reed
Among this multitude of hills,
Crags, woodlands, waterfalls, and rills;
Which soon the morning shall enfold,
From east to west, in ample vest
Of massy gloom and radiance bold.

The old Hall of Threlkeld has long been in a
state of ruinous dilapidation, the only habitable part
having been for many years converted into a farmhouse; but when it is entirely gone, the remembrance
of it and its kind-hearted owner will survive perhaps
in these lines.

The Castle Rock, in the Vale of Legberthwaite,
between High Fell and Great How, is the fairy
castle of Scott's *Bridal of Triermain.* "Nathdale
Fell" is the ridge between Naddle Vale and that of
St. John, now called High Rigg. The remaining
local allusions in the poem are obvious enough;
Castrigg is the shortened form of Castlerigg, the
ridge between Naddle and Keswick.

The mists, that o'er the streamlet's bed
Hung low, begin to rise and spread;
Even while I speak, their skirts of gray
Are smitten by a silver ray;
And lo!—up Castrigg's naked steep
(Where smoothly urged the vapours sweep
Along—and scatter and divide,
Like fleecy clouds self multiplied)
The stately waggon is ascending.

Expressing his regret at the close of the poem
that the "living almanac" and "speaking diary,"
which the old Waggoner supplied to the whole of
the district, had disappeared, Wordsworth says—

Yes, I, and all about me here,
Through all the changes of the year,
Had seen him through the mountains go,
In pomp of mist or pomp of snow,
Majestically huge and slow:
Or, with a milder grace adorning
The landscape of a summer's morning;
While Grasmere smoothed her liquid plain
The moving image to detain;
And mighty Fairfield, with a chime
Of echoes, to his march kept time;
When other little business stirred,
And little other sound was heard;
In that delicious hour of balm,
Stillness, solitude, and calm,
While yet the valley is arrayed,
On this side with a sober shade;
On that is prodigally bright—
Crag, lawn, and wood—with rosy light.

The passing of Great How, in this journey with
the Waggoner, recalls the poem entitled *Rural
Architecture.* It was on the top of this How that
the three boys of Legberthwaite built their giant

"stone-man;" and when it was tossed down by the wind, the next day built up another.

Another allusion to the road between Grasmere and Keswick occurs in the *Evening Walk*, where Wordsworth tells us that the following image—

Waving his hat, the shepherd from the vale,
Directs his winding dog the cliffs to scale,
The dog, loud barking, 'mid the glittering rocks,
Hunts, where his master points, the intercepted
    flocks—

was suggested to him when he was "an eye-witness of it, while crossing the pass of Dunmail Raise."[1]

The Song at the Feast of Brougham Castle, which was written at Coleorton in 1807, refers mainly to the Skipton district of Yorkshire, but in it there are naturally allusions to localities about Threlkeld, between Keswick and Penrith.

The boy must part from Mosedale groves,
And leave Blencathara's rugged coves,
And quit the flowers that summer brings
To Glendermakin's lofty springs.

The gaps in the side of Sadleback are here referred to, and the ragged patches of hawk-weed, golden rod, and white water-ranunculus in the pools of Glendermakin : while Bowscale Tarn, in which the two undying fish were supposed by the country people to swim for ever, is to the north of Blencathara. The lines however by which this *Song* is best known are these—

Love had he known in huts where poor men lie,
His daily teachers had been woods and rills,

[1] I. F. MS.

The silence that is in the starry sky,
The sleep that is among the lonely hills.

Comparatively few of the poems describe, or refer directly to, Keswick and the Derwentwater district. But there are two lines in Wordsworth's *Evening Walk*, referring to Lodore, which are worth more than the whole of Southey's well-known poem on that cascade—

Where Derwent rests, and listens to the roar
That stuns the tremulous cliffs of high Lodore.

A sonnet was composed at Applethwaite, near Keswick, in reference to Sir George Beaumont's gift of a small property there, which the poet made over to his infant daughter Dora. It was presented by Sir George, Wordsworth tells us, "with a view to the erection of a house upon it, for the sake of being near to Coleridge, then living, and likely to remain, at Greta Hall, near Keswick. . . . This little property lies beautifully upon the banks of a rill that gurgles down the side of Skiddaw; and the orchard and other parts of the grounds command a magnificent prospect of Derwentwater, the mountains of Borrowdale, and Newlands;"[1]

Beaumont ! it was thy wish that I should rear
A seemly cottage in this sunny Dell,
On favoured ground, thy gift, where I may dwell
In neighbourhood with One to me most dear.
That undivided we from year to year
Might work in our high Calling—a bright hope
To which our fancies, mingling, gave free scope
Till checked by some necessities severe.
And should these slacken, honoured BEAUMONT !
    still
Even then we may perhaps in vain implore

[1] I. F. MS.

Leave of our fate thy wishes to fulfil.
Whether this boon be granted us or not,
Old Skiddaw will look down upon the spot
With pride, the Muses love it evermore.

And in the next sonnet he says—

Pelion and Ossa flourish side by side,
Together in immortal books enrolled:
His ancient dower Olympus hath not sold;
And that inspiring Hill, which did divide
Into two ample horns his forehead wide,
Shines with poetic radiance as of old;
While not an English Mountain we behold
By the celestial Muses glorified.
Yet round our sea-girt shores they rise in crowds:
What was the great Parnassus' self to Thee,
Mount Skiddaw?   In his natural sovereignty
Our British Hill is nobler far; he shrouds
His double front among the Atlantic clouds,
And pours forth streams more sweet than
      Castaly.

Some sentences on Skiddaw, by Coleridge and
Southey respectively, may be compared with
Wordsworth's poem on that mountain.

In July 1800 Coleridge wrote : " Right before me
is a great *camp* of single mountains—each in shape
resembles a giant's tent! and to the left, but closer
to it far than the Bassenthwaite Water to my right,
is the lake of Keswick, with its islands and white
sails, and glossy lights of evening, crowned with
green meadows ; but the three remaining sides are
encircled by the most fantastic mountains that ever
earthquakes made in sport ; as fantastic as if Nature
had *laughed* herself into the convulsion in which
they were made.   Close behind me, at the foot of
Skiddaw, flows the Greta.   I hear its murmuring
distinctly, where it curves round almost in a semi-

circle, and is now catching the purple light of the scattered clouds above it, directly before me."

Again, in September 1800, Coleridge wrote to William Godwin: "I know of no mountain in the north equal to Snowdon, but then *we* have an *encampment* of huge mountains; in no harmony perhaps to the eye of a scene-painter, but always interesting, various, and, as it were, nutritive. Height is assuredly an advantage, as it connects the earth with the sky by the clouds that are ever skimming the summits, or climbing up, or creeping down the sides, or veiling or bridging the higher parts or lower parts of the waterfalls . . . Mountains and mountainous scenery put on their immortal interest first, when we have resided among them, and learnt to understand their language, their written characters, and intelligible sounds, and all their eloquence, so various, so unwearied. Then, you will hear no 'twice-told tale.' I question if there be a room in England which commands a view of mountains, and lakes and woods, and vales, superior to that in which I am now sitting. . . . Here, too, you will meet with Wordsworth, 'the latch of whose shoe I am unworthy to unloose.'"

In August 1817 Southey wrote: "Summer is not the season for this country. Coleridge says, and says well, that there it is like a theatre at noon. There are no *goings-on* under a clear sky; but at other seasons there is such shifting of shades, such islands of light, such columns and buttresses of sunshine, as might almost make a painter burn his brushes, as the sorcerers did their books of magic when they saw the divinity which rested on the apostles. The very snow, which you would perhaps think must monotonise the mountains, gives new varieties; it brings out their recesses, and designates all their inequalities; it impresses a better feeling of their height; and it reflects

R

such tints of saffron, or fawn, or rose-colour, to the evening sun. *O, Maria Sanctissima!* Mount Horeb, with the glory on its summit, might have been more glorious, but not more beautiful, than old Skiddaw in his winter pelisse. I will not quarrel with the frost, though the fellow has the impudence to take me by the nose. The lake-side has such ten thousand charms : a fleece of snow, or of the hoar frost, lies on the fallen trees on large stones ; the grass points, that just peer above the water, are powdered with diamonds ; the ice on the margin with chains of crystal, and such veins and wavy lines of beauty as mock all art ; and, to crown all, Coleridge and I have found out that stones thrown upon the lake, when frozen, make a noise like singing birds ; and when you whirl on it a large flake of ice, away the shivers slide, chirping and warbling like a flight of finches."

In the poem composed *At the Grave of Burns, seven years after his death* (1803), Wordsworth says—

> Huge Criffel's hoary top ascends
>   By Skiddaw seen,
> Neighbours we were, and loving friends
>   We might have been.

Of the Greta, near Keswick, he writes—

>   Oft as Spring
> Decks on thy sinuous banks, her thousand
>   thrones
> Seats of glad instinct and love's carolling,
> The concert, for the happy, then may vie
> With liveliest peals of birthday harmony :
> To a grieved heart, the notes are benisons.

Another sonnet, entitled *Nun's Well, Brigham,* may be read in connection with this and the already quoted address to the Derwent.

The cattle crowding round this beverage clear
To slake their thirst, with reckless hoofs have trod.
The encircling turf into a barren clod ;
Through which the waters creep then disappear,
Born to be lost in Derwent flowing near;
Yet, o'er the brink, and round the limestone cell
Of the pure spring (they call it the " Nun's Well,"
Name that first struck by chance my startled ear)
A tender spirit broods—the pensive Shade
Of ritual honours to this Fountain paid
By hooded Votaresses with saintly cheer ;
Albeit oft the Virgin-mother mild
Looked down with pity upon eyes beguiled
Into the shedding of " too soft a tear."

Coleridge wrote to Sir Humphrey Davy, Oct. 1800 :
" Fronting out our house" (he then lived at Greta
Bank, Keswick), "the Greta runs into the Derwent.
Greta, or rather Grieta, is exactly the Cocytus of the
Greeks, the word, literally rendered in modern
English, is 'the loud lamenter'; to griet, in the
Cumbrian dialect, signifying to roar aloud
for grief or pain ; and it does roar with a
vengeance."

In 1835 Wordsworth wrote : " Many years ago,
when I was at Greta Bridge, in Yorkshire, the
mistress of the inn, proud of her skill in etymology,
said that the name of the river was taken from the
bridge, the form of which, as every one must notice,
exactly resembled a great 'A.' Dr. Whittaker has
derived it from the word of common occurrence
in the North of England, '*to greet*' signifying to
lament aloud, mostly with weeping : a conjecture
rendered more probable from the stormy and rocky
channel of both the Cumberland and Yorkshire rivers.
The Cumberland Greta, though it does not among
the country people take up *that* name till within three
miles of its disappearance in the river Derwent may

be considered as having its source in the mountain
Cove of Wytheburn, and flowing through Thirlemere,
the beautiful features of which lake are known only
to those who, travelling between Grasmere and
Keswick, have quitted the main road in the vale
of Wytheburn, and crossing over to the opposite
side of the lake, have proceeded with it on the right
hand.   The channel of the Greta, immediately above
Keswick, has, for the purposes of building, been in
a great measure cleared of the immense stones
which, by their concussion in high floods, produced
the loud and awful noises described in the sonnet."

In 1833 Wordsworth went on a tour to Scotland,
which he memorialized in verse.   He seems to have
started for the border *via* Keswick, and near Keswick
wrote the following sonnet to the Greta—

Greta, what fearful listening! when huge stones
Rumble along thy bed, block after block;
Or, whirling with reiterated shock,
Combat, while darkness aggravates the groans;
But if thou (like Cocytus from the moans
Heard on his rueful margin) thence wast named
The Mourner, thy true nature was defamed,
And the habitual murmur that atones
For thy worst rage, forgotten.   Oft as Spring
Decks on thy sinuous banks, her thousand thrones,
Seats of glad instinct, and love's carolling,
The concert, for the happy then may vie
With liveliest peals of birthday harmony;
To a grieved heart, the notes are benisons.

Southey is buried in the churchyard of Crosthwaite parish, and in the church there is a monument
to his memory, with the following inscription by
Wordsworth, who was one of the few mourners
from a distance who attended his friend's funeral—

Ye vales and hills, whose beauty hither drew
The poet's steps, and fixed him here, on you
His eyes have closed !   And ye, loved books
        no more
Shall Southey feed upon your precious lore,
To works that ne'er shall forfeit their renown,
Adding immortal labours of his own —
Whether he traced historic truth, with zeal
For the State's guidance, or the Church's weal,
Or Fancy, disciplined by studious art,
Improved his pen, or wisdom of the heart,
Or judgments sanctioned in the Patriot's mind
By reverence for the rights of all mankind.
Wide were his aims, yet in no human breast
Could private feelings meet for holier rest.
His joys, his griefs, have vanished like a cloud
From Skiddaw's top; but he to heaven was vowed
Through his industrious life, and Christian faith
Calmed in his soul the fear of change and death.

Derwentwater suggests the Inscription *For the
spot where the Hermitage stood on St. Herbert's
Island*—

.   .   .   .   .   .   Not unmoved
Wilt thou behold this shapeless heap of stones,
The desolate ruins of St. Herbert's Cell.
Here stood his threshold; here was spread the
        roof
That sheltered him, a self-secluded Man,
After long exercise in social cares,
And offices humane, intent to adore
The Deity, with undistracted mind,
And meditate on everlasting things,
In utter solitude.—But he had left
A Fellow-labourer, whom the good man loved
As his own soul.   And, when with eye upraised
To heaven he knelt before the crucifix,
While o'er the lake the cataract of Lodore

Pealed to his orisons, and when he paced
Along the beach of this small isle and thought
Of his Companion, he would pray that both
(Now that their earthly duties were fulfilled)
Might die in the same moment.

Other lines amongst these " Inscriptions" were
entitled *Near the Spring of the Hermitage*—

> Troubled long with warring notions
> Long impatient of Thy rod,
> I resign my soul's emotions
> Unto Thee, mysterious God!
>
> What avails the kindly shelter
> Yielded by this craggy rent,
> If my spirit toss and welter
> On the waves of discontent?
>
> Parching Summer hath no warrant
> To consume this crystal Well;
> Rains that make each rill a torrent
> Neither sully it nor swell.
>
> Thus, dishonouring not her station,
> Would my Life present to Thee,
> Gracious God, the pure oblation
> Of divine tranquility!

The following, in a different strain, are *Inscriptions supposed to be found in and near a Hermit's Cell.* They may be associated with the home of the Solitary at Blea Tarn, or with the island at Derwentwater—

> Hopes, what are they?—Beads of morning
> Strung on slender blades of grass!
> Or a spider's web adorning
> In a straight and treacherous pass.

What are fears but voices airy?
Whispering harm where harm is not;
And deluding the unwary
Till the fatal bolt is shot?

What is glory?—in the socket
See how dying tapers fare!
What is pride?—a whizzing rocket
That would emulate a star.

What is friendship?—do not trust her,
Nor the vows which she has made;
Diamonds dart their brightest lustre
From a palsy-shaken head.

What is truth?—a staff rejected;
Duty?—an unwelcome clog;
Joy?—a moon by fits reflected
In a swamp or watery bog;

Bright, as if through ether steering,
To the Traveller's eye it shone:
He hath hailed it re-appearing—
And as quickly it is gone;

Such is Joy—as quickly hidden
Or mis-shapen to the sight,
And by sullen weeds forbidden
To resume its native light.

What is youth?—a dancing billow,
(Winds behind, and rocks before!)
Age?—a drooping, tottering willow
On a flat and lazy shore.

What is peace?—when pain is over,
And love ceases to rebel,
Let the last faint sigh discover
That precedes the passing knell!

The *Floating Island*, on which Dorothy Words-worth composed some lines which have a melancholy interest, is in Derwentwater. Her brother tells us that she "took a pleasure in repeating these verses, which she composed not long before the beginning of her sad illness."

Going up Borrowdale, the poem of all others which will most probably occur to the reader of Wordsworth is that which he called *Yew Trees*. It has some of the grandeur of Greek Tragedy; the actual cluster of trees suggesting "an ideal grove, in which the ghostly masters of mankind meet, and sleep, and offer worship to the Destiny that abides above them, while the mountain flood, as if from another world, makes music to which they dimly listen."[1]

The path to these yew-trees breaks to the left from the Honiston road at Seatoller, about a mile from Rosthwaite, in Borrowdale. It is the track leading to Seathwaite, and thence over the Sty Pass to Wastdale. The grove is soon reached on the west side of the beck that comes down from Styhead, and on the flank of Greyknotts.

In the great winter storm of December 1883 this "brotherhood of venerable trees" was irreparably injured. One of them was uprooted, another had some of its leading branches wrenched from the trunk. I saw it a few days after the disaster, when the ground for a wide space was strewn with the wreckage; to those who remember the grandeur and solemnity of the old "fraternal four," there is no doubt that the Borrowdale grove is a thing of the past.

There is a Yew-tree, pride of Lorton vale,
Which to this day stands single, in the midst

---

[1] Stopford Brooke's *Theology in the English Poets*, p. 259.

Of its own darkness, as it stood of yore;
Not loth to furnish weapons for the bands
Of Umfraville or Percy ere they marched
To Scotland's heaths; or those that crossed
        the sea
And drew their sounding bows at Azincour,
Perhaps at earlier Crecy, or Poictiers.
Of vast circumference and gloom profound
This solitary Tree! a living thing
Produced too slowly ever to decay;
Of form and aspect too magnificent
To be destroyed.   But worthier still of note
Are those Fraternal Four of Borrowdale,
Joined in one solemn and capacious grove;
Huge trunks! and each particular trunk a
        growth
Of intertwisted fibres serpentine
Up-coiling, and inveterately convolved;
Nor uninformed with Phantasy, and looks
That threaten the profane;—a pillared shade,
Upon whose grassless floor of red-brown hue,
By sheddings from the pining umbrage tinged
Perennially—beneath whose sable roof
Of boughs, as if for festal purpose, decked
With unrejoicing berries—ghostly shapes
May meet at noontide; Fear and trembling
        Hope,
Silence and Foresight; Death the Skeleton
And Time the Shadow;—there to celebrate,
As in a natural temple scattered o'er
With altars undisturbed of mossy stone,
United worship; or in mute repose
To lie, and listen to the mountain flood
Murmuring from Glaramara's inmost caves.

The "pride of Lorton Vale," referred to at the
beginning of this poem, still survives, majestic in
decay; and although the Borrowdale yews have

suffered irreparable injury, they may yet live for hundreds of years.

As we ascend towards this grove of yew trees the Great Gable is visible, to which allusion is made in the poem of *The Brothers*, but which more specially refers to the Pillar Rock in Ennerdale—

> You see yon precipice :—it wears the shape
> Of a vast building made of many crags ;
> And in the midst is one particular rock
> That rises like a column from the vale,
> Whence by our shepherds it is called THE
>   PILLAR.

This is the only poem of Wordsworth's which refers to Ennerdale.   The height from which James Ewbank is supposed in the poem to have fallen is not, however, the Pillar Rock—which is a crag rather difficult of ascent—but a spur of the Pillar Mountain.   The "airy summit crowned with heath" could not be the top of the Pillar Rock.   It is not likely that Wordsworth ever ascended the latter.

There is not much room for localization in the *Stanzas suggested in a Steamboat off St. Bees Head, on the Coast of Cumberland*, nor in others referring to the western coast, such as the *View from the top of Black Comb*.   On his sixty-third birthday, however (Easter Sunday, April 7th, 1833), he wrote some lines *On a light part of the Coast of Cumberland*, between Moresby and Whitehaven, which have an interest from his description of the sea—

> The sun, that seemed so mildly to retire,
> Flung back from distant climes a streaming fire,
> Whose blaze is now subdued to tender gleams,
> Prelude of night's approach with soothing dreams.
> Look round ;—of all the clouds not one is moving ;

'Tis the still hour of thinking, feeling, loving.
Silent and steadfast as the vaulted sky
The boundless plain of waters seems to lie :—
Comes that low sound from breezes rustling o'er
The grass-crowned headland that conceals the
    shore?
No; 'tis the earth-voice of the mighty sea,
Whispering how meek and gentle he can be.

In the same year he wrote, at Moresby, White
haven—

The sun is couched, the sea-fowl gone to rest,
And the wild storm hath somewhere found a nest :
Air slumbers—wave with wave no longer strives,
Only a heaving of the deep survives,
A tell-tale motion ! soon will it be laid,
And by the tide alone the water swayed.
Stealthy withdrawings, interminglings mild
Of light with shade in beauty reconciled—
Such is the prospect far as sight can range.

CHAPTER IX.

THE PENRITH DISTRICT, ETC.

AT the close of the Scottish tour of 1833, with
Henry Crabb Robinson, and his son John, Words-
worth returned leisurely from Carlisle to Rydal
Mount; and several of his poems, written in memory
of that tour, describe the district around Penrith.
One addressed to *The River Eden, Cumberland,*
may refer to almost any part of its course between
Carlisle and Corby; although the "bold rocks"
referred to are finest in its upper reaches, beyond
Appleby.

Eden ! till now thy beauty had I viewed
By glimpses only, and confess with shame
That verse of mine, whate'er its varying mood,
Repeats but once the sound of thy sweet name:
Yet fetched from Paradise that honour came,
Rightfully borne; for Nature gives thee flowers
That have no rivals among British bowers;
And thy bold rocks are worthy of their fame.
Measuring thy course, fair Stream ! at length I
    pay
To my life's neighbour dues of neighbourhood;
But I have traced thee on thy winding way
With pleasure sometimes by this thought
    restrained,—
For things far off we toil, while many a good
Not sought, because too near, is never gained.

In Wetheral Church, at Corby, he composed two sonnets on the *Monument of Mrs. Howard,* by Nollekens. The first is as follows—

Stretched on the dying Mother's lap, lies dead
Her new-born Babe; dire ending of bright
    hope!
But Sculpture here, with the divinest scope
Of luminous faith, heavenward hath raised that
    head
So patiently; and through one hand has spread
A touch so tender for the insensate Child—
(Earth's lingering love to parting reconciled,
Brief parting, for the spirit is all but fled)—
That we, who contemplate the turns of life
Through this still medium, are consoled and
    cheered;
Feel with the Mother, think the severed Wife
Is less to be lamented than revered;
And own that Art, triumphant over strife
And pain, hath powers to Eternity endeared.

At Nunnery, a few miles higher up the stream, which he used to visit when a boy—an easy day's excursion from Penrith—and which is named after a Home for Benedictine Nuns, established there by William Rufus, he wrote—

The floods are roused, and will not soon be weary;
Down from the Pennine Alps [1] how fiercely sweeps
CROGLIN, the stately Eden's tributary!
He raves, or through some moody passage creeps
Plotting new mischief—out again he leaps
Into broad light, and sends, through regions airy,
That voice which soothed the Nuns while on the
    steeps
They knelt in prayer or sang to blissful Mary.

[1] The chain of Crossfell.

That union ceased; then, cleaving easy walks
Through crags, and smoothing paths beset with
　　danger,
Came studious Taste; and many a pensive
　　stranger
Dreams on the banks, and to the river talks.
What change shall happen next to Nunnery Dell!
Canal, and Viaduct, and Railway, tell!

On his way south to Penrith, he revisited *The
Monument commonly called Long Meg and her
Daughters, near the river Eden*, on which, in 1821,
he had written a memorial sonnet.   This Druidical
circle is—after Stonehenge, Stennis, and Caller-
nish—perhaps the most remarkable in Britain.
It is a perfect circle, eighty yards in diameter, and
the stones now above ground are seventy-two in
number.   Long Meg herself is a high block of
unhewn stone, detatched from the rest, and is
eighteen feet high.   The following is the sonnet
which this Druidical remain suggested.

A weight of awe, not easy to be borne,
Fell suddenly upon my Spirit—cast
From the dread bosom of the unknown past,
When first I saw that family forlorn.
Speak Thou, whose massy strength and stature
　　scorn
The powers of years—pre-eminent, and placed
Apart, to overlook the circle vast—
Speak, Giant-mother! tell it to the Morn
While she dispels the cumbrous shades of Night;
Let the Moon hear, emerging from a cloud;
At whose behest uprose on British ground
That Sisterhood, in hieroglyphic round
Forth-shadowing, some have deemed, the
　　infinite,
The inviolable God, that tames the proud!

From Penrith passing on to Lowther Castle—
Lord Lonsdale's residence—Wordsworth was
stirred to write a sonnet upon it. The present
castle was begun in 1808. The arched corridors
surrounding the staircase—sixty feet square by
ninety feet high—justify the description in the
sonnet.

Lowther! in thy majestic Pile are seen
Cathedral pomp and grace, in apt accord
With the baronial castle's sterner mien;
Union significant of God adored,
And charters won and guarded by the sword
Of ancient honour; whence that goodly state
Of polity which wise men venerate,
And will maintain, if God his help afford.
Hourly the democratic torrent swells;
For airy promises and hopes suborned
The strength of backward-looking thoughts is
    scorned.
Fall if ye must, ye Towers and Pinnacles,
With what ye symbolise; authentic Story
Will say, Ye disappeared with England's Glory!

In the earlier Scottish tour of 1831—memorialized in the volume which Wordsworth called
Yarrow Revisited, etc.—there are several poems
referring to the Penrith district. One was *Suggested
by a view from an eminence in Inglewood Forest*—
an extensive tract enclosed, he tells us, within his
own memory.

The forest huge of ancient Caledon
Is but a name, no more is Inglewood,
That swept from hill to hill, from flood to flood:
On her last thorn the nightly moon has shone;
Yet still, though unappropriate Wild be none,

Fair parks spread wide where Adam Bell might
    deign
With Clym o' the Clough, were they alive again,
To kill for merry feasts their venison.
Nor wants the holy Abbot's gliding Shade
His church with monumental wreck bestrown ;
The feudal Warrior-chief, a Ghost unlaid,
Hath still his castle, though a skeleton,
That he may watch by night, and lessons con
Of power that perishes, and rights that fade.

In this Inglewood Forest there was a famous
sycamore called Harts-horn Tree, which stood,
single and conspicuous, on a height near Penrith.
It was always called the "Round Thorn," and
Wordsworth in his sonnet called it an oak,
although it was himself who mentioned to Miss
Fenwick that it was a sycamore.   It has now
perished, although its site is known.

Here stood an Oak, that long had borne affixed
To his huge trunk, or, with more subtle art,
Among its withering topmost branches mixed,
The palmy antlers of a hunted Hart,
Whom the Dog Hercules pursued—his part
Each desperately sustaining, till at last
Both sank and died, the life-veins of the chased
And chaser bursting here with one dire smart.
Mutual the victory, mutual the defeat !
High was the trophy hung with pitiless pride ;
Say, rather, with that generous sympathy
That wants not, even in rudest breasts, a seat ;
And, for this feeling's sake, let no one chide
Verse that would guard thy memory, HARTS-
    HORN Tree !

On the high road between Penrith and Appleby,
about two miles out of Penrith, stands a weather-

worn pillar called the Countess Pillar.   It has the
following inscription :—

"This pillar was erected, in the year 1656, by Anne, Countess
Dowager of Pembroke, etc., for a memorial of her last parting
with her pious mother, Margaret, Countess Dowager of
Cumberland, on the 2nd of April 1616 ; in memory whereof
she hath left an annuity of 4*l*. to be distributed to the poor of
the parish of Brougham, every 2nd day of April for ever,
upon the stone table placed hard by.   Laus Deo !"

While the poor gather round, till the end of time
May this bright flower of Charity display
Its bloom, unfolding at the appointed day ;
Flower than the loveliest of the vernal prime
Lovelier—transplanted from heaven's purest clime !
'Charity never faileth:' on that creed,
More than on written testament or deed,
The pious Lady built with hope sublime.
Alms on this stone to be dealt out, *for ever!*
'LAUS DEO.'   Many a stranger passing by
Has with that Parting mixed a filial sigh,
Blest its humane Memorial's fond endeavour ;
And, fastening on those lines an eye tear-glazed,
Has ended though no Clerk, with 'God be
        praised !'

It is an octagonal pillar.   The inscription is in
capital letters, and is let into the stone in a copper-
plate, thirteen and a-half inches by ten and a-half
inches.
    The final memorial poem in this series refers to
Roman Antiquities.   At Voreda, some six miles
from the present town of Penrith, there had been
an old Roman Station—a camp of the third class.
The relics discovered in it are now at Lowther
Castle.

How profitless the relics that we cull,
Troubling the last holds of ambitious Rome

S

Unless they chasten fancies that presume
Too high, or idle agitations lull!
Of the world's flatteries if the brain be full,
To have no seat for thought were better doom,
Like this old helmet, or the eyeless skull
Of him who gloried in its nodding plume.
Heaven out of view, our wishes what are they
Our fond regrets tenacious in their grasp?
The Sage's theory? the Poet's lay?—
Mere Fibulæ without a robe to clasp;
Obsolete lamps, whose light no time recals;
Urns without ashes, tearless lachrymals!

CHAPTER X.

WORDSWORTH has described the Duddon Valley,
and memorialized it, both in verse and prose. The
allusions in the poems were traced out some years
ago, during successive visits, by Mr. Herbert Rix;
and although there may be room for difference of
opinion in one or two points, a subsequent visit to
the valley has not led me to differ from Mr. Rix,
except in two instances. I therefore think it best to
give his localization in full. To this Mr. Rix has most
kindly consented. The following chapter is his—

I.

Not envying Latian shades—if yet they throw
A grateful coolness round that crystal Spring,
Blandusia, prattling as when long ago
The Sabine Bard was moved her praise to sing;
Careless of flowers that in perennial blow
Round the moist marge of Persian fountains
    cling;
Heedless of Alpine torrents thundering
Through ice-built arches radiant as heaven's
    bow;
I seek the birthplace of a native Stream.—
All hail, ye mountains! hail, thou morning light!
Better to breathe at large on this clear height

Than toil in needless sleep from dream to dream :
Pure flow the verse, pure, vigorous, free, and bright,
For Duddon, long-loved Duddon, is my theme !

The Duddon rises on Wrynose Fell, though
whereabouts on Wrynose Fell it rises is not so
easy to determine. James Thorne, indeed, in his
pretty little book, *Rambles by Rivers*, has furnished
a picture of the source of the Duddon, and given
directions for finding it, warning his readers at the
same time that the "real source" may easily be
overlooked and the wrong spot selected. But his
woodcut is so vague and featureless, that the
traveller who tries to identify the spot which it
represents, will find in this wild waste of rocks and
rivulets any number of combinations which exactly
suit it. Following, however, the stream which lies
most nearly in a line with the lower bed of the
river, it will be found to rise in a spot which commands a wide prospect : the valley of the Brathy,
from Langdale Tarn to the head of Windermere, being
in the foreground, and, in the background, wave
upon wave of distant mountain ranges. Geographi-
cally speaking, this appears to me to be the source
of the Duddon.

Poetically speaking, however, a different beck
may be selected as the infant Duddon. As you go
from Fell Foot to Cockley Beck, turn sharply to
the right at the Three-Shire Stones, and you will
come, at the distance of 200 yards, to a deep cleft,
draped on either side with bracken and parsley-fern,
and over-arched by two mountain ashes, which
spring from the rock on either side, and interweave
their branches midway. Just above this grotto the
stream divides. The branch on the right hand, as
you go towards the source, is the rill leading to
the geographical source, but the left-hand branch is
that which the poet is more likely to have followed

when he sought "the birthplace" of the Duddon.
It is somewhat the larger of the two, and decidedly
the more picturesque.

Following this stream we find it rising at a point
whence neither the Brathy nor the Duddon Valley
can be seen.   We are surrounded by a perfect
wilderness of huge hill-tops, and the spot, with its
surroundings, answers well to the description given
in the second and third sonnets.   We are in the
midst of a "lofty waste," haunted by the spirit of
"Desolation;" the "whistling blast," which is never
wanting in Wrynose Pass, sweeps bleakly by, and
the "naked stones," such as the poet chose for his
seat, are scattered all around.

As to the "tripping lambs," which supply a simile
in the third sonnet, it is truly wonderful where
those fell lambs will climb to! Not only do you
encounter them on these lofty and desolate fells,
where it seems almost strange to meet with any
living creature, but, if you look upward, you will
see them high above you, almost on the crown of
Pike o' Blisco.

III.

How shall I paint thee?—Be this naked stone
My seat, while I give way to such intent;
Pleased could my verse, a speaking monument,
Make to the eyes of men thy features known.
But as of all those tripping lambs not one
Outruns his fellows, so hath Nature lent
To thy beginning nought that doth present
Peculiar ground for hope to build upon.
To dignify the spot that gives thee birth,
No sign of hoar Antiquity's esteem
Appears, and none of modern Fortune's care;
Yet thou thyself hast round thee shed a gleam
Of brilliant moss, instinct with freshness rare;
Prompt offering to thy Foster-mother, Earth!

"A gleam of brilliant moss" refers, no doubt, to the *Sphagnum*, or Bog-moss, which grows here in large patches, very noticeable among the sombre ling and heather, and which shines like gold when the sunlight is upon it.

IV.

Take, cradled Nursling of the mountain, take
This parting glance, no negligent adieu !
A Protean change seems wrought while I
      pursue
The curves, a loosely-scattered chain doth
      make;
Or rather thou appear'st a glistering snake,
Silent, and to the gazer's eye untrue,
Thridding with sinuous lapse the rushes, through
Dwarf willows gliding, and by ferny brake.
Starts from a dizzy steep the undaunted Rill
Robed instantly in garb of snow-white foam;
And laughing dares the Adventurer, who hath
      clomb
So high, a rival purpose to fulfil;
Else let the dastard backward wend, and roam,
Seeking less bold achievement, where he will!

The "parting glance" of this sonnet would naturally be taken just before rounding the brow of the hill. The path drops somewhat suddenly, so that two or three steps brings the traveller from a level whence the "sinuous lapse" of the stream may be seen for some distance, to a stage where it is entirely hidden from view. The Duddon, which, since it reached the level of Wrynose Gap, has gently wound its way through bracken and rushes, now suddenly descends to the valley by a quick series of falls, as by a flight of steps. The first of these falls—a very pretty cascade—is doubtless the "dizzy steep" mentioned in the sonnet.

V.

Sole listener, Duddon! to the breeze that
    played
With thy clear voice, I caught the fitful
    sound
Wafted o'er sullen moss and craggy mound—
Unfruitful solitudes, that seemed to upbraid
The sun in heaven!—but now, to form a
    shade
For Thee, green alders have together wound
Their foliage; ashes flung their arms around;
And birch-trees risen in silver colonnade.
And thou hast also tempted here to rise,
'Mid sheltering pines, this Cottage rude and
    grey;
Whose ruddy children, by the mother's eyes
Carelessly watched, sport through the summer
    day,
Thy pleased associates:—light as endless May
On infant bosoms lonely Nature lies.

Sonnet v. is generally taken to be descriptive of
Cockley Beck.   Here as we emerge from Wrynose
Bottom, the first *trees* meet the eye, after a full two
miles of monotony and stones, and here, too, is the
first *cottage*, where the " ruddy children " of another
generation " sport through the summer day."   The
cottage itself is not indeed surrounded at the present
time by " sheltering pines "—that is a feature which
applies better to another cottage half a mile lower
down the stream.   The pines may, of course, have
disappeared since Wordsworth's day ; or more probably, one spot furnished him here, as in other
poems, with the main idea, while accessory features
were borrowed from other quarters, or created by
the imagination.

VI.

FLOWERS.

Ere yet our course was graced with social trees
It lacked not old remains of hawthorn bowers,
Where small birds warbled to their paramours;
And, earlier still, was heard the hum of bees;
I saw them ply their harmless robberies,
And caught the fragrance which the sundry
    flowers,
Fed by the stream with soft perpetual showers,
Plenteously yielded to the vagrant breeze.
There bloomed the strawberry of the wilderness;
The trembling eyebright showed her sapphire
    blue,
The thyme her purple, like the blush of Even;
And if the breath of some to no caress
Invited, forth they peeped so fair to view,
All kinds alike seemed favourites of Heaven.

The little rill, described above in the note on
Sonnet i., has worn for itself a channel deep enough
to shelter the "sundry flowers" (line 6) which form
the subject of Sonnet vi. The "trembling eyebright" (line 10), and the "purple thyme" (line 11),
still grace the Duddon, even in these "unfruitful
solitudes;" and in addition to these, there may be
found, in the same little gully, the Spearwort, the
Milkwort, the Small Beadstraw, *Euphrasia offici-
nalis*, and *Potentilla tormentilla*.

VIII.

What aspect bore the Man who roved or fled,
First of his tribe, to this dark dell—who first
In this pellucid Current slaked his thirst?
What hopes came with him? what designs were
    spread

Along his path?   His unprotected bed
What dreams encompassed?   Was the intruder
      nursed
In hideous usages, and rites accursed,
That thinned the living and disturbed the dead?
No voice replies;—both air and earth are
      mute;
And Thou, blue Streamlet, murmuring, yield'st
      no more
Than a soft record, that, whatever fruit
Of ignorance thou might'st witness heretofore,
Thy function was to heal and to restore,
To soothe and cleanse, not madden and
      pollute!

This probably does not refer to any particular
spot, but to the whole of the upper valley of the
Duddon.   There is nothing that can, strictly speaking, be called a "*dell*" anywhere between Cockley
Beck and Birks Brig.   The term is merely used
as an equivalent for *dale*, and includes the whole
space between the two ranges of fells which here
bound the valley.

This part of the river-valley is certainly quite
of a character to have inspired the sonnet.   It is
almost treeless, and the ground on either side of
the stream is covered with bracken and loose blocks
of granite, while the fells rise steeply on either hand,
and are capped by naked crags.   The epithet
"dark" (line 2) is not inappropriate, inasmuch
as the valley just here runs due north and south, so
that it gets neither the early morning nor the
evening sun.

As to the epithet blue (line 10), the cerulean colour
of the Duddon is one of its most exquisite characteristics, and is due, as Wordsworth has himself
explained, to the hue of the rocks and gravel seen
through the "perfectly pellucid" water.

IX.

THE STEPPING-STONES.

The struggling Rill insensibly is grown
Into a Brook of loud and stately march,
Crossed ever and anon by plank or arch;
And, for like use, lo! what might seem a zone
Chosen for ornament—stone matched with
     stone
In studied symmetry, with interspace
For the clear waters to pursue their race
Without restraint. How swiftly have they
     flown,
Succeeding—still succeeding! Here the Child
Puts, when the high-swoln Flood runs fierce
     and wild,
His budding courage to the proof; and here
Declining Manhood learns to note the sly
And sure encroachments of infirmity,
Thinking how fast time runs, life's end how
     near!

X.

Not so that Pair whose youthful spirits dance
With prompt emotion, urging them to pass;
A sweet confusion checks the Shepherd-lass;
Blushing she eyes the dizzy flood askance;
To stop ashamed—too timid to advance;
She ventures once again—another pause!
His outstretched hand He tauntingly with-
     draws—
She sues for help with piteous utterance!
Chidden she chides again; the thrilling touch
Both feel, when he renews the wished-for aid:
Ah! if their fluttering hearts should stir too
     much,
Should beat too strongly, both may be betrayed.

The frolic Loves, who, from yon high rock, see
The struggle, clap their wings for victory!

There are three principal sets of stepping-stones
across the Duddon. The first set is between
Cockley Beck and Birks Brig, a little below a farmhouse called Black Hall ; the second set, called by
the natives of the district the " Fiddle Steps," is in
a deep hollow between Birks Brig and Seathwaite,
at a point where the footpath to Eskdale crosses the
Duddon ; and the third is just opposite Seathwaite.

Of these, the second may be disregarded ; they
are little known, and there is nothing to be said in
favour of them. The question lies, then, between
the first and third, which we will call respectively
the *upper* and the *lower* stones.

James Thorne has fixed upon the upper stones as
those of Wordsworth's two sonnets, and has given
a picture of them. His woodcut is very rude, but
is sufficiently defined by the number of the stones,
the gate on the right, and the distant cottage on
the left, all of which indicate the upper stones as
those which he intends to represent. Miss Mar-
tineau, on the contrary, in her *Survey of the Lake
District*, appears to regard the stones opposite
Seathwaite as *the* stones ; and this is the traditional
view. Any inhabitant of Seathwaite or Ulpha, if
asked for " Wordsworth's stones," would at once
direct the stranger to the *lower* stones.

There is something to be said for each of these
views. The upper stones fit in with the order of
the sonnets, coming after the sonnet about Cockley
Beck, and before the sonnets about the Faery
Chasm, Seathwaite Chapel, and Ulpha Kirk. But
the lower steps answer better to the description of
the scene. The " zone chosen for ornament " and
the " studied symmetry " are much more applicable
to the lower than to the upper stones ; and " yon

high rock" (Sonnet x. I. 13) is wholly inapplicable
to the upper stones, as there is no rock of any sort
at hand, while the lower stones are overshadowed
by Wallabarrow Crag.

Then, again, the upper stones are in the highroad; anybody driving up the valley must pass
close to them, and Wordsworth must have seen
them again and again in his visits to this region,
while the lower stones have to be looked for and are
approached by a narrow footpath which leads off
the road and crosses two considerable fields before
the Duddon is reached. But, on the other hand,
the very beauty of the lower stones, once seen,
would fix them in the poet's mind for ever.

In respect of beauty there is indeed no comparison between the two spots. The lower stones
are approached down a flowery slope and through a
grove of larches, and crossing the stream by them,
you are landed in a coppice through which the
footpath winds most prettily, while the upper
stones are approached from a perfectly level bit of
rough pasture, and land you face to face with a
bare stone wall. The *lower* stones are eighteen in
number, counting only the principal ones, or you
can make twenty-one of them; they are of a bluish
tint, are set at equal distances, and form a beautiful
curve down the stream, looking to a fanciful eye
as though they were bending with the current.
The *upper* stones are nine in number, or you
may make eleven of them, and they are in a
straight line.

Perhaps, taking all things into consideration, the
most probable view is that Sonnets ix. and x. were
originally inspired by the beauty of the lower stones;
but when the Duddon Sonnets, written at various
times, came subsequently to be strung together, the
place given to these two sonnets was either acci-
dentally, or of set purpose, determined by the position

of the upper stones. The series being arranged
from memory of the order in which the scenes occur,
it is very possible that this misplacement may have
been accidental ; but it is not at all impossible that
it may have been intentional, and for this reason:
The emphasis of the earlier sonnets in general, and
of the opening lines of Sonnet ix. in particular, is
on the growth of the "struggling rill"—a thought
which would be rather out of place if it came later
in the series. In short, the motive of the sonnet
best suits the position of the upper stones, while
some of the descriptive features may be taken from
the lower or traditional stepping-stones.

XI.

THE FAERY CHASM.

No fiction was it of the antique age:
A sky-blue stone, within this sunless cleft,
Is of the very footmarks unbereft
Which tiny Elves impressed ;—on that smooth
    stage
Dancing with all their brilliant equipage
In secret revels—haply after theft
Of some sweet Babe—Flower stolen, and coarse
    Weed left
For the distracted Mother to assuage
Her grief with, as she might!—But, where, oh!
    where
Is traceable a vestige of the notes
That ruled those dances wild in character?—
Deep underground? Or in the upper air,
On the shrill wind of midnight? or where floats
O'er twilight fields the autumnal gossamer?

Adopting the view explained in the last note

as to the stepping-stones, the position of the "Faery Chasm" becomes perfectly clear. It is sometimes looked for below Seathwaite, whereas it is considerably above Seathwaite, and is, in fact, the very next striking feature that occurs after the stepping-stones at Black Hall are passed. It is the chasm which is crossed by Birks Brig.

The stream is here precipitated down a series of falls, and at the same time is forced into a much narrower channel than it has hitherto occupied. In its downward course it is thrust from side to side in a series of some half-dozen rebounds. The effect is that the flood is churned into a mass of foam, while the rocks between which it is driven are worn into the most fantastic shapes. They are scooped into basins and niches, and caverns and arches, and carved into pillars of all shapes, some having an odd spiral twist. Anything of a more elfin character could hardly be conceived.

There is a rock of blue granite cropping up from the bed of the stream below the bridge, which might very well do for the "sky-blue stone" (line 2).

There is no faery tradition associated with the place.

XII.

HINTS FOR THE FANCY.

On, loitering Muse—the swift Stream chides
    us—on
Albeit his deep-worn channel doth immure
Objects immense portrayed in miniature,
Wild shapes for many a strange comparison!
Niagaras, Alpine passes, and anon
Abode of Naiads, calm abysses pure,
Bright liquid mansions, fashioned to endure
When the broad oak drops, a leafless skeleton,
And the solidities of mortal pride,

Palace and tower, are crumbled into dust !—
The Bard who walks with Duddon for his
        guide,
Shall find such toys of fancy thickly set ;
Turn from the sight, enamoured Muse—
        we must ;
And, if thou canst, leave them without
        regret !

Immediately after leaving Birks Brig the stream
plunges into a gorge - the "deep-worn channel" of
this sonnet. By dint of wading and clambering,
all the picturesque features described in the sonnet
may be seen, though it is not possible to penetrate
the gorge to any very great distance, and the traveller
is forced at last to resume the road. The channel is so deep and confined that the stream
cannot be seen from the road, and this is
the first time since leaving the source that
the Duddon is lost to sight. It is this fact
which gives rise to the concluding lines of the
sonnet.

XIII.

OPEN PROSPECT.

Hail to the fields—with Dwellings sprinkled
        o'er,
And one small hamlet, under a green hill
Clustering, with barn and byre, and spouting
        mill !
A glance suffices ;—should we wish for more,
Gay June would scorn us. But when bleak
        winds roar
Through the stiff lance-like shoots of pollard
        ash,

Dread swell of sound! loud as the gusts that
    lash
The matted forests of Ontario's shore
By wasteful steel unsmitten—then would I
Turn into port; and, reckless of the gale,
Reckless of angry Duddon sweeping by,
While the warm hearth exalts the mantling ale,
Laugh with the generous household heartily
At all the merry pranks of Donnerdale!

In determining the spot to which this sonnet
belongs two conditions have to be satisfied.   In the
first place, Seathwaite must be seen from it; and, in
the second, there must be an open prospect of
fields.   Now, from Cockley Beck to Ulpha there is
no single spot upon the road satisfying these two conditions. With one possible exception, there is only
one station in all the valley which supplies them, and
that is the summit of a rock called in maps and
guide-books "Pen Crag," but which the dalesmen
always call simply "The Pen."   There are two
additional reasons for regarding the Pen as the
station whence Wordsworth viewed his "open
prospect."   The first is, that the point from which
the ascent of the crag is most conveniently made is
identical with the point where the Duddon makes
his second plunge into a rocky abyss, which plunge
is signalised in the very next sonnet (xiv.).   Thus,
at the very point where the poet is enabled to gain
a view of "the haunts of men," "some awful Spirit"
impels the torrent "utterly to desert" those haunts,
and to make a second plunge into the wilderness.
An increased significance is thus given to each of
the sonnets (xiii. and xiv.) by the juxtaposition of
the localities which they describe.
    The second reason for fixing upon the Pen is
derived from Sonnet xvii., which belongs to the same
group. The Pen is almost the only place from which

Hardknott, with its Roman camp, and Stoneside, with its Druid circle, can both be seen at the same time. The one lies far up the valley, the other far down it, and from nearly every point of view whence one can be seen, the other is hidden by the intervening Pen; but from the Pen itself both are clear in view. It may be inferred, therefore, that Sonnets xiii. xiv. xv. xvi. and xvii. all refer either to the Pen or to the gorge of which the Pen forms one wall. And it is to be noted that immediately below the Pen we drop into Seathwaite, which is the subject of Sonnet xviii.

It should be explained, in connection with this, that the Pen stands in the centre of the valley a prominent and inviting look-out, and that the easy slope, by which it is on one side ascended, rises from the high-road, so that anybody who cares for views at all—and Wordsworth above all people—would not think of passing by without climbing to such an obvious 'coign of vantage.'

The only other possible place is the point on the Coniston road, mentioned by Wordsworth in his note on Sonnets xvii. and xviii. The view from that point, so exquisitely described by the poet in this note, may possibly be the "open prospect" of Sonnet xiii. Even supposing that Seathwaite, Newfield, the Old Mill, Stoneside, and Hardknott —all of which are mentioned or alluded to in this group of sonnets—are simultaneously visible from the Coniston road as they are from the Pen, probability still seems to incline to the Pen as the spot referred to, because it is on the Duddon, while the other is far away, and quite out of the line which has hitherto been followed.

The "one small hamlet" (line 2) is Seathwaite, which lies just below the Pen.

The "barn and byre" (line 3) must have belonged to Newfield, the only farmhouse in the foreground.

T

The "spouting mill" (line 3) is now a ruin. In Wordsworth's time it was in full work. Later (in the autumn of 1842), when it was visited by James Thorne, the wheel was broken, the machinery decaying, and the roof partly fallen in. At the present time, wheel, machinery, and roof have totally disappeared, and there is nothing to indicate that it ever was a mill. These ruined walls standing by the Beck represent that "mill for spinning yarn," of which Wordsworth says that it calls to mind "the momentous changes wrought by such inventions in the frame of society." The ruin stands on the Tarn Beck, a few yards below Seathwaite Chapel, and on the other side of the stream.

The last three lines of the sonnet are probably an allusion to the inn which, in Wordsworth's time, was to be found here. This is now a farmstead. It is called Newfield, and is just below Seathwaite Chapel. In Wordsworth's day it was inn and farm combined.

XV.

From this deep chasm, where quivering sun-
    beams play
Upon its loftiest crags, mine eyes behold
A gloomy NICHE, capacious, blank, and cold;
A concave free from shrubs and mosses grey;
In semblance fresh, as if, with dire affray,
Some Statue, placed amid these regions old
For tutelary service, thence had rolled,
Startling the flight of timid Yesterday!
Was it by mortals sculptured?—weary slaves
Of slow endeavour! or abruptly cast
Into rude shape by fire, with roaring blast
Tempestuously let loose from central caves?

Or fashioned by the turbulence of waves,
Then, when o'er highest hills the Deluge
    passed?

The "deep chasm" of this sonnet is identical
with the "passage cleft through the wilderness"
of Sonnet xiv.   It lies between the Pen on the left
hand, and Wallabarrow Crag on the right.   As to
the *niche*, which forms the subject of the sonnet, it
cannot now be identified.   There are, of course,
plenty of such niches in the crags which tower
above the Duddon just here, but none is more
striking than the rest.   From the fact that it was
"free from shrubs and mosses grey," one may
perhaps infer that it was a place in the cliff from
which a mass of rock had recently fallen.   The
bed of the stream is a chaos of such masses of
rock, some of them being of enormous size.

XVIII.

SEATHWAITE CHAPEL.

Sacred Religion! "mother of form and fear,"
Dread arbitress of mutable respect,
New rites ordaining when the old are wrecked,
Or cease to please the fickle worshipper;
Mother of Love! (that name best suits thee
    here)
Mother of Love! for this deep vale, protect
Truth's holy lamp, pure source of bright effect,
Gifted to purge the vapoury atmosphere
That seeks to stifle it;—as in those days
When this low Pile a Gospel Teacher knew,
Whose good works formed an endless retinue:
A Pastor such as Chaucer's verse portrays;
Such as the heaven-taught skill of Herbert
    drew;
And tender Goldsmith crowned with deathless
    praise!

Seathwaite Chapel has been rebuilt. It may be worth mentioning that there is a woodcut of the original structure, at page 23 of Thorne's *Rambles by Rivers* (12mo, London, 1844), and a good engraving in the Rev. Canon Parkinson's *Old Church Clock* (5th edition, 1880, p. 99). The Parsonage, too, has been enlarged. It was formerly a mere cottage, with a peat-house at one end and an out-house of some kind at the other. These have been removed, and additions made to the dwelling at both ends. The brass in the church to the memory of Wonderful Walker was taken from the tomb-stone—the gap left by it is on the under side. The stone has been turned over, and a new inscription cut.

XIX.

TRIBUTARY STREAM.

My frame hath often trembled with delight
When hope presented some far-distant good,
That seemed from heaven descending, like the
    flood
Of yon pure waters, from their aery height
Hurrying, with lordly Duddon to unite;
Who, 'mid a world of images imprest
On the calm depth of his transparent breast,
Appears to cherish most that Torrent white,
The fairest, softest, liveliest of them all!
And seldom hath ear listened to a tune
More lulling than the busy hum of Noon,
Swoln by that voice—whose murmur musical
Announces to the thirsty fields a boon
Dewy and fresh, till showers again shall fall.

The "tributary stream," which forms the subject

of this sonnet, is the Tarn Beck, which joins the Duddon just below Seathwaite. Seathwaite Chapel is not itself on the Duddon, but on the Tarn Beck. The sonnet gives a perfect description of its leading characteristics.

XX.

THE PLAIN OF DONNERDALE.

The old inventive Poets, had they seen,
Or rather felt, the entrancement that detains
Thy waters, Duddon! 'mid these flowery
    plains—
The still repose, the liquid lapse serene,
Transferred to bowers imperishably green,
Had beautified Elysium! But these chains
Will soon be broken;—a rough course remains,
Rough as the past; where Thou, of placid
    mien,
Innocuous as a firstling of the flock,
And countenanced like a soft cerulean sky,
Shalt change thy temper; and, with many a
    shock
Given and received in mutual jeopardy,
Dance, like a Bacchanal, from rock to rock,
Tossing her frantic thyrsus wide and high!

The term *Donnerdale* (now usually spelt *Dunner-dale*) is strictly applied to the district on the east bank of the Duddon from Broughton up to Ulpha Bridge, and extending thence parallel to Seathwaite, from which it is divided by fells. Guide-books sometimes apply the term to the whole valley of the Duddon, but this is entirely wrong; the term is never used by the inhabitants as applicable to the upper or confined part of the valley. Donner-dale does not join the Duddon valley until you get below Seathwaite, and is therefore correctly used by Wordsworth to indicate the open plain of the lower stream.

Hall Dunnerdale, sometimes shortened into *Dunnerdale*, is a hamlet on the highroad between Seathwaite and Ulpha. From a bridge just below this hamlet the characteristics of the stream at this part of its course may best be noted. Indeed, so strikingly does the scene at this point agree with the description of Sonnet xx. that one is tempted to think that from this bridge the sketch must have been made. The water on each side of it is perfectly still; a little way up the stream and down it is just broken into ripples, and that is all—a great contrast to the Duddon as we have hitherto known it! The banks are thickly wooded with oak, ash, beech, alder, sycamore, and larch; the hills are lower and greener than the fells farther up the valley, and for the moment we might almost think we had been transported to the banks of the Wey, and were looking upon a Surrey landscape. But this, as the sonnet says, is not to last long—"a rough course remains, rough as the past." Before we reach Ulpha bridge "suspended animation is again succeeded by the clamorous war of stones and waters, which assail the ear of the traveller all the way to Duddon Bridge." [1]

XXII.

TRADITION.

A Love-Lorn Maid, at some far-distant time,
Came to this hidden pool, whose depths surpass
In crystal clearness Dian's looking-glass;
And, gazing, saw that Rose, which from the
    prime

[1] Green's *Comprehensive Guide to the Lakes.*

Derives its name, reflected, as the chime
Of echo doth reverberate some sweet sound:
The starry treasure from the blue profound
She longed to ravish;—shall she plunge, or
    climb
The humid precipice, and seize the guest
Of April, smiling high in upper air?
Desperate alternative! what fiend could dare
To prompt the thought?—Upon the steep rock's
    breast
The lonely Primrose yet renews its bloom,
Untouched memento of her hapless doom!

This tradition appears to have completely died
out. The scene of the tragedy is not, however, very
difficult to identify. There are few "hidden pools"
in this part of the stream : it is mostly a shallow,
brawling brook. Carefully tracking the stream
from Donnerdale Bridge to Ulpha Bridge, only two
places can be found which will at all answer to the
description given in the sonnet.

If the traveller from Seathwaite to Ulpha will
keep to the bank of the stream instead of taking the
road, he will come at length to a waterbreak where
there is a fall of six or eight feet and a plank bridge
across the stream. In order to reach this place he
will have to climb some very high walls or go
round some very large fields, but once reached, by
hook or by crook, the way is clear. From this
point there is a footpath along the left bank of the
stream which will lead him to a set of stepping-
stones. He must not cross these, but must keep
along the left bank, and he will come at length to a
place where a sudden bend in the stream reveals,
with something of a surprise, a long straight corridor, with perpendicular walls of slate on either hand.
Half-way down this corridor a little rill tumbles
into the Duddon by a miniature cascade, and on the

other side of this rill there is a rock some twelve or
fifteen feet in height overhanging a deep and placid
pool, sheltered and darkened by oak and beech.
There is a similar pool a little lower down the
stream, exactly opposite the "Traveller's Rest" inn,
and these are the only two places which fulfil the
conditions of Sonnet xxii.

If we take the upper one as the scene of the
tragedy, the succeeding sonnets fall into order.

XXVII.

Fallen, and diffused into a shapeless heap,
Or quietly self-buried in earth's mould,
Is that embattled House, whose massy Keep,
Flung from yon cliff a shadow large and cold.
There dwelt the gay, the bountiful, the bold;
Till nightly lamentations, like the sweep
Of winds—though winds were silent—struck a
    deep
And lasting terror through that ancient Hold.
Its line of Warriors fled;—they shrunk when
    tried
By ghostly power:—but Time's unsparing hand
Hath plucked such foes, like weeds, from out the
    land;
And now, if men with men in peace abide,
All other strength the weakest may withstand,
All worse assaults may safely be defied.

Sonnets xxiv. to xxvii. appear to be written in
one spot—some "nook—with woodbine hung and
straggling weed." No particular "nook" can be
fixed upon as the one referred to. There are
plenty of such "grottos" or "arbours" at this part
of the stream. The only condition to be satisfied
is, that there shall be a distant view of the "Old
Hall"—which forms the subject of Sonnet xxvii.—

and this condition is satisfied by a score of grottos, as the "cliff" where the "Old Hall" stands is one of the most prominent features in the landscape.

Of the Castle itself (Sonnet xxvii.) there is scarcely anything now remaining—less even than in Wordsworth's day, for a woman living in a cottage close by it assures us that she could remember when there was much more of it standing than at the present time. The cause to which she assigns its rapid disappearance is not, however, the same as that assigned in the first two lines of the sonnet. According to her, natural decay has had less to do with it than the destructive hands of the dalesman, who pulled the stones down to mend the fell-walls with. A native of Ulpha adds that a new barn was built for the adjoining farmhouse some little time since, and that there is little doubt a great part of the materials came from the old ruin.

There is still one room standing. The walls of it are 3 feet 6 inches to 4 feet in thickness. There are three small square windows, and one larger one, none of which have arches, but flat tops, formed by one large slab of stone to each window. They are splayed inwards. There is a fireplace about 6 feet long by 12 feet high, with a wide chimney.

The building, of which this is the only fragment remaining *in situ*, is said to have been the seat of the Lords of Ulpha.

As to the ghostly tradition embodied in Sonnet xxvii., Wordsworth himself has explained that it was borrowed from Rydal Hall. But the "Old Hall" has a weird tradition of its own, for near it there is a well, called "The Lady's Dub," where in old times a lady was killed by one of the numerous wolves which formerly infested the region. This is, in fact, the origin, according to some of

the inhabitants, of the name "Ulpha" ("Wolfa").
But a more likely derivation seems to be from Ulf,
the father of Ketell, the father of Bennett, the
father of Allan.   Ketell lived in Henry III.'s reign,
and Bennett in King John's, and to their ancestor
Ulf the lordship of "Ulphay" was granted.[1]

XXIX.

No record tells of lance opposed to lance,
Horse charging horse, 'mid these retired domains
Tells that their turf drank purple from the veins
Of heroes, fallen, or struggling to advance,
Till doubtful combat issued in a trance
Of victory, that struck through heart and reins
Even to the inmost seat of mortal pains,
And lightened o'er the pallid countenance.
Yet, to the loyal and the brave, who lie
In the blank earth, neglected and forlorn,
The passing Winds memorial tribute pay;
The Torrents chant their praise, inspiring scorn
Of power usurped; with proclamation high,
And glad acknowledgment, of lawful sway.

Leaving now the pool described in the note on
Sonnet xxii., and keeping along the left bank of
the Duddon, the traveller will presently be stopped
by an insurmountable stone wall.   Let him turn
his back upon the stream, and follow this wall for
some distance, till he comes to a little square
enclosure, with two old fir-trees and a quantity of
laurels.   Here let him pause, for this, there is little
doubt, is the scene of Sonnet xxix.

The enclosure in question is near a farmhouse,
called New Close, and it is known to the country

---

[1] Mr. J. Denton, quoted in Whellan's *History and
Topography*, p. 410.

people as The Sepulchre (pronounced by them
Se*pul*chre). It is an old burial place of the Society
of Friends, none having been interred here since
1755, when a Friend from Birker, a small hamlet
about four miles distant, was buried.[1]

The following lines literally describe the condition of the little burial-ground—

> Yet, to the loyal and the brave, who lie
> In the blank earth, neglected and forlorn.

The earth is "blank," because there is not a single
tombstone, and the graves are (at any rate at the
present time) most literally "neglected and forlorn,"
for the place is a tangle of rank grass and un-
trimmed bushes, and the cattle are kept from it
only by some rough pieces of wood nailed across
the gap where the gate once hung.

About the year 1842 it was planted with fruit-
trees, but when Wordsworth saw it, it probably
presented much the same appearance as at present.

The opening lines—

> No record tells of lance opposed to lance, etc.,

and indeed the whole sonnet obtains a new significance from the association of the spot which it
describes with the *men of peace.*

XXX.

> Who swerves from innocence, who makes divorce
> Of that serene companion—a good name,
> Recovers not his loss; but walks with shame,

[1] *Furness and Furness Abbey*, by Francis Evans (8vo,
Ulverston, 1842), p. 180.

With doubt, with fear, and haply with remorse:
And oft-times he—who, yielding to the force
Of chance—temptation, ere his journey end,
From chosen comrade turns, or faithful friend—
In vain shall rue the broken intercourse.
Not so with such as loosely wear the chain
That binds them, pleasant River! to thy side:—
Through the rough copse wheel thou with hasty
    stride;
I choose to saunter o'er the grassy plain,
Sure, when the separation has been tried,
That we, who part in love, shall meet again.

Just beyond the "Sepulchre" is a track which
leads to a woodland path, passing through which
you come into open hay-fields. The river, however,
still pursuing its way between thickly-wooded banks,
is hidden from sight. This juxtaposition of copse
and meadow (the river choosing the wood, and the
traveller the meadow) will, if the place bore the
same appearance in Wordsworth day, account for
Sonnet xxx. being assigned to this position in the
series.

XXXI.

The KIRK of ULPHA to the pilgrim's eye
Is welcome as a star, that doth present
Its shining forehead through the peaceful rent
Of a black cloud diffused o'er half the sky:
Or as a fruitful palm-tree towering high
O'er the parched waste beside an Arab's tent;
Or the Indian tree whose branches, downward
    bent,
Take root again, a boundless canopy.
How sweet were leisure! could it yield no more
Than 'mid that wave-washed Churchyard to
    recline,

From pastoral graves extracting thoughts
      divine;
Or there to pace, and mark the summit's hoar
Of distant moonlit mountains faintly shine,
Soothed by the unseen River's gentle roar.

Ulpha Kirk is situated on a rock, the base of
which is washed by the Duddon.   From time
immemorial its walls have been whitewashed, so
that on a sunny day it *literally* "shines" from its
exalted position.   It is best seen from the hay-
fields mentioned in the previous note (xxx.).   These
fields lie low, and the church perched on its rock
seems lifted higher than from any other point of
view.

In 1882 the carpenters were at work restoring
the church of Ulpha.   But in 1881 the interior,
as well as the exterior, still kept the appearance
which it wore in Wordsworth's day.   The pulpit
(with sounding board) was in the middle of one
side, and to the right hand thereof was a magnificent lion and unicorn, and "G. III. R."   The
font was up against the wall, near the door, with
a ladder hung above it.   There was no vestry;
the surplice was kept in a cupboard near the
door, and the clergyman donned and doffed it
behind a screen which only partially hid him.   The
pews were square and high, and the people sat all
round them, with their backs to the four points of
the compass; but when the hymn was sung they
turned their backs to the altar, and their faces to
the choir.

The sonnet called *After-Thought* concludes the
Duddon Series, and with it this book may fitly
close.

XXXIV.

AFTER-THOUGHT.

I thought of Thee, my partner and my guide,
As being past away.—Vain sympathies!
For, backward, Duddon! as I cast my eyes,
I see what was, and is, and will abide;
Still glides the Stream, and shall for ever glide;
The Form remains, the Function never dies;
While we, the brave, the mighty, and the wise,
We Men, who in our morn of youth defied
The elements, must vanish;—be it so!
Enough, if something from our hands have
     power
To live, and act, and serve the future hour;
And if, as toward the silent tomb we go,
Through love, through hope, and faith's tran-
     scendent dower,
We feel that we are greater than we know.

THE END.

www.ingramcontent.com/pod-product-compliance
Lightning Source LLC
Chambersburg PA
CBHW020850020726
47497CB00005B/1345